HUNT THE HIGH AIR

"It's not war," Amarson said. "I'm sending my cubs up to kill Draks who are hunting food. My people of the Marches, you Valley People, you River People—we are all simply *food*! You harvest the giant Riverfish, for food, even as the Drak harvest the land people. The Riverfish fight back with the only weapons they have, even as we have done for millennia . . ."

Amarson flexed his claws, then went on:

"Now with these new Fliers we have been able to do a little stalking on our own account. Should the Riverfish ever develop weapons to carry the fight beyond the riverbeds, even as we now hunt the high air, would that then be war—or survival? As your priest said, we're paid to kill Draks; we're proud to kill Draks . . .

"But it's not *war*!"

SOLO KILL

S. KYE BOULT

A BERKLEY MEDALLION BOOK
published by
BERKLEY PUBLISHING CORPORATION

**To Jeanne, Jamie, and John
who once asked me to motivate a war.**

Berkley Publishing Corporation
200 Madison Avenue
New York, N.Y. 10016

SBN 425-03560-3

*BERKLEY MEDALLION BOOKS are published by
Berkley Publishing Corporation
200 Madison Avenue
New York, N.Y. 10016*

BERKLEY MEDALLION BOOK ® TM 757,375

Printed in the United States of America

Berkley Medallion Edition, NOVEMBER, 1977

Sections of this novel were originally
published in *Analogue* as short stories.

Contents

SOLO KILL

ONE

A Little Edge

1.

Baron Amarson always heard a silent fighting scream from the stuffed Drak head whenever he turned up the lights and saw it come out of the darkness. His ears pointed rigidly, the hair on the back of his neck, head and around his mouth stiffened as the fear instincts armed his nerves and bloodstream for combat. The tight alertness was not a bad feeling for the start of the day and Amarson always enjoyed the emotions, even if they were unnecessary. He was in his war room at Flight Base XII, many miles from the nearest live Drak. The one he was looking at had lost all interest in killing and eating Amarson two years ago when it became a trophy instead of a deadly enemy.

The Drak head, mounted over the war map board, glared down out of malevolent oval eyes. It was mounted with the feathers on the sides of the head sleeked back as though by a wind. The head was cocked to one side and the curved orange beak was half open. The effect was of a Drak diving to attack anyone who stood in front of the war board. In this case, this morning, it was Amarson and Ambass| dor Theiu of the River People to the south.

Amarson was in uniform, the leather of a flight leader. His

1

jacket was a deep brown, only a shade darker than the skin of his head and hands. It bore an insignia of arms that told his family rank and the shoulder badges of a Flight Commander. The ambassador was a civilian, dressed in a pale blue coverall over a silver grey skin that looked slightly wet. He was visibly nervous.

"You will forgive a guest, Baron Amarson," he said, "but that is a barbaric trophy."

Amarson looked down at the round grey head beside him. The Riverman was less than half his height.

"Trophy, Ambassador Theiu?" He had been studying the map intently and did not understand.

"The Drak," said the little man. "It looks ready to kill." He pulled a flask from a pocket in his coverall and sprayed water over his head, nervously wiping his flat nose and wide eyes with one hand. The hand was webbed.

"Oh, yes," Amarson looked up. "The taxidermist was a genius. Makes you want to fight just looking at it, doesn't it?"

"You perhaps, Baron." The ambassador used his spray again. "I am forced to remember that the Draks consider me very good to eat. I would rather be in a deep pool.

"Do you always use this . . . thing, to inspire your combat flight?"

"Yes, Amarson said. "There is the enemy and the land he controls. I can stand in front of one wall and hate them both.

" Don't worry about this Drak, Ambassador. See, we have clipped his wings." He gestured across the top of the map. The Drak's two great leather wings, severed from his body, were spread against the wall.

"Forget the trophy and look at my map. There in the north, the mountain peaks marked with purple striping, is the great Alp stronghold of the Draks. My fliers cannot get at them in those canyons and peaks. Below that is the jungle barrier. It also shows as Drak territory, although we can send ground troops, our Jungle Patrols, into that area."

"As soon as you leave the Draks fly back in, and then attack the Valley farms," the ambassador finished. "I have read the complaints."

"The only thing I can hold is the air over the Valley. My

2

bases are the triangles." Amarson indicated a curve of numbered triangles arcing between the jungle and the valley plain. "Bases Number One and Number Two cover your River People in the east. I have two more flights based west of me here on the coast of the Mud Sea. Base XII is nearest to the Drak mountain passes."

The ambassador became paler at that reminder of his danger. At the tip of each of the mounted Drak wings he could see the large metal XII's—the number of Amarson's own field.

"We hold the air, when the Draks fly hunting patrols," Amarson said. "The people of the plain and your cities to the south are getting all the protection we can give them."

"You have cities in the plain, too, Baron."

"Yes, and they are on the frontier, close to the Drak," Amarson growled. "The Draks hunt us for food, too, Ambassador."

"But they don't find you so easy to pick up and carry away." The ambassador sprayed his head again. "We are small and light."

"And *we* tend to fight back," Amarson snapped, then he went on contritely. "Sorry, Ambassador, that was unworthy. Your Rivermen craftsmen give us the weapons to fight Draks and we have made treaties to fight Draks for you and the Valley People. Well, that's where our honor lies. We fight Draks, kill Draks. My business is fighting back.

"And fighting back is what I am going to do today."

With a quick movement Amarson drew a straight yellow line from the Number XII triangle, east and north, across the coast and out into the Mud Sea, behind the mountains. At the end of his line was a group of islands, Drak held. He wrote course numbers and times along the line and then signed his name directly below the triangle: *Leon Amarson Baron Rufus, Commanding*.

"That's the first attack order I've signed in three months," he said. "Defensive patrols! The best of my men are getting killed on defensive patrols."

"You know we must have the Draks driven away during these months," the ambassador said. "I was against your

3

flight when it was proposed. An attack now may bring them down on us during the harvest. I know you need to try this new weapon, but the Valley Harvest and our Fish Catch are vital to the war at this time. We must be supplied before the Draks swarm.''

"Holding the Valley and the River is not my idea of war.'' Amarson's lips parted in a snarl along the length of his long nose and head. His ears twitched up and his eyes narrowed. He clenched his fists and moved his feet inside his flight boots. The leather of his flight gear creaked as his leg muscles tightened and relaxed.

The ambassador shifted away from him a bit. For a moment the expression on Amarson's face was very much like the one on the mounted Drak head. The ambassador was remembering old legends about the time when Amarson's people had also found the small Rivermen very good to eat. The memories did not help his nervousness.

"May I disagree, even as a guest, Baron," he said. "The Draks are not at war. It takes two sides opposed in national pride to make a war. The Draks are only hunting. They consider us a food supply only, Baron. They harvest us the way we harvest the riverfish; without thought, communication, warning, or declaration of war. They simply kill to eat. Your fliers, I suspect, are considered an especially dangerous kind of game animal.

"Oh, I know they wear armor, use weapons, and can think and fight, but they truly are not making war.''

"War!'' Amarson growled. "What we do isn't war either. The Draks are back there in the hills breeding, now. In three months they will swarm out. Every Drak that can fly will head south looking for food. Then you'll get your war, Ambassador, as we have every season. They will fly to kill and we will be driven back to the river. War? That's not war!

"Look at the map. I can't get into the mountains to finish the fight. My fliers can't stay in the air in the passes and canyons. The Draks only come out in small groups to hunt or to attack my fliers. Then they swarm. They kill us in the air with swords and spears, but it isn't war. I kill Draks because they always attack and will kill me if I don't, but it isn't war!''

He slammed his hands together to control his anger.

"For six years now, I have fought them like this, futilely. I have seen cooked, half-eaten bodies left by the Draks after the swarm. Permit me my honor, Ambassador. There is no honor in being someone's reluctant supper. I have more honor fighting a war to kill all Draks, everywhere. So I must call our fight a war. I am a warrior, not just an angry food animal!"

A clear bell rang three times. Amarson shook his head and relaxed visibly.

"It is almost sunrise. Will you come to the Shrine with me, Ambassador? Our chants this morning dedicate us to combat, but you are welcome.

"This war of ours has little honor in it except the protection of the lives of the Valley and River People. The Shrine pledges us to that, even when we use the Warrior's Rites."

Without waiting for a reply he turned and walked into the adjoining Shrine. Time enough for brooding and philosophy later; this morning he had to lead an attack to kill Draks.

2

All of his flight were kneeling before the Shrine, waiting for the first light of the Father Sun to shine on the altar.

Above the altar were the representations of the two suns and the World, hanging in the divine three-body position. The Father Sun was a great disk of red crystal fully as large as the golden globe of the planet behind it. The Younger Sun was a small ball, barely two fingers in diameter. It caught the light of the altar fires and sparkled as it turned. At the ritual time the sunlight from the Younger Sun would turn it into a golden ball of flame.

The adjutant, as eldest-to-them-all, began the chant of the rising. The silver hair along his mouth and beside his ears gleamed the honor of his age as he lit the new altar flames for his prayer.

Suddenly Amarson whirled, brushed the ambassador out of his path, and strode out of the stone Shrine onto the flight field. The artificial emotion of the Shrine made his breath stop in his throat. His moodiness, the talk with the ambassador, demanded a return to basics. He wanted to dedicate himself to the rising ritual out here in the open. He wanted to see the physical rise of the Father Sun, the brightness of the Younger Sun, and wait with upraised eyes for the Rite of Pausing, as the Younger Sun stopped in the sky. Today was a day for greeting the Father Sun in the open and alone. This morning the Flight flew to attack Draks and some of his men would die. It would be under his leadership that they died, and he wanted to feel that they died as men, warriors, not as food for obscene winged Draks. So he felt a need for the old rituals, out here in the open, under the sun, as it was done before man learned to fly into the red and yellow sky of the dual suns.

The deep darkn ss gave way slowly to the dim red glow that preceded the rising of the giant red sun. The Father Sun rose first of the two suns. It came up slowly, ponderously. It literally covered the horizon as its giant size was magnified by the thick air near the ground.

Amarson picked up the chant from inside the Shrine. The deep red light glowed on the silver disks at his shoulders as he passed his hands over them and across his heart, then back to his lips in the ritual of the morning greeting. Inside the Shrine, Amarson's men performed the same ritual as the red light glowed in the disk of the Father Sun above the altar.

Before Amarson, Base XII became visible in the morning light. He faced a wide square field of open ground planted with multicolored grasses to confuse Drak eyes and hide it from the air. To his left crouched a line of five fliers, their motors rumbling in the stillness. Beside the wings of these fliers stood a group of groundsmen. Amarson felt them

6

watching him intently, even though he did not permit himself to look at them.

Slowly he knelt on both knees and held out his arms in the old gestures of the ancient ritual. Out of the corner of his eye he saw three of the older men follow him to their knees, then he could see no more. The small yellow Younger Sun rose. It jumped swiftly over the hills and arced up one-eighth of the way to the zenith. There it appeared to stop and hang in the sky to wait for the stately rise of its giant partner. This was the Rite of Pausing.

At first the yellow light filled Amarson's eyes, then as the sun rose, the light from it shrank until the sun was a pale, moon-like star at the pausing. The fading yellow light left the deep red color of the Father Sun to bathe the field and buildings. The Father rose higher.

The kneeling figures continued the movements of the ritual. The ceremony was an ancient challenge to the Drak. A warrior kneeling in the open like this would be instantly attacked by the first Drak to see him. It had been a way for untried warriors to kill Draks and gain much honor.

Even now, Amarson found himself looking at the sky with all his senses alert. There would be instant, unthinking combat if a Drak flew over. The nearest Drak was in the jungle at the base of the Alps, but the instinct to kill Draks burned violently during the ritual. Amarson's pulse pounded in time with the chants.

Guided by the words of the chant, Amarson lowered his eyes to his hands. The skin on his closed fists had turned a pulsing blood red in the light of the sun. Slowly he opened his fists and let the red palms face the sun.

"The blood of my enemies on my hands, before your next light," he chanted, for so the old ritual ran.

"Blood from the Father will be returned in blood."

He ran out the claws on his finger tips. The red light covered them with blood also. His skin shivered as he forced an outward calm against the racing pulse and rising emotions that swelled in him.

Aargh, a really barbaric ritual, he thought. *The little*

ambassador must be washing his face continuously at this. I wonder if he's ever seen our rituals before.

"Father, bring me to the blood for my hands. Blood that only stains the hands!"

He completed the ritual and sheathed his claws. Already the light was fading, as the Father Sun moved up through the thicker air on the horizon and the morning light took on its normal orange-yellow color.

Amarson overrode his pounding heart, calmed his thoughts and stood up. He forced himself to walk slowly over to the line of waiting fliers.

Emeran, the chief groundsman, came to meet him. The man's hair was iron-white even in the morning light, and like the adjutant the hair at his mouth was bearded as an indication of age as well as rank. The knees of his uniform were spotted with two disks of dust. Amarson noted the dust and knew his own uniform was marked the same way. This old soldier would be one of the ones to kneel in the old ways, of course he would. The pride of men like this was to be expected; counted on.

"How many fliers do you have for me today, Chief?" He held his voice to an even conversational tone.

"Five on the line, Baron." The groundsman flung a hand in a wave to indicate the flapping tents hidden in the trees. "Seven in the tents for repairs, three out by mid-passage and the rest before dark. The tents will be empty and ready for these five when you bring them back, my lord."

"I may not bring them all back, old man," Amarson said. "But have the other fliers ready for tomorrow. We will use them."

The groundsman swung his hand upward and placed it on Amarson's shoulder insignia in a salute to acknowledge the order.

"The men know you cannot bring them all back, sir," he said. "They follow you to fight the Draks. Still they follow you; you still lead the pack, Baron."

"I still lead," Amarson nodded. "And I lead men, not cubs. If they were cubs, I would bring them all back. Because they are men it is part of my honor to spend their lives."

"The fact that they are men, sir, that gives them lives to spend with honor. They fight Draks like demons."

"I know, Chief," Amarson smiled. "I can't complain about the men I lead." He shook his head sadly. "I only complain about the lack of fliers. It's not a very heroic thought, no honor in it at all, but I would spend more lives if I could bring back the fliers. We have more demon men of honor, than machines of war."

"The blood only stains the hands."

"The blood only stains the hands," Amarson repeated the ritual. "But what stains your hands, old man? The lubrication of these fliers, heh? You treat them like cubs." He smiled to emphasize his joke.

"Perhaps I do," the chief laughed. "But these I have for you today are no cubs. Come look at the claws the Rivermen have built for them."

"I want to see them, and so does the Riverman Ambassador," Amarson turned and beckoned the small grey man over to him. "Come with me, Ambassador Theiu," he said. "We are going to look at your toys now."

"We have taken the rocket racks off entirely," the chief indicated the nearest flier. They walked over to look up at the wings. "The Design College has ordered your whole Flight equipped with these dart throwers, Baron." He pointed to the upper wing panel. Fitted onto its under surface was a belt of woven wire holding hundreds of short darts. The belt came out of a hopper in the fuselage and ran out to a flat mechanism outboard of the braces holding the wingtips at their flight spacing.

"That's the launcher?" Amarson asked.

"Yes, my lord. They are all very well made. The best Riverman work. We had no trouble fitting them." The chief raised his voice to include the rest of the men who had come up behind Amarson. "The launcher is located outboard of the wing-tip braces for two purposes." His voice droned into a parade-ground lecturing tone. "Purpose one: To stabilize your flier when the launcher fires. There is a recoil with the mechanism. Purpose two: To provide a wide base necessary for aiming at a flying target. The missiles ejected from the

9

launcher will cross two hundred meters ahead of your flier. This is a Margroth Mark II Cyclic Launcher. Its rate of fire is sixty darts per heartbeat. Thus, you see, we have an advancing wedge of darts, two hundred meters ahead of you, as you fly into the attack. . . ''

"Darts? No rockets?"

"Sixty darts a. . . "

"How does it work?"

The chorus of questions broke against the air.

"As you were!" Amarson stopped them as they bounced around the wing tips. "Listen to the Chief, you cubs!"

"Can we kill Draks with these?" somebody asked, as they quieted and considered the new weapon.

"Yes, you can kill with these," the chief said. "We hope you can kill at a distance." He motioned to his crew. They came forward and lifted the tail of the flier up on a trestle to put it in flying position. Four of them carried a large, white square out onto the field and placed it at a marked spot.

"This launcher system is aimed as you point the flier," the chief went on as he climbed up to lean into the seat space. "The darts trail a smoke pellet as they are launched so you can correct your aim. The arming switch is located on your panel. It must be turned on before you go into combat. To fire the launchers, you press the red button on the control column.

"Stand clear of the flier, please."

When he had made sure that the area to the target was clear, the chief reached in and turned on the arming switch.

"Arm the launcher. Aim your flier at a Drak. Fire."

He pressed the button. There was a rattling clatter as the darts moved into the launcher and were thrown out at the target. Over a hundred darts rushed through the air before the chief released the button, but no one counted the heartbeats. They all stood in shocked silence staring at the gaping hole in the white target, two hundred meters out on the field.

"Brutal. I had no idea. . . " the ambassador said. Amarson felt the wetness of the spray against the back of his hands.

"The blood only stains the hands," Amarson said. "I think we can kill Draks with this toy, Ambassador. Yes, I do.

"Orders, my cubs!" he went on, commandingly. "Five of

you follow me this morning to test these launchers. Did you get your courses?'' They had. ''Very well. Now, hear me. We fly to see how these launchers work. *That* is our mission. Avoid single combat. Stay away from the Draks. Don't give them a chance to use their spears or swords. This thing kills at a distance. Learn how to use it.

''When we sight the first Drak flight I will signal the group into a single line. Stay lined up. Don't get ahead of the flier on either side of you. I want all of those darts to go into Draks, not into my fliers.

''After the first engagement, we may break up into pairs. Watch for my signals and stay together. Understand? Don't get pulled into pack fights, or boarded. Your honor is in these launchers and the way they kill. Let's leave the Draks hungry!'' He looked at each of the five men. Yes, they understood.

''Your honor, my cubs, is in these launchers and the way they kill. When we get back I will begin a regular schedule of practice flights against targets. You five men will act as teachers for the rest of the command.

''But the Rivermen made these launchers to kill Draks, so let's go kill Draks.

''Thank Ambassador Theiu for your new toys and get your fliers in the sky!''

3

The five men saluted the ambassador with laughing thanks, ran to their fliers, and began to start the engines. Amarson waited until the ground crew lowered his flier down from the trestle, then he too saluted the ambassador, climbed into the seat and tightened his flying straps.

"My Lord," the chief was at his side. "You will be low on darts near the end of the combat. I used nearly a hundred."

Amarson nodded, his voice murmuring the starting ritual prayers. The ground crew plugged the long nose of the starting cart into the engine and waited for the end of the ritual. Amarson soon finished and called out, "Power to start! Controls back!"

The man on the starter fired the charge. A flaming blast of gases shot into the engine and slammed against the single cylinder, spinning it in the combustion chamber. The engine caught smoothly and ran with its usual throbbing roar. The crew pulled away the cart and the chief followed them.

Amarson looked down the line of fliers. All five of the engines had started. He held his hand in the air to question whether they were ready. Five hands were lifted in answer. Amarson looked back to where the chief groundsman stood. The old man raised his arm to signify that his men were clear, then he turned the upraised hand over and opened his fingers, extending his claws, the old religious salute of the warrior.

"The blood only stains the hands, old man," Amarson shouted into the engine noise. "I will bring you my kill."

He dropped his hand and shoved the power control to take-off power. The flier began to move, rolling out on the grass-covered field. Halfway down the field, the flier reached its first speed point and slid smoothly into the heavy air. Caressing the controls, Amarson held the flier parallel to the ground until the speed reached the second point, then he climbed steeply up the sky and turned to head for the sea.

The flier climbed out swiftly. It seemed to be in a hurry to get out of the heavy air near the ground and up into the lighter sky.

Amarson was hurrying, too. There was a long way to go. He wanted to try out these new Rivermen weapons over the island chain where he could expect Draks in small hunting parties, but not chance meeting a bigger swarm.

He looked around him for the first time. The five fliers rode the sky behind him. He had expected them to follow him in a single file; instead they were fanned out three to the left and two to the right. He frowned, then smiled, as he realized that none of the men were flying behind another flier. The demonstration with the target had made an impression. He glanced back again, at the unconscious pattern the fliers had assumed. It might be a good combat pattern for these new launchers. All the fliers could fire at once.

He shrugged the idea into the back of his mind and turned to his flying. He had almost reached the height of the thermocline. Ahead of him was the barrier between the heavy air and the light air of the upper sky. Soon his wings would be fighting to break through the turbulent layer where they met.

He advanced the power control and tightened his grip on the flight controls. With the swiftness that the snarling gutterals demanded, he began to recite the penetration ritual. The words tightened his muscles, quickened his reflexes, and brought his blood pulsing to meet the air storm. His timing was good. He was chanting the final stanza when the flier hit the barrier. The heavy, near solid, thermocline threw the flier up and rolled it violently to the left. Without the stimulus of the ritual, the flier would have stalled over on its back. As it was, his hands moved strongly on the controls and held the flier boring through into the calm, lighter air above.

The engine sang a new higher pitch and lifted up into the air. He steadied on his course and looked back to see how the others had come through. Their formation was wider, but they closed it as he watched. There was no worry with these men.

Amarson turned to look ahead. The coastline was below him now. To the south the water of the River spread for miles along its delta and disappeared into the shimmering wet mud surface of the sea. The Mud Sea stretched off north and west as far as he could see. The high peaks of the alps were behind him to the north. Ahead, on the very edge of the sky, was the island group that was the home of the Drak clutch he was seeking. Now, for a time, their flight would be safe. The Draks flew on their own wings, and their hunting parties did not fly out over the Mud Sea. No Drak could land on the soft, almost liquid mud and live. Amarson's fliers carried fuel range to let them make the approach across the sea and return,

13

but they wouldn't meet the Draks until they got closer to the islands.

Amarson reached his flying height and came out of the climb. For a few moments he busied himself balancing the flier, for the long flight ahead; setting the engine power at the precise point to give him the most thrust against the thin air, with the smallest amount of fuel. He adjusted the muscles of his legs and arms to control the flier with tiny, relaxed movements, in just the right attitude for maximum range. These were things he set his mind and body to do smoothly and automatically as a first discipline of flight.

The ritual words for doing this drill were torn from his lips by the wind of the flight and blended with the roar of the motor. He knew he said them out loud and briefly, in the beginning, he heard himself; then his ears tuned to the sound of the motor and he did not hear. Soon he did not hear the motor. As the ritual action of his mind and body welded him spiritually with the flier he would be able to hear other things outside the flier, other motor noises, sounds from the ground, even the combat screams of the Draks when they were contacted. The ritual would free his senses to concentrate on anything that was not normal to the operation of his flier.

Behind him, the other fliers flew smoothly through the air, and the sea of mud slid below them. The arrow point of the five fliers held its shape under the red glow of the Father Sun. It was the time of mid-passage. The Younger Sun sank down the sky behind them and set. It would rise again when they were over the islands. Amarson had planned his flight so that the swiftly traveling Young Sun would light the combat zone and silhouette the flying Draks as they rose to meet him. Draks were hard to see, small, man-size, and Amarson didn't want them to get in too close. The yellow sun would help. Amarson was well satisfied with his timing.

He let his mind relax and slide down into the trance of flight. His pulse slowed and his controlling became instinctive. For a time he seemed to sleep, flying on and on, with no conscious thought, conserving and building his strength for the combat that would come.

The islands on the horizon grew in size and the first one of

14

the chain slid under his wings before he moved again. A shudder seemed to run through his body and the flier rocked in response. He checked his flier with eyes that saw again and ears that were keenly alert. The engine was running smoothly. The fuel load was well above the half weight point. Good. If any rising Draks wanted to come hunting, Amarson's flight was at the combat zone and ready for them.

He unlocked the trigger switches on the dart launchers and reached forward to loosen the short, curved knife fastened across the front of his instrument panel.

Suddenly, the flier just behind him roared its engine and slid up beside Amarson. Its wings rocked frantically.

Amarson sat up straighter and turned his head to see where the danger lay. Nothing was behind them.

Then he saw a group of flying figures below them, lifting from a point of a large island. He swung his hand flat over his head to signal his flight into the line formation he had planned for the combat. The fliers slid smoothly into place, but the man nearest Amarson was still rocking his wings and making negative motions. The nose of the flier lifted up and the man pointed forward and up.

Amarson scanned the sky ahead of the group. Nothing.

Then he saw it. Far off, against the bottom of a cloud bank, a gigantic round object was hanging in the sky. Swarming around it were small, black dots that could only be flying Draks. Draks already in the air, and at combat altitude; even higher! This was new.

Except for the swarming season the Draks had very little endurance in the air. Always they rose from the ground to attack. Now, they were already in the air, waiting.

Amarson tilted his flier to get a better look at the Draks coming up at them from the ground. Quickly he measured the distance.

"No," he said out loud, the wind whipping the words away.

The Draks below were no menace. By the time they rose to fighting height, Amarson's group would be very near to that great ball and its swarming escort. Waving his arm in the no-combat signal, he lifted the nose of his flier and began to climb toward the new enemy. The rest of the group rode up and down on the air waves as they lifted with him. The entire fighting line pivoted to head onto the new course and then the men dropped back into the arrowhead formation.

4

Good men, Amarson smiled with pride. No cubs, these. No one screamed off to accept the fight with the lower Draks. They had all made the same decision. The unknown thing in the sky ahead was more important than a small pack fight.

Amarson went to one-half combat power on his engine. A stream of dots had broken away from the ball and was headed toward him. Amarson held his speed and climbed. Just before he met the Draks he intended to pour on all the power he could get and fly right through their attack. He wanted to get up close to whatever that was, hanging there in the sky.

Amarson signaled his men, bringing them up into the single line formation again. When they were in position he went to full combat power. The flier pulsed under him and lifted to meet the enemy. They were closing rapidly. He could see the short spears they carried and the gleaming markings on their harness.

They were close enough.

"Now!" He yelled and triggered the dart launchers. Four of the stubby missiles leaped forward, the racks rattled, and four more were launched. The noise startled him, and before he could loose the trigger, eight more darts were launched.

The other fliers had fired with him. The air ahead was filled with the darts, each streaming a tiny trail of smoke. Amarson had time to notice that all of the fliers had fired; then the Draks flew into the cloud of darts. The result was brutal. The Draks were hit and hit hard. Two of them spun into a third. More tumbled in the sky. They didn't have a chance.

Amarson lifted his flier to avoid the swarming mass and saw one Drak go rolling past. His body bristled with four darts and two more pinned his wings together. He was still clutching his fighting spear, his eyes and beak gaping wide with shock.

Then they were through the Draks and climbing beyond them. Quickly Amarson checked his men. All there. He looked behind him. The Draks were a jerking, falling group. Not one spread his wings to turn and fight. They were falling. Five, twelve, fifteen, Amarson counted. All dead or dying.

He shouted a prayer to the Rivermen. Glory to the maker of those dart launchers! What a weapon! This was the edge of a War Sword. Now the fight could be carried to the Draks. Now I can truly talk about war, little Ambassador Theiu. Spray your head!

And the whole group firing at once like that. A good tactic for the first clash of combat. It wouldn't do to try it more than once, though. The Draks were good fighters, they would learn fast.

He signaled the group to pair up and they wheeled out into two-flier fighting units. All of them headed on up toward the rest of the Draks. Amarson led his wingman out wide and up near the cloud. He wanted to see what they faced here in the sky. The thing hanging mysteriously in the clear air.

As he came nearer the ball became a brightly colored shape of painted fabric. Its strange colors made its outline hard to see; even this close. Hanging under the great ball was a wide wooden platform on which a number of Draks stood. Around the platform more Draks flew. There must be at least a hundred of them.

Ah, this was indeed a new weapon for the Draks. Here they could rest their wings, high in the air. The thing was a hunting camp in the sky. It could hold Draks and extra fighting spears. Yes, there they were, bundles of them, racked there. A dangerous weapon, indeed.

Amarson pulled his flier up and over the top of the ball.

17

How did it stay up in the air. . . and stationary?

There were no engines on the platform. The cloth ball was holding it up. He could see the ropes. A sail like a boat? No, it must be filled with something like smoke. Yes, smoke from a fire lifted straight up in the morning air. Hold the smoke in a bag and it would lift the bag. That must be it.

But no more time. His men were going in to attack the Draks and here came two he could get. He rolled out at the top of his looping climb, checked that his wingman was in position, then tilted his flier over and slid down the sky at them. He loosed off four of his darts as he dove.

Ahiee, they missed. The Draks were moving across his path and he saw his darts smoke by behind them. His wingman fired and they were past, and diving down at the colored ball.

He twisted his head back and saw one of the Draks spin on his wings and throw his spear. The other Drak was falling. Good, his wingman got one of them.

Amarson took his flier down past the platform under the ball. The platform was empty. All of the Draks were in the air. That was bad.

A Drak swooped up in front of him and Amarson triggered his dart launchers. The Drak crumpled in the air. It hadn't even thrown its spear.

Speed was the way to use these dart launchers. No more hovering and letting the Draks come in close. The Rivermen had done that much. *Now, we have a sharp edge to our sword, Draks! Come and feel it!*

Amarson continued on up around the other side of the ball and tilted to his left to see how the others were doing. They were doing badly. The air below him was filled with Draks.

As he watched, four of them hit one of his fliers. They flew right at it and clutched its wings and body. Their stabbing spears flashed in the sun. Amarson saw the pilot swing his knife and then the flier flipped over on its back and was gone.

"Aiiyee! Shrine Rite for one of us. Blood only stains the hands."

Three swiftly moving fliers caught his eye, as they darted through a pack of Draks, and winged up and over to dive back again. Somebody else had learned the trick of speed. Hit and run and let the dart launchers kill. Good men. Quick.

But there were too many Draks. We have to break off. Get out of here. Get away from this flying fort.

Amarson put his flier into a flat dive and unclipped the signal gun beside him. As he flashed through the thick of the melee, he fired the bright, white, recall flares to order his men out and away home. He saw three of the swift fliers peel away and start back, his wing man had separated, and the others still had to fight their way out. The Shrine might have other banners on it before those three got clear.

As he went by the platform again, a group of Draks landed on it, snatched up spears and dove off again. That platform! He'd better do something about that.

He pulled around in a tight turn and held the trigger down as the raft came in front of him. The Draks coming up to rearm died, but the big fat ball still hung there. Amarson pulled up around its curve and climbed above it. Turning harshly, he flew right at the thing and triggered his dart launchers. He saw his darts tear at the cloth of the ball and he kept the trigger down as he closed in. He held it; kept the darts rattling off his wings, until the great colored ball filled the sky. At the last minute, he swerved away, cursing.

The sky exploded!

Amarson's flier was driven down and over on its back by a mighty blast. Amarson had one swirling glimpse of the great bag exploding in a roiling ball of red fire, shot with black, then his flier was tumbling out of the sky. The exploding bag drove a shock-wave across the sky. The flier shook and rolled ahead of it. Control was gone and Amarson waited for the crack of breaking spars and the rip of fabric.

The Rivermen's skill, the power of their gods, or the strength of their materials fought for him. The flier held onto its wings and wavered into a diving slide. A correction on the controls fought the nose out of its wild dive and Amarson turned back to gain altitude.

The flaming wreckage was still falling past his altitude and

19

so were Draks. Some of them were on fire and some were caught in the wreckage, but the swarm of the hunting party was gone. The sky was almost clear.

Amarson pointed the nose of his flier for home and climbed for altitude.

5

Suddenly there was a Drak above him, diving. The flier shuddered with the impact as the Drak landed on the wing above Amarson's head, rolled off and grabbed at the body frame behind him. Amarson jerked his war knife out of its clips and cut at the Drak. There was a shock of pain in his arm and the Drak's head was split open in a spray of blood.

The flier rolled over on its back and the dying Drak fell off, tearing his short spear from Amarson's arm as it fell. The muscles of Amarson's arm jerked with the pain of the wound, and the arm dropped uselessly over his head as the flier flew inverted. The fighting reflex of his claws dug into the knife handle, and it did not drop. He continued the roll, and brought the ship right side up again. The knife, a dead weight in his numb hand, flopped back aboard, almost cutting his leg in the process. Amarson pried his claws loose, and put the blade back in its clips, while the flier carried him up past another group of Draks at full combat power.

None of them followed him. In seconds his speed carried him beyond them, and he was safe.

He pulled the power level back to control his fuel and leveled the flier onto the course for his base. He looked around, but the other fliers were out of sight. The Draks were all going down. He had the sky to himself.

"All the sky I need," he snarled out loud. "I have killed, and the sky is mine!

"Maybe more sky than I'll need," he continued as he checked the fuel weight. It was low. Very low.

He probed his arm carefully, but there was nothing he could do about it here in the air. There was not much bleeding. The fighting reflexes of his body were sealing off the torn veins. Not serious there, but his arm wouldn't work. Well, that would have to keep. The trouble was the fuel weight and getting back. Forget about the arm and start to work on that job.

Amarson settled the flier in a very shallow climb and began the relaxing ritual chant to ease the combat tensions in his body. The flight home must be smooth and controled. His fuel reserve was gone and the weight of fuel left would take all of his skill just to get the flier across the Mud Sea. There would be no room for jerky flying mistakes.

He was planning his flight with a gradual climb to give him as much height as he could get near the end. With height, he could float down the wind for a few more miles when the engine ran out of fuel. That hope, and an engine throttled back to minimum power, was all he could do now. That and wait. Wait, and guide the flier smoothly through the air, to take advantage of every foot of distance he could get out of the fuel weight.

Any thoughts of a landing in the Mud Sea, or engine failure, or combat weakness in the flier's structure, were useless now. The ritual chant drove these worries from his mind and he lapsed smoothly into the flier's trance. He flew on and on, through a sky empty of clouds and Draks.

At last, a portion of his mind that had been counting the miles and time with relentless accuracy, aroused him.

Swiftly he became aware of his surroundings. The flier still flew, the engine still pulsed, and the height indicator showed a good altitude. All was well. The engine still ran, although the mental trigger that had stirred him was the ending of the time allotted for his fuel weight. But the engine still ran, no matter why.

Amarson looked down ahead of him. The red sun was covering the horizon below his wings, almost setting. Behind him the yellow sun was above the horizon again and follow-

21

ing swiftly. It would pass overhead and meet the red sun, just as they both dipped below the horizon. The third passing of the Younger Sun was very swift and ended in the almost instant starless darkness that was the night.

Amarson strained his eyes and made out the low, red shadow of the coast. It was there ahead of him, just on the limit of visibility. It was close, and the engine still ran. The Father Sun still watched over him. He might make the coast. He just might.

The engine sputtered and missed. Amarson glanced quickly at the fuel weight instruments. They showed nothing left. Next to them, the little tube with its fluttering vane still indicated fuel flowing to the engine.

Careless now of his fuel weight, Amarson ran the engine to combat power and pulled up in a steep climb. For a few heartbeats the flier responded, angling quickly up into the sky. Th: n the engine stopped. The fuel weight was gone.

Amarson dropped the nose and began his long drop back to the Mud Sea below him. His job now was to make that fall as long as possible. To make it last until he passed over the shore line. Now his life and honor flew along the narrow edge of a sword. A crash in the jungle on the mainland was a chance at life. A crash on the mud meant a sinking death.

He caressed the flier's controls, gliding it as shallowly as he dared. He had to keep it flying, and that meant speed. A loss of flying speed now could mean a fall of several hundred feet. Altitude must be traded for distance, but smoothly, gently. He began to talk to the flier. He told it how to fly; held it in the air with his fingertips and sang to it. The Rivermen had made a wonderful flier and it balanced through the air without a flaw. He did everything his skill taught him to do to lengthen his glide, but the coastline was still a long way off.

He hit the thermocline, and fought his way through it, with the flier right side up. The rough air gave him a little boost. The heavy air beneath it let him flatten the glide a little. The flier didn't sink so fast now.

Down here in the thick air he could see the wet shiny surface of the Mud Sea. It gleamed crimson in the light of the setting Father Sun. The mud was almost the same color as when he had flown out across it this morning.

Now he could see the shadow of his flier on the sea. The yellow sun was arcing above him on its way to meet with the red sun. The shadow flitted across the mud and gave him a different picture of his height. The instruments told him the figure, but the shadow pictured the true danger. He was very low.

The coast was nearer now. Close, but Amarson, using his flier's shadow as guide, let his eyes follow the path of the flier. With skilled instinct he saw the slanting path through the air ahead of him. Here was the sword edge he envisioned, straight and true, like Riverman metal, with his life balanced on its edge. It pointed to the mud. The end was as certain as a Drak's spear through the heart.

He kept on flying his shallow dive. Holding the flier off the wet mud as long as he could. Death would come when he hit the orange-red patch of sea up ahead, but not sooner. His honor held his life on the sword as long as possible.

The groundsman at sunrise had taken it for granted that his Baron would lead the flight home. What would the old fighter think now, when the flight came home without. . . ?

How many would come back? Amarson had seen one go down. . . and somewhere, he had lost a wingman before he attacked the gas bag. Two gone; no, three. He smiled. He wasn't coming back, either. The Riverman Ambassador would get his weapon evaluation from some other. The seven fliers in the tents would need some new pilots tomorrow.

"The fact that they are men gives them. . . " the old chief had said.

"The fact that *I* am a man lets me lead myself to death," Amarson growled. "Yet I'm going out like any cub, in an orange mud puddle.

"Well, I won't!" he yelled. "The mud is my enemy and the blood stains the hands!"

He began to chant a warrior battle song. His hands turned on the firing switches as he noticed four darts in the launcher racks.

"When I hit the mud I'll fire. The warrior will die in combat and so will the flier."

23

• • •

Suddenly, he stopped talking to himself and sat rigid in the seat. Three times he had seen the orange spot ahead of him, and each time it was closer. Now, as he looked, the yellow sun passed across the Father Sun and the light was all crimson on the sea.

The patch ahead didn't glisten.

"By the Father Sun, it looks dry." He was amazed. In fact he could see a wide strip of odd-colored mud in the slanting light. "The mud must be shallow, and dried out.

"Maybe I can land after all. The wheels won't roll. The mud couldn't be that dry. I'll have to crash, but the flier won't sink. If the mud is dry enough to hold the flier, I can walk on it." Suddenly, the sword edge of death was a little wider. His honor held him on it, facing life again, standing firm with no thought of falling.

In quick jumping thoughts his mind planned the landing. The flier would be gliding, slow, but still too fast. He couldn't trust the wheels to roll. The best he could hope for was that the flier would not flip. If the wheels caught, the flier would flip over, burying him under it.

The flier was on top of the mud patch and the dry section was just ahead. No more time for plans.

He lifted the nose of the flier to slow it down and it fell out of the air. He felt it sink under him. Still too fast; got to kill the forward speed, or die! How?

His eye caught the arrowed points of the darts in the wing launchers.

"*Eeagh!*" A battle cry screamed out of his throat as he snatched at the trigger and fired all the darts.

The launchers gave a racking rattle. The recoil hit the slow-moving flier and stopped it in the ai . It hung nose up, then dropped straight down on its wheels in the mud. There was a ripping crackle and the wheel supports tore away. The body and lower wing slammed into the ground and came to a halt.

Amarson turned off his switches by reflex. There wasn't enough fuel in the flier to start any blaze, but his body was moving in trained reactions. He freed himself from the straps and climbed out on the wing. He crouched there and jerked his fighting knife out of its clips.

Then he froze, as his reason took over. He had been about to run away from the wreck. That led out onto the mud. He stopped himself and didn't move. Out on the mud was death, if the mud wasn't dry.

He looked down at the wing, where it lay on the mud. It wasn't sinking. The mud was dry enough to support the flier. He turned to look out in front of the flier. There was a gleam in the yellow-red light. He saw the pattern of his fired darts sticking in the mud. They were standing upright, just as they had struck. . . and beyond them. . . a pile of solid rock and a point of land rising out of the mud. He laughed harshly. The sword of death had turned and he was standing on the flat of the blade. If the dry mud would hold the darts, it would hold him.

The color of the sky and the mud deepened, suddenly, to a dark red. He looked up in alarm. The Younger Sun had set and the red Father Sun was low on the horizon. In minutes it would be dark. There was no time to lose.

He gripped his knife tightly and stepped off the wing onto the mud. His feet sank into the surface, but it held him. Quickly, he began to walk toward the darts, then he broke into a run. The mud was dry, but not hard. If he walked, his feet sank. If he stood still, it might still suck him down. So he ran. He ran toward the rack and the point of land. The fight with his enemy, the mud, was not over yet.

He bent and plucked four of the darts out of the mud as he passed. These he would take back to the Riverman Ambassador.

Riverman, he thought. *I'll spray your head myself for this day's work; then you can have these darts for a proper trophy, little man.*

The dart launcher was a great killer of Draks, but this last . . . Amarson had used these darts to save his life. He was going to give these darts to the Riverman as a trophy and the ambassador would take them proudly, with much water spray. His honor would let him hang these four life-saving darts in his house. That Riverman was quite a warrior in his own way. As good as the weapons he made.

The red light of the setting sun deepened and darkened as Amarson ran. The mud tugged at this legs and he stumbled and fell. His fighting claws slid out as he pulled himself up and stumbled on.

The red light was now so deep he could not see far. In seconds it would be dark.

He fell again, but this time his hands slammed against rock with a biting pain. Rock! He was on the point! On the land!

The Father Sun set and the perfect black night closed around him. He couldn't see, but he was on land. Free of the Mud Sea. He'd won.

Amarson pulled himself upright and raised his knife in the air. His voice cracked in a victory chant. Then the night's blackness folded around him. . . Blackness, and something else.

Six points of light flickered and danced off there to the left, down the coast. His chant roared in triumphant volume. That could only be a Jungle Patrol. The Draks didn't use lights. They didn't fly at night. It was a Patrol, safety in six men, and they would find him in the morning.

His skin tingled and he felt his thoughts swim away into the night. He was falling unconscious, but his last feeling was the shock of his shoulder and face hitting the hard, rocky ground. The pain was a triumph. He had won his fight. He was on dry land. The Patrol was out there. He had driven his honor up on another sword edge. This time it was the sword of life and this time he would stay on its edge. The darkness would go away when the sun came up.

TWO

Solo Kill

1

Amarson was kneeling in the meadow, waiting for the Draks to attack. The wide sleeves of his ceremonial costume weighed at his arms and shoulders. His eyes and ears were bound by a jeweled helmet. He was all alone—waiting.

The costume was a fake. His chest and torso were bare, the wide sleeves were slit to free his arms, and the helmet would fly off with a flick of his head. The costume was bait, magnifying his solitary position here in the meadow, far from the trees at the jungle's edge.

He clenched his hands to control his nerves and felt his claws run out against the grass. He cleared his lips back away from his teeth to put a fighting grin on his long jaws. The costume was bait, and so was the picture of his unarmed helplessness.

In the sky, high above the edge of the meadow, the three Draks changed their flight from a straight flyway course to a circle. One of them began to spiral down. The trap was set, baited and about to be sprung.

The Drak flapped its long wings and slowed its spiral. The red glow of the rising Father Sun shone from its armor and turned the skin of the heavy-muscled wings purple when they beat in an upstroke. The Drak was being cautious, but it was coming down the sky. Amarson's helpless posture, alone in the meadow, had lured it out of a hunting sweep. Soon the bait would become too inviting, and the Drak would dive down for a solo kill. The slowly beating wings carried the Drak out of Amarson's sight behind his back. He held his position, motionless. The Drak would not attack from back there. The yellow Younger Sun was up in front of Amarson, to his right, almost at the point where it poised in the sky. With both suns low in the morning sky, the Drak would dive out of the light of the yellow sun. Amarson was facing in that direction.

The Drak wheeled back into the helmet's line of sight. The yellow sunlight caught the point of its hunting spear with a flash of brilliance. The Drak was a flying hunter. It flew on its own wings; long, muscled wings of furless skin. It used the spear as a thrusting weapon when it dived.

The spear was one of the weapons Amarson had to face; the spear and the Drak's own fierce beak. The beak was curved and thick for tearing flesh; the hunting spear was one meter of triangular metal blade and a short half-meter shaft. The Draks used both to kill the animals it hunted for food.

Amarson was one of those *animals* the Draks considered food. He ran his claws out again at the thought.

The Rivermen, in their city, and the Valley People, in their safe, crop-filled fields, have forgotten this fear; his thoughts ran quickly. They have been safe too long. By the Ancient Compact we have kept the Drak out on the Jungle Marches with our air and jungle patrols, while they, the town dwellers, have forgotten fear. They should send men out here, so that they could learn to be food again. Then there would be new fliers for my cubs to use—to carry killing into the air, and death to the Draks.

Amarson snarled at the thought. He should be leading his fliers from Base XII against these Draks in the air, not kneeling on the ground in an open meadow. But someone had revived an old ritual and used it against him. Someone who knew that Amarson fostered the old prayers and rituals at his Base.

28

The Drak turned in the yellow sun and began its dive. Amarson started the fighting chant. The rapid guttural cries brought his blood pressure up and quickened his nerve speed, but he held himself still; kneeling in apparent helplessness as the Drak fell toward him.

At the last second, the Drak's wings snapped open, spread wide to brake its dive.

Timed by the flap of the wings, Amarson straightened his legs and jumped straight up at the Drak. His voice yelled the combat cry that mingled with the scream of the Drak.

One hand batted the Drak's tearing beak aside and the other struck at the Drak's throat. His claws ripped and tore.

Amarson threw his weight sideways and down, pulling the Drak over on one wing, pinning the wing and the spear arm beneath him as he jerked the Drak to the ground.

The one free wing beat and whipped across his back as he drove his knees into the Drak's body and crushed it to the meadow. The wing struck him again, and again, then snapped back against the grass and was still.

The Drak was dead.

Amarson's reflexes began to come down from their peak. The helmet was gone, but the costume robe had protected his back. He had hardly felt the wing blows. There was a hot burning pain in his right leg. The spear had hit him! A sense of wet blood came through to him. He started controlling the skin and muscles in his hurt leg to stop the bleeding. The blood on his hands—no pain there. That was Drak blood. Hah! *Blood only stains the hands!*

The Drak was still beneath him. He realized that he was kneeling on its body, holding the beak closed in one hand, while the other hand was at the Drak's throat. The throat was gone, shredded by the fighting sweeps of Amarson's claws.

The Drak was dead.

He felt a movement of bodies near him and reared backward, his right hand arcing to strike.

"Baron!" The Jungle Patrolman yelled once. He took Amarson's blow on a leather-covered forearm with a grunt. He caught the blow precisely, as if he had expected it, then he simply held Amarson's arm, and waited for the fighting passion to pass.

Amarson saw the Patrolman as he started his blow and retracted his claws at once. The blow landed with only an open-wide hand and Amarson's rolling weight behind it. Amarson heard the grunt and gripped the friendly, solid arm tightly as he struggled to control his heartbeat and nerve speed down to normal.

A roar of flier engines filled the meadow and two of Base XII's standby fliers swept over the trees. One slid into a low turn and began to circle the meadow protectively. The second lifted and headed into the yellow sun, climbing vertically on combat power.

"Can you walk, Baron?" the senior Patrolman asked. "He's going up after the other two Draks. The spent darts will start coming down soon."

Amarson threw his head back and caught the gleam of Drak weapons. High in the air, the two Draks had circled to dive out of the sun. They had been unable to break their hunting habit. This time the habit meant death.

The flier was climbing to intercept them before they could dive. There! He was firing his darts, right overhead. . . . "Darts!" Amarson choked, his breath still gasping. He lurched to his feet and began to run. A wild, hot pain cramped his right hip, and his leg gave way after three steps.

A Patrolman was at his side, the senior Patrolman still supported his left arm, and between the two of them they half-carried Amarson to the forest edge without a pause. They had undercut a bank into a command post dugout, and they hurried Amarson into the protective cover. The three other Patrolmen stumbled up, carrying the body of the Drak and dumped it on the ground. They faded away to right and left in the jungle.

The falling darts arrived. Dropping spent from the flier's dart launcher, they covered a wide area on the ground.

The *swak* and *thunk* when they hit the meadow was like rain; then they tore through the leaves and branches above the dugout and bits of forest drifted down. The whole thing lasted

30

less than a hundred heartbeats, and impressed Amarson with its impersonal deadliness.

"That's the end of it," the senior Patrolman announced. "Here come the fliers back."

The two fliers slanted down low across the meadow and the leader blipped his engine.

"Mardon, give him a flare," the senior Patrolman called. "Then check out the meadow."

A flare blazed up out of the trees.

"That tells them you made your kill and are alive, sir." The senior Patrolman turned to Amarson and held out a metal bottle. "Better have a drink. It's Valley *frooge* and not very old, but drink it anyway. My thought is: it's got power. I want to look at your leg." He began untying the panels and skirt of the costume.

"While I'm doing this, you can tell me why my squad is risking their lives protecting a Baron Flight Commander while he plays cub tricks in the jungle. You command Base XII, don't you? Can't you find enough Draks to kill in the air?"

"I crashed my flier in the Mud Sea, last patrol, and walked home. Somebody decided I was *Inhacru*, a Warrior-who-has-lost-his-weapons. Somebody with more knowledge of the ancient rituals than is good for him; or me."

"The Warrior's Code?" the senior Patrolman asked. "My thought is: we were more modern than that. You should find your 'somebody' and tell him to sleep with his claws out."

"I suspect *he* is a Riverman. The orders came from there."

"And there is no honor in killing a Riverman!" the senior Patrolman grinned. "They pay us, by the Compact, to guard their Marches and keep them safe. My thought is: they don't pay for killing Draks one at a time."

"There was support for the Code in our own people, Senior. . ." Amarson drank from the bottle. "Superstitions die hard.

"Base XII was grounded; not allowed to fight, until I had regained my 'battle honor'!"

"Well, you've done that and with a wound to cap it. Nice work, too. I've never seen anyone move so fast. Glad I saw it. My thought is: it's good to know you can kill a Drak with your claws if it gets close. Fine thing to know.

"I'm going to have to cut this uniform.

"Not much blood, it can't be too bad. Ah, no, just a clean graze on the inside leg muscle. Any pain?"

"Not much, " Amarson gasped. The two swallows of *frooge* made speaking difficult. *Aaargh*, it was hard to breathe.

"My leg. . . just wouldn't work. . . folded up.

"Aiyha! I can feel your fingers, Senior. If you want to cut the leg open use a knife, not your thumb. Or let me finish this bottle, and you can use a dull rock. Power, aha!"

"No need, Baron." The senior Patrolman laughed and took back his bottle. "You have the bleeding stopped. The Drak lance must have gone between your legs. The cut is small and clean. Your fold up was shock, my thought is, and drop out of battle tension. It's no big thing.

"Try moving the leg."

Patrolman Mardon stuck his head in the dugout.

"The meadow is clear," he said. "Lots of *frooge* tonight. We each got a double handful of darts." He held up a bundle of the small metal missiles from the flier's launcher. "A real good day. How is the Baron?"

"Bring in your aid kit: leg wound," the senior Patrolman ordered.

The Patrolman slid into the command post and looked at Amarson's leg. 'Hm-m-m," he said, professionally. He shoved the bundle of darts into his kit with one hand, and brought out a field dressing with the other.

"A real hero's wound, sir." He began to apply the bandage. "No blood, no call for surgeons, and you'll be able to limp with honor and dignity. Best of all the only time you can show such a wound is in bed with a woman.

"And a woman who will want to look at a wound there. . . . Why she will. . . . Ahh, me, she certainly will."

"That's where the hero part comes in, obviously," Amarson joined the banter. The *frooge* was warming his tongue.

"You talk too much, Mardon," the senior Patrolman said. "Snap it up, or I'll give *you* a wound."

"All done. Ready to move. Do you want trophies, Baron? Head or wings?" Mardon pulled a wicked skinning knife.

"Neither, Patrolman." Amarson's voice became curt. "We take the whole body.

"The Riverman ambassador has requested a fresh-killed Drak brought to him. I don't know what he wants it for, but he gets this one."

"Calm down, Mardon," the senior Patrolman said. "You've got enough darts to keep you drunk for a week. Don't be greedy. Get out there and put some poles under that Drak so we can carry it fast and quietly. We go as soon as the Baron wants to walk."

"You trade darts for liquor?" Amarson stood up, half-crouched in the dugout. His leg seemed to want to work.

"That weapon is brand-new, not more than ten fliers carry the launchers. How could a trade develop so fast? What do the Valley People want with launcher darts?"

"Your *pilots* buy them back, Baron. They say it brings them good luck. Maybe. My thought is: that any chance of having your fliers run a pack fight over a ground patrol, and anybody not getting hit by the spent darts, or attacked by Draks; then finding a bitty dart. . . . Well, my thought is: the luck is all on our side."

"All ready, Senior," Mardon reported promptly. "The patrol is already formed."

"We should go, Baron." The senior Patrolman backed out of the dugout. "We are still ten kilometers outside our perimeter, and this is a Drak flyway."

"I can walk, Senior." Amarson came out of the dugout and demonstrated, to himself as much as to the patrol.

"Mardon, out and front!" the senior Patrolman ordered. "Let's move that Drak out of here!"

Mardon moved past Amarson and handed him the short Drak lance. The jungle patrol closed up around Amarson and he recognized that he was still being protected. Only the bright grin and the shine in Mardon's eyes when he passed the spear, told the change in the character of the protection.

33

Mardon had remembered the reason for the ritual killing in the meadow. Mardon had closed the ritual and given him back his honor and a weapon. A warrior's weapon, captured by killing.

Amarson carried his honor and followed the patrol into the jungle.

2

The next morning, Amarson's Second Commander woke him.

"Draks, Baron!" he said, shaking the bed. "Wake up! Draks!"

The words snapped Amarson up out of bed, standing. Then he realized the sound of the alarm bell was missing and sat back down on the bed. His eye caught the empty bottle of *frooge* on the floor. He kicked it sourly and growled away the sickness in his head and mouth.

"*Aarrgh!* That's a dangerous way to wake me, Mitch."

"I had to, Baron. I meant it. The Draks are here. A giant mating swarm. Over the field and as far south as we can see. I've canceled all regular operations. We've forted up. SOP."

"What!" Amarson was awake, now. He struggled into his uniform and headed for the outside door.

"Not that way!" Mitch stopped him. "The Draks will strike at anything moving on the ground. Come inside, to the ops. room. You can see across the field from there."

"Go! I'm right behind you. Run!"

The two went out the corridor from Amarson's quarters and up the stairs to the windowed operations office. Inside the operations room, Amarson slowed to a walk and began to put on his shirt absently. His eyes were focused out the window.

"They came in just as the Father Sun rose," Mitch said. "The Chief Groundsman held the morning patrol. He got two fliers in the big hangar and shut up the base. Damn good man. But he's seen that before, I expect."

"That" was the sky over Base XII. It, the sky, was filled with Draks, hundreds of them. Amarson literally couldn't see across the field. They were not screaming, fighting Draks, the kind he was used to seeing. These moved slowly through the air, barely flapping their wings to gain height. They drifted and glided into wide spiral patterns and flew around and around.

Suddenly, with no reason, a single Drak would fold its wings and strike at the ground, recover, and beat clumsily back up to where it could join a spiral again.

The Draks, all of them, moved sightlessly, trance-like, through the air; not seeming to avoid one another, but never touching.

"Both males and females," Mitch said. "I've only seen them swarm like this twice before myself—and that was way south, on the mountain shoulder. . . but never so many."

"How many?"

"No way to guess. Thousands, at least," Mitch said. He handed his baron a warm drink. "Breakfast behind you, when you want it, Baron. I launched one combat flier from inside the big hangar—catapult. He had orders to scout the edge of the swarm and see how big it is. Aahh! It was weird to watch him fly through that—" He pointed outside. "None of them touched him, or noticed him. They just got out of his way."

"As long as he's in the air with them," Amarson said nodding. "Be absolutely sure you brief anyone else who flies. Don't fire on them. If they think they are menaced they will mob the flier. They have females to protect and there are just too many. Live and let live while the swarm lasts, even if we don't like the idea."

"Of course, anything else is suicide," Mitch agreed.

"The groundsmen are working with a covered truck to get ropes on the fliers out by the tents and pull them over to the big hangar. We can launch them two at a time, from there,

35

but I can't crowd the hangar floor."

"Right. That's our only landing field. Better get the crash crews doubled up. If anybody misses a landing, they'll have to clear away fast."

"Understand." Mitch nodded. "We've already taken one flier in."

"What? Who?"

"A courier. He came in from Base III. We flagged him into the hangar before he could make the mistake of landing and trying to taxi. He made a good landing, but he's got the shakes. Too many Draks.

"He brought in a written order for you. You are ordered to Riverton: conference with Ambassador Theiu."

Amarson picked up the order form Mitch indicated, and read it.

"New weapons, heh? Most personal contact; and urgent. Do you suppose they knew about that. . .?" he waved at the window.

"I don't see how," Mitch said. "I've had your flier spotted on the catapult. Do you want it called down?"

"No. I'll go. You aren't in any danger here. All those Draks make you want to climb a tree, but they aren't dangerous if you take proper precautions.

"I'd double up the scout patrol, though, and keep everybody under cover. Don't let them shoot, just keep them out of sight."

"Sightseers *will* be a headache!"

"They'll get killed if a Drak sees them," Amarson growled. "They do strike at the ground while they are swarming; they're not all that safe.

"This spiraling should go on all day, maybe into the night. . . and they will be back tomorrow. Two days, then they will all go to ground to mate. *That* they will do in the hills— higher up.

"Two days. I'll be back before that."

3

The flight to Riverton was not long, but at the end of it he had to come down and fly in among the circling Draks again. It was an eerie feeling to lose height into that mass of deadly wings; to have a full armed hunter match course and height with him; to fly wingtip to flapping wingtip with a Drak that was not screaming to kill.

They ignored him as they had done when he climbed away from Base XII. They flew lazily out of his path and ignored him.

But, he was conscious of the killing power of those beaks and weapons. The wound in his leg tightened and ached whenever the sunlight glinted from one of the hunting spears.

Amarson eased his grip on the controls and flew lower across Riverton. Some of the streets he could see below had covered walkways. A hasty plank structure had been thrown up on the waterspray system the Rivermen used for comfort in their town. How? Who? A Drak swarm like this was new to Riverton. They couldn't have seen one—since before the Ancient Compact. . . . Oh, of course, Jungle Patrolmen. On duty in Riverton, they would have spread the word. . . organized. . . .

He circled the converted rivership yard that Theiu called his *weapons factory*, to find it deserted. The two buildings and the open yard where the fliers were built were closed and locked. They had no protective cover for the workers. With the Draks swarming, the factory had to be shut down.

A flag waved at him from the big hangar, signaling him into land. It was the wrong sort of signal, but the Rivermen's intent was clear. The doors of the hangar began to slide open and the flag-waver signaled frantically.

Amarson threaded his way around a spiraling formation of Draks and dropped down to line up with the hangar. He took his flier down steeply, rolled it out and held the nose high to kill his speed. He flew with one hand, the other he held near his fighting knife. The Draks were leaving him alone in the air, but as he tried to land, one of them might rush him. If he was attacked, his knife was his only weapon, this close to the ground.

The ground came up to meet him. He held the flier off the field until just before he got to the big hangar doors. He touched down right in front of the doors and flashed inside; completing his landing roll down the center of the long hangar.

As he went by the door threshold, he caught a glimpse of two Jungle Patrolmen manning a dart-throwing installation. They were guarding the door in case a Drak followed him into the hangar. Theiu was well organized.

Amarson completed his landing, still inside the hangar. He had managed to slow his flight enough in the air before touchdown, so that his rollout was short. He cut off his engine and heard the big hangar doors slide shut behind him.

A Riverman fire patrol came up with parking blocks. They explained that the shutdown was to let everybody work the riverfish harvest, and not due to the Drak swarm.

"We were expecting you, Baron," the leader said. "Ambassador Theiu left a direction plaque to his hunting boat at the docks. We will look after your flier."

Amarson took the hand-size square of wood and checked the map printed on it. The factory was not far from the river, he'd seen that from the air, so the directions were brief and simple. Amarson allowed himself to be conducted to the factory gate and set off to the docks. The walk took only a few minutes. The direction plaque kept him on covered walkways all the way, so he was in no danger. The Draks were only black shadows gliding on the street and buildings.

The fire leader had said that Theiu was down at the docks with the fishing fleet, but he hadn't said anything about the ceremony.

Fifty or sixty boats crowded the finger piers under the

spreading dock sheds. The dock area had been roofed against Drak hunting parties early in the post-Compact period and the fishing docks were the safest place in Riverton during this swarm. To Amarson's eyes it seemed that all of Riverton was here, under the shed.

As he watched, four of the hunting boats left the tip of the finger piers and slid out into the water. They sank as they went out, so that they were submerged by the time they cleared the protective roof. Another group of five boats was cast loose, with much singing, chanting and movement, and maneuvered slowly toward the deeper water.

Amarson watched them submerge and wondered how he was going to find Theiu in all this. He was not used to seeing Rivermen, didn't see enough of them, to be able to pick Theiu out of a crowd.

He went over to the nearest boat, where a Riverman was sitting on the low deck with his feet in the water.

"I am looking for Theiu, the Ambassador to the Jungle Marchlands," he called. "Do you know where I can find him?"

"Theiu? Ah, yes." The Riverman was a little startled by Amarson's size. He picked up a handful of water and poured it over his head, nervously. "Yes, I know him. His boat is just down the float. Three fingers that way." He pointed.

"Thank you," Amarson said. "Will these floats hold my weight? I would not want to damage the dock."

"They will hold you. We bring our fish cargo up on them."

Amarson nodded and went down onto the float and along to the finger piers. The floats had a movement of their own under his feet and he was a little uncomfortable. He evidently made the Rivermen uneasy too, for they moved away from him and quickly left any dock float he was standing on.

Theiu saw him coming and saved him the need of further questions by jumping off the deck of a boat and coming down the finger to meet him.

"Baron Amarson," the Riverman called. "This way. Come see my boat. The dock out here is private. The townspeople will leave you alone, out here."

39

Theiu's words were strange. Amarson turned back to look at the crowd. In his anxiety over the swaying dock, he had missed the look on their faces; missed the reason they had avoided him. They were angry. His fighting instincts now felt the hate and anger; smelled the fear in the crowd. The hair on his head stiffened and his ears erected alertly.

"This way. This way," Theiu said. "You got here just in time."

Amarson followed the Riverman down the dock float. With an effort, he retracted his claws and forced himself to relax. He deliberately sat on a convenient box, in full sight of the crowd. He made no attempt to board the boat.

The boat was long enough, sixty meters or so, and wide enough to support his weight, but the curved deck was only inches above the water. The boat was visibly rocking in the harbor chop, so Amarson had no intention of trusting it as a fighting base. Instead he sat balanced on the dock and, in an exaggerated fashion, for the benefit of the crowd, admired the boat from a distance.

Like all Riverman machines, it was simple and uncluttered in its design. A small curved cabin and covered deck were mounted aft, and the whole forward deck was taken up with six hunting sleds. These were clamped into depressions in the deck and Amarson noted the familiar shapes of dart launchers under their weather covers. These were the water weapons the Rivermen used in their fish hunting.

"You recognize the weapons, Baron?" the Riverman said. "They are basically the same as the ones on your fliers, except these do not operate by pressurized air as yours do. These are water weapons and we use pressurized water to work the mechanisms. They are all completely water-proofed, of course. We have some massive corrosion problems here in the river-delta waters. The water is filled with mineral salts of every kind. Any material we use on our boats has to be tested extensively."

"I recognize them," Amarson said. "But I was surprised at the size. I would have thought they would be bigger. Don't you need more force to propel the darts through the water?"

"Actually, it's about even, Baron. Your flier's mounted

40

launchers were designed for lightness, of course, so they are smaller in that respect, but the speed at which your fliers move through the air dictates the propelling force behind the darts. My designers tell me the air is very much like water at these speeds. Then, too, we are compressing and accumulating water for the charging mechanisms. We can work with much higher pressures. When we went to the air system in the flier units some of the components had to be made bigger for safety. Storing really high-pressure air is very dangerous, you know.

"As you can see, the size of the two launchers came out amazingly close. Once we had developed a dart launcher small enough to be handled by one man on a hunting sled, the task of converting it to your airborne fliers was not difficult." The little Riverman sprayed his head with water.

"Do they kill riverfish as well as mine kill Draks?" Amarson asked.

"Oh, yes. They are quite lethal up to fifty meters. We can't see much further than that underwater, so they are perfect. Your air launchers are actually more brutal in shocking power, Baron. We were quite amazed at your report of tearing up a Drak hunting platform—on your first combat patrol—with them. We had never test-fired them against solid targets. The impact energy is very high. Our ordinancemen were breaking up boxes for days after your report came in. They tell me, at two hundred meters, a dart will penetrate four inches of ship timber. Amazing! They must kill a Drak instantly, from shock."

"They do that. My cubs are out hunting whenever they can get a launcher-equipped flier off the ground. The groundsmen have to steal the control levers in order to service the engines properly. We need more fliers fitted with them.

"But that is what you called me down here for, isn't it? You said, last week, you might have new weapons. New fliers?"

"Not out here, Baron." The Riverman turned his head and looked up the dock. He worked his water spray, nervously. "A bit later, please. We are going to have company in a

41

moment, and there are people in Riverton who do not believe in new weapons.

"In fact, they are marshaling much political force to stop me arming you with dart launchers."

"What! They must be mad!" Amarson was stunned. "Theiu, that must not happen. Why, for the first time, we can fly out and kill Draks when and where *we* want to; without waiting until they go hunting. We *must* stay aggressive, Theiu! It is the only way!" He stopped and glanced up at the dock roof, thinking of the Drak swarm, that he could neither control nor attack.

"Yes, I know," Theiu said. "They swarm at a bad time. We are getting our boats away and underwater as fast as they can dive here in the harbor, but we have lost lives. The big boats cannot go deep until they clear the channel." Theiu sighed.

"They are coming, now," he said, looking up the dock. "Say nothing, I ask you. Please, Baron. Control yourself. Be patient until after the ceremony. We will have our meeting then, I promise you. There is another person I want you to meet. . . ."

Amarson looked up the dock. A religious procession was coming rapidly down the float ramp. The faction that Theiu was talking about must be religious. Then the arguments against new weapons would be emotional, not practical. Let Theiu handle his own negotiations on that level. . . .

"Very well, Ambassador," Amarson agreed. "I will be good."

The little Riverman sprayed himself with water.

"Good. Just until after the ceremony, you understand."

The procession was headed at Theiu's boat. The priest leading the group was angry. At least there was anger in his walk and the way he carried his hands. The rest of the group seemed peaceful, if a little bit harried. They were chanting a prayer of good hunting for the riverboats, but they had chanted it too many times this morning. The rhythm was hurried and off count.

The priest came down the float ramp and stopped to stare up at Amarson. He was fat for a Riverman, and the robes he

42

wore made him look square. His robe was jeweled with an ornate design of the yellow Younger Sun on the left and the red Father Sun on the right side. The two designs overlapped on the front of the robe to symbolize the mid-passage rites.

A young assistant hurried into position and sprayed the priest with water. Another brought up a large orrery made of jeweled metal and mounted on a pole so it could be carried above the crowd. The orrery pole was grounded with a ritual thump and flourish and the mechanism of the symbolic two suns began to rotate past the jeweled disk of The World.

The priest did nothing until these symbols were in place, then he glanced back at a group of four men standing behind the singers. They wore solid-color robes: red of the Father, yellow of the Younger, black of Night and the motley of The World. Amarson saw anger and fear on their faces. These, then, would be part of the anti-weapon faction: elders of the priest's church, to judge by their robes of ceremony.

The priest turned back to Amarson again. A flash of anger showed in his eyes and faded quickly. Amarson had a twinge of sympathy for the man. The priest was being pushed into something by the elders. . . .

"Your badge of rank and your presence here with Theiu tell me that you are the Baron who attacks Draks." He paused, was sprayed with water, then went on in a loud voice: "My people speak to you, Baron. They say you are not welcome here. They say you provoke the Draks into flying. . . . Provoke them by your senseless killing. Draks fly over our rivercity. Our people are being killed. All because you attack the Draks.

"My people cry against you, Baron!"

"The Jungle People of the border Marches are killed by the Draks, too," Amarson said. He held his voice tight. "Killing Draks is my profession, Priest. Your rivercity pays for my skill against the Draks. The Valley grainfood; the Rivercity factory and riverfish; a fair share of food and craft: all pay for the killing skill of our jungle patrols and my cubs in the air.

"Stay with your religious ceremonies, my friend. The Jungle People will guard the Marches in their own way, according to the Ancient Compact, as they have done since

43

the aging of the Father Sun began to turn our seas to mud.

"In any case, let us have peace between us," Amarson forced his voice to calm tones. "I'm sure this is a peaceful rite you celebrate."

"This is a food-gathering ceremony!" The four elders called, their phrases coming one behind the other, hissing with anger.

"You are not welcome!"

"Do we need a border beast. . .?"

". . . . To teach us how to kill the riverfish for our children's bellies?"

I can teach you fools! Amarson's anger flared. He was irritated by the insecurity of the dock and startled by the verbal attack. "I have seen the Draks kill and prepare Rivermen for their food supplies. . . to fill the bellies of *their* children. I can teach killing. I am well-qualified." His claws ran out. "Who will be my first student?" he growled.

"There will be no students in Riverton!" the priest said. He spoke to Amarson, but he was facing the four Rivermen, glaring his displeasure at them. "My people have spoken out in ceremony, despite their promise to me. You have heard the words of my people, Baron. Listen; do not teach.

"If you are proud of killirg, Baron. . . proud of being paid to kill Draks, then go and kill Draks. Do not spend your time walking in our city. . . ."

"Holiness," Theiu interrupted, "will you come aboard my boat?" He shoved himself between Amarson and the priest so as to maneuver the priest into facing the boat. "We have new barrier nets this season. Will you come aboard and sanctify them, Holiness?"

The priest looked down at the boat. One of his staff quickly handed him a water sprayer on a ceremonial ribbon and set it swinging. The priest began to chant the required prayers. The ceremonial group closed in around him and took up the chorus of the chant.

Amarson heard the anger leave the priest's voice as the professional tones took over. The priest worked the water sprayer and began spraying the boat, then stepped aboard and went aft to the cabin, preceded by a sanctifying mist of water.

44

Amarson's own control began to dampen his quick anger. There was no reason to sustain it and it drained from him quickly, to be replaced by amusement. He was amused at the four Rivermen who were still standing, mutely antagonistic, behind the chanting group. Their anger was so futile; the swarming Draks overhead made it futile. Like it or not, the Compact between the Rivermen and the Jungle People would stand. The Draks were a constant menace and killing them was a political and military decision. Religious emotions meant little to a hunting Drak; killing Draks was all that mattered.

The sanctifying sprays of water squirting from the cabin ports and openings seemed to indicate that the priest was turning *his* emotions into a rainstorm. Rivermen always had to get things wet.

Last month, when Theiu had visited Base XII to watch Amarson fly the new dart launchers in combat, the Riverman had sprayed himself every minute or so. That had been Amarson's first close experience with the Rivermen's psychological need for a wet skin. He had recognized the need and tolerated it. He had never considered the philosophy of advancing that need to a religious ritual—and one covering a superstitious need for luck in hunting, at that—until today.

Even as he smiled tolerantly at the sanctifying of the nets, a picture rose in his mind of his own combat flights; and himself, kneeling in the red light of the rising Father Sun to hold his hands and claws into the blood-red sunlight.

"By the holy suns! It's the same thing," he muttered.

"*The blood only stains the hands!* We are all slaves to the old rituals, no matter how modern we get." He shook his head from side to side. These Rivermen became more interesting as he came to know them.

The ritual on Theiu's boat came to an end. The chanting stopped.

Amarson put his hands behind his back and prepared himself to be peaceful and absorb any future insults. Unless he held himself in check, these religious Rivermen could goad him into a killing fight. Amarson had no delusions about what would happen if he killed a priest, here in Riverton, but aside from that, he really had no reason or desire to test the courage of the short, fat Rivermen. Least of all because four richly-clad fools had chivvied him into striking. The priest was brave enough. Considering the differences in size, and weight, and Amarson's claws, the priest had already shown his courage.

Courage, heh! Amarson said to himself. *I won't fault a Riverman there. I wonder how many of my high-flying hero cubs could get on a hunting sled and go diving deep in the water for a riverfish.*

I wouldn't want to! The thought of groping around in the murky river for a riverfish made his muscles tighten. These fish—teeth, tail and size—were as deadly in the water as the Draks were in the air. The riverfish actually out-weighed the Rivermen, kilo for kilo, and the need for the dart launchers was obvious. The Rivermen had no natural weapons either—Amarson'. claws twitched out and back in—just a habit of courage. That they did have. Rivermen had been eating riverfish for a long time.

The priest came back on the dock and looked at Amarson. He gave his sprayer a sudden movement and sprayed Amarson with water.

Amarson's ears flattened and his eyes blinked closed, but he kept his fingers locked behind his back. He bowed.

The priest turned and walked toward his retinue. He handed the sprayer to the assistant and began to take off his robes. He beckoned and two of the chanters came forward to help him, folding the robes reverently for carrying.

"The ceremony is over. Return to the temple!" the priest ordered. "I will walk alone for a while before my prayers. Go!"

The procession left, moving to its own rhythm and taking the four belligerent Rivermen with it as unwilling leaders.

Amarson felt the float rock under his feet and looked up. The riverboat was already pulling away from the dock, its crew moving purposefully around the hunting sleds on the bow. Theiu was standing on the float watching Amarson and the priest.

"No, I'm not going, yet, Theiu," the priest said, unnecessarily. "Let the boat get a little further out in the stream and then I want to talk to Baron Amarson."

They watched the boat slide under the water as it left the covered dock. A Drak screamed and broke his dive just above the water. Two dartbows twanged from the sinking cabin, but there was no damage; either way. The Drak missed his kill, too.

"Theiu will take you presently to look at a new weapon, and meet the man who designed it," the priest said abruptly. "He will tell you what you want to know, then. . . ."

"Why did the two of you want my Drak?" Amarson asked, trying for a shock reaction.

"Heh?" Theiu turned to look at him. The change of subject was unexpected, but it evidently meant something to the Riverman. "Yes, I'll tell you about that," he said. "The Drak is a most important part." He sprayed himself. "Most important." He glanced at the priest.

"I agree," the priest said. "But save the telling for later, my Theiu.

"For now. . . .

"Baron Amarson, I am Dell Paudre, Priest of Riverton. . . ." He paused. "I am a man who must say things, in public, before certain people, that I would not say in private—nor believe. The compact is as real to me, your job of killing Draks as vital, as. . . my prayers—or the swarming, black-winged evil over our city. They are things real beyond doubt.

"Those four who challenged you are leaders in my church. I am its priest, but they govern and, to an extent, they govern me. . . What I say. . . . What I said to you."

"*Blood only stains the hands,*" Amarson said. The priest was trying to apologize. Amarson relieved him of the strain.

"The old rituals are very useful," the priest said. "Thank you." He reached for Theiu's sprayer and wet his head and eyes.

"Now we can leave here," he announced. "Walk with us, Baron. Down to the end of the docks."

They walked in silence for a while, Theiu bringing up the rear.

"Baron Amarson," the priest said, again opening the

conversation abruptly. "This morning you risked your life because of a sense of honor. You call it *Warrior's Code,* I believe. Would you risk your life again, against the Draks, if the possibility existed that there would be no *honor* in the mission?"

"A mission to kill Draks?"

"Yes, that I can promise, although not killing them in the way you have been killing them."

"Priest Paudre, killing Draks is my job. There is no *Code* attached to the task. I do it wherever, and however, I can. The Warrior's Code does not apply to Draks. Tell me how you want them killed—forget such thoughts as honor and code."

"How do I want them killed? Secretly, Baron, without the knowledge of any of those four; especially their leader, the one in red—Domne."

"Is that his name? Well, agreed, and easily. Keeping secrets from that one comes without effort."

"Don't underestimate him. He studies the old rituals and has ambitions of becoming Riverton's Priest in my place. He *must not* know. None of them must know. That means that Theiu and I must hide our plans from half of Riverton, too."

"The pressure to stop arming my fliers comes from this Domne?"

"Yes. He also had the orders sent that resulted in your ritual kill yesterday. So you see, he has power."

"Aargh!" Amarson showed his teeth. "And he still picked a fight with me just a while ago. He is braver than I would have believed; shouting from the safety of a crowd. Still, he may have heard our Jungle saying; *There is no honor in killing a Riverman.*"

"It wasn't bravery. Domne believes he is powerful enough to direct the fighting on the Marches. It was power he was displaying on the dock; not bravery."

"Perhaps." Amarson smiled. "However, the next time you see him, tell him I said, *Sleep with your claws out*. If he knows the old rituals, he will know the meaning of that."

"I will tell him," Theiu said. He sprayed his head again. "But if you agree to this mission, I plan to spend most of my

48

time avoiding Domne, officially, privately, and, if possible, religiously."

"There, I can help a great deal," Paudre said, laughing. "Our riverfish season is a time of long ritual and many prayers, for me. I can and will keep Domne by my side through most of the ceremony. That *I* can do, willingly.

"But we are here, at the mole, and I must leave you, Baron. As much as I may want to, I cannot come with you. As Riverton's Priest I cannot be publicly connected with the new weapons. Not publicly. As I said, Baron, Domne governs my church. Perhaps later. . . ."

The priest looked at Amarson for a moment, as if he wanted to say more, then he looked at Theiu and nodded.

"Baron," he said. "Thank you for accepting my mission on faith. Theiu will tell you more—brief you, is the term, I believe—on the new weapons. We will meet later, perhaps, but for now, good-bye. Good luck."

He turned quickly and walked away.

"Let's hurry a little, Baron," Theiu said. "The Patrolmen are waiting and I want to cross the mole as soon as possible."

4

Their walk had brought them to the end of a long mole jutting out into the river. The mole was not covered and three Jungle Patrolmen were setting up one of Theiu's dart throwers on a high post mount. The pressure bottles and charging motors for the firing system were strapped neatly on a small two-wheel truck.

At the other end of the mole was a square block of buildings, dominated by a squat, round tower. The cluster of stone was an island in the river, except for the heavy stones of the

49

mole. They, the stones, were not natural. They had been placed there by the Rivermen and they looked newly cut. The mole was not very old.

It was also not covered; exposed to the Draks.

From the presence of the dart thrower crew, Amarson judged the next plan of Theiu's was a run along the mole under the covering fire of the Patrolmen.

He stepped near the edge of the dock roof to look at the sky—judge the Drak swarm.

The senior Patrolman took two steps to his side and put a fighting knife in his hand. Amarson took the knife and stepped clear of the roof.

The sky above the mole was clear. The main Drak swarm was behind them, over the city, in three high, spiraling flights.

"Clear, except for some isolated Draks on the fringe," Amarson reported. "The weapons and the man you want me to see are out there?" He looked at the tower.

"Yes," Theiu said. "Be patient with me a little longer, please."

"Doesn't Domne like him, either?" Amarson wanted to know. "That looks like a prison."

"No, it's not a prison," Thieu managed to laugh. "The man we are going to see likes privacy. Also he sometimes has explosions and makes vile smells in the night. His neighbors in Riverton were delighted to help him build his island.

"Senior, when you are ready, we will run."

"Ready now," the Patrolman said. "Baron, here is a dartbow. I'll yell if anything gets past us on your back. Keep the knife."

"I won't even look around," Amarson said. He took the bow. "The trophies will be all yours." He slid his claws out and felt his stomach tighten.

"Stand by." The senior Patrolman exposed himself to check the sky and then snapped: "Go!"

Theiu started off across the mole. Amarson matched his run and checked the sky above and ahead of them.

They neared a barred gate; a Drak hunting scream broke out in the air behind them. The clatter of the dart launcher cut

50

it off. Amarson rushed Theiu through the gate, across an empty courtyard and through the heavy, wooden door of the tower.

At the door, Amarson turned and looked back through the gate. The Drak—knocked out of the sky by the launcher crew—had fallen on the mole. The senior Patrolman already had a man out collecting darts and the head and wings.

Amarson returned the senior Patrolman's wave. They were good with that dart launcher. Amarson's leg and stomach muscles began to relax. His claws disappeared. He turned and closed the door. It moved on well-oiled hinges. The gate had opened smoothly, too. The privacy of the tower's owner was evidently maintained by some other means than locks and gates.

Inside the doorway, Amarson found himself in the ground floor room of the tower. The room was largely empty; seeming to serve as an entry hall for the rest of the buildings. The stairway to the rest of the tower, above, circled the right wall to a wooden balcony.

The only article of decoration, or furniture, was a large orrery in the center of the hall. It was larger than a man, about twenty meters tall and strangely designed. The proportions of The World and the two suns were all wrong—and so were the movements.

Theiu was not going any further. He stood waiting for someone, spraying himself and looking at the orrery. It was the only thing to look at, so Amarson watched it, too. His eyes followed the arms and gears of the movement and he realized the the only orrerys he was familiar with were all religious symbols, luck charms, altars. His contact with the priest this morning had made him sensitive to religious symbols. This orrery was different.

Of course! This one must be a scientific instrument, scaled accurately, to be used in time-keeping and sun predictions.

The Rivermen would be able to make such a thing. . . and this man—the owner of the tower—must be a major scientist among them, to need such a large orrery. If size meant accuracy; this was a precision tool.

Now, he was definitely curious about the different size and

51

motion relations he was watching. The World was small, barely large enough to contain the gears that made it turn as it circled the Father Sun. The yellow gem of the Younger Sun was set in the matrix of a looped track about the shape of Amarson's thumb, but wider at one end. The wide end was toward the disk of the Father Sun and the small end pointed at The World, but was separated from it by a space as wide as Amarson's hand. The yellow sun gem moved in and out along this looped track. As it did so, the mechanism of the orrery caused the small end of the loop track to move in a path around the spinning World.

The center representation of the Father Sun, was a dull red disk, not a ball at all, and the distance between the Father Sun and the system of The World and the Younger Sun was what made the orrery so big. Well, that was explainable. You could go outside and see that the Father Sun was *big*. It covered half the horizon when it rose.

Amarson went back to watching the yellow sun move around The World, until the complex movement made him a little dizzy.

"The movements are too complicated for anyone to understand," a deep voice said. "That is why we make charts and tables for the course plotters."

Amarson turned to see a tall Riverman standing in the archway at the back of the hall. He came forward slowly, without the usual darting appearance of a Riverman's walk. He was dressed in a common coverall and was wearing a dark cape with a cowl. His face was long and lined with either age or the effects of illness. The large brown eyes, and the webbed hand he raised in greeting marked him as a Riverman, but he was a full head and shoulder taller than Theiu. His height, thinness and the slowness of his movements gave him a massive air of dignity.

"We who watch and weigh the movements of the two suns," he said, "spend long hours marking their movements into diagrams and columns of figures so that our technicians can devise machines to guide the hunting boats on the river, and your fliers in the air. We spend long watching hours. Even so, we still do not know why there is a period of darkness in the rhythm of the Father Sun.

"But I am a bad host." He turned to Theiu. "One of the things I do know is why you are here, and my reason tells me who you are, but. . . . Introductions are a social convention. Ambassador Theiu, will you be social?"

"Certainly," Theiu sprayed his face and spoke formally. "Scientist Lewyll, may I present Flight Commander Leon Amarson, Baron Rufus, Comanding Flight Base XII. Baron Amarson, Scientist Lewyll is the man I have brought you to see. He has developed the new weapon."

"Scientist Lewyll," Amarson bowed to acknowledge the introduction.

"Welcome to my tower, Baron," Lewyll's voice relaxed into a deep whisper. "What you have come to see is in the room above us. I have just been confirming my experiments in the lower chamber. I won't ask you down there. I have butchered the body of your Drak and several riverfish. It is not a pleasant-smelling place."

"My Drak?"

"Please follow me." Lewyll started up the stairs. The whispery quality of his voice was evidently normal, not any attempt at secrecy. "Yes, Baron. The Drak you killed yesterday in your ritual combat. Delivery was prompt. I have had a standing request for a new-killed Drak for some time. Theiu has told you of it. This one was brought in most quickly. Your senior Patrolman was most helpful.

"Tell me, Baron, why are you so dedicated to Drak killing that you risk your life in a ritual?" The scientist didn't wait for an answer, but went on up the stairs.

Amarson followed and found himself shepherded into a room that the scientist used for the chemical laboratory. Amarson didn't recognize the equipment, but his nose told him the purpose of the room. He shut off his sense of smell to protect his stomach.

One thing in the room was familiar to him, however. A large-scale combat map covered one wall. He walked directly to it and looked at the codings marked on it. The arc of protective flier bases; the colored paths of the main Drak hunting parties—strike corridors down which the Draks flew to kill the Valley People; yesterday's combat strikes, the details were all there.

"This map is as accurate as mine at Base XII," he said. "Not many Rivermen know so much about our fight against the Draks."

"One of your liaison types comes over every afternoon," Lewyll said. "He provides me with data and some very good recruiting speeches."

"Recruiting?"

"He tells me how wonderful the war is, now that we have begun to attack and kill Draks."

"He is a fool!"

"The Baron does not like to call Drak-fighting a war, Scientist," Theiu put in as explanation.

"Oh? Then what is your dedication, Baron, if not war with the Draks? The senior Patrolman who delivered your Drak kill was pretty basic about *his* business of killing."

"And so am I," Amarson gestured at the map. "All that these pretty pictures show is a series of pack fights. Oh, we're good at it. Dedicated! We still fly rocket fire against the Drak jungle camps, when the ground patrols find them, and your new launchers, Theiu, are giving us more kills in the air. Air fights are no longer knife and spear melees. We *are* attacking the Draks and killing them and with almost no losses. My flying cubs are very, very happy with *their* business of killing.

"But it's not war, gentlemen. I am still sending my cubs up to kill Draks who are out *hunting food*! My people of the Marches, the Valley People, you in Riverton, are simply good to eat, and the Draks fly in to hunt us. They like to hunt and kill my cubs in the air and they stalk us whenever we fly near one of their hunting parties. My cubs kill Draks willingly, but also because the Draks *always attack* and will kill a pilot if he doesn't strike first.

"Again, with these new launchers we have been able to do a little stalking on our own account. We kill Draks! In the process we are guarding the Valley and protecting your riverfish harvest in the way we have always done.

"You harvest the riverfish, for food, even as the Draks

54

harvest the land people. The riverfish fight back with the only weapons they have—even as we have done for millennia. . . .''

Amarson flexed his claws.

"Should the riverfish ever develop weapons to carry the fight beyond the riverbeds, even as we now hunt the high air, would that then be *war*—or survival? I have no time for philosophy. As your priest, Paudre said: We're paid to kill Draks; we're proud to kill Draks. . . .

"But it's not war!''

"You have stopped the Drak's deep penetration flights,'' Lewyll said. "The Valley harvest is almost complete.''

"We accomplished that much when we first started fighting the Draks in the air with the fliers you built for us,'' Amarson said. "But the Draks still fly and they still hunt and *feed*!''

"Can't you be satisfied with that?''

"No! It's not enough . . . . Stopped their deep hunting flights, you say,'' Amarson swung his finger in an arc along the length of the Valley, beyond his bases. "Inside our base perimeter I can cut them out of the air. Your riverfish harvest is usually safe, here along the delta. . . .

"This swarm—Draks have never swarmed this far down the plains before—I hope it is unusual. If it becomes seasonal. . . . I don't know. There isn't a thing I can do about a Drak swarm. We don't dare attack them.

"Up to now, your fishing has been safe in deep water. Up stream, too far. . . I can't say that. Without special air patrols over your boats, the danger is still great. The toe of the great mountains comes down here, and we cannot fly into the Drak mountain passes.''

He stopped and looked intently at a group of course lines marked on the map.

"Your liaison is posting false data,'' he snapped. "There have been no patrols here. That's right in the center of the alps. The peaks around there are higher than our fliers can climb.

"I'll have him disciplined. There's no reason for jokes like that.''

"Relax, Baron," Lewyll said. "I marked that course, myself. That is your next combat flight." His voice went to a lower tone. "This flight might even qualify as *war*."

"Can't do it," Amarson cut in. "Our fliers won't . . ." He let his voice die away as he remembered that Theiu's reason for bringing him here was bound up in a new weapon. Those course lines and the tall Riverman must mean that they had some way of getting there. He turned his back to the map and stopped being irritated.

"Tell me," he said. He even managed a smile.

"We have six new fliers that will go to that height," Ambassador Theiu said. "They are being delivered to your Base XII by truck today. By truck, armed against the Drak swarm and in force enough to fight their way through. By truck, so that no one in Riverton can see what they look like, until you fly them."

"Have they been tested?"

"Yes, I trucked them up to Base II, so the test flights were all over the mountain jungle. They've been test-flown and dismantled. A Riverman assembly crew is with the trucks."

"That is not all," Lewyll said. "Getting a flier to that height would be useless unless the Draks could be attacked. "I doubt that the Draks fly that high. I'm certain they can't. What you will find in those mountains are the Drak camps, gathering places, and their main water supply. But these camps will be in a deep central valley, or a high plain in the mountains."

He went over to a bench and put his hands on two polished wooden boxes.

"Now, as to why I want you to go there—

"About a year ago a Valley village on the Delane River designed a new nutrient fluid for their fields. They sprayed it on the ground and improved the crop. In the Delane, however, the results were death."

"The Delane is the breeding ground for a type of fish we harvest, some of them we supply to your base, the *lenief*," Ambassador Theiu explained.

"Very tasty, I like them," Amarson nodded. "Go on."

"We maintain a fish count and watch station at the mouth

56

of the Delane. Hatch time came and passed. The fingerling count was twenty percent of normal. The fish watch called an alert and we sent Scientist Lewyll in with a team, looking for some new predator in the area.''

"Predator! Hah, I found the worst one there is,'' Lewyll said. "The hatch was still in the breeding pools. All up and down the river. The eggs were unfertilized; dead. Dead? They had never lived.

"The water and the valley nutrient!" He put his hand on one box. "The nutrient killed the *lenief*. . . still is killing them. The fingerling count is one percent, this year. We don't even know where they are coming from. Some tributary of the Delane, not the river itself.''

"Has it got to any other riverfish?'' Amarson asked the obvious question.

"No!'' Lewyll clapped his hands together. "That was the wonderful part. Completely selective!'' The Riverman was almost gleeful. "In fact it was the selectivity that made me see a great discovery in this disaster on the Delane.

"I brought specimens of the original nutrient and the water back here and started to work on a line of chemical change. It worked, Baron. Theory said it should, and I have proved it.

"I got final confirmation this morning from your fresh-killed Drak, and my work is complete. Here it is.''

He opened the wooden box and took out a glass cup filled with a blue liquid.

"This will kill Draks!'' The scientist held the cup up and looked at it. "Spray this nutrient on the ground, and near the water supply of the Drak camps, and they will not breed. The next generation of Draks will die like the *lenief*; unfertilized and unhatched.''

"That is the combat mission we want you to fly—using the new fliers, Baron,'' Ambassador Theiu said. "They have tanks in them to hold many liters of this nutrient. The Valley People are making it for us right now.''

"You should appreciate the irony of the situation, Baron,'' Lewyll said, slowly. "Yesterday you, alone, killed a single Drak. This afternoon, I am asking you to kill a whole generation. We make progress in our weapons when we serve Death, don't we?''

"Death for Draks, Scientist." Amarson matched his intensity. "I am tired of seeing Drak food camps and butcher points on the Marches. I am sick of being *food* for Draks.

"If your way of killing is Death for them, you have my help."

"I guarantee it, Baron." Lewyll held up the glass cup. "This is Death."

"Very well.

"But I see why the church elders would oppose you. Death of a whole generation is a terrible thought.

"Are you certain the priest, Paudre, sides with you in this?"

"Absolutely," Theiu answered.

"His aid has been valuable," Lewyll said.

Amarson nodded. He wasn't so certain, however, about a man who had two voices: one public, one private.

"He does not know about killing Draks. The Compact has kept it from him—safe on the border Marches, until now. . . . " He lifted his hands and ran his claws out and back in.

"A whole generation. A terrible thought. But against Draks. . . ?

"You have my aid! *Blood only stains the hands*!"

"This will mean secrecy, Baron," Theiu said. He worked his sprayer. "Not only about the new flier, but about the purpose of that deadly nutrient."

"Hm-mmm. Secrecy. I don't know." Amarson looked at the map; not really seeing it. "That means assembling the fliers, training six pilots and crews, flying them. . . . My pilots would have to have test flights. . . a new flier. All in secret?"

"More than that," Lewyll put in. "The Valley People, the ones making the nutrient, will deliver and fill your tanks from trucks. They must stay at Base XII until you fly. Also you will need six more men. . . to fire the dart launchers. The fliers are built for two men."

"Show him the flier, Lewyll," Ambassador Theiu broke in. "You have the model, there."

Lewyll put the cup of nutrient back in its container and opened the second wooden box. Amarson came across the room to look closely at the polished quarter meter model.

"It has one large wing," Theiu began describing it without needing to see it closely. His factory had made the model and his designers had shown it to him many times.

"The wing is thick and wide to lift heavy loads. The body is really just a big tank. The pilot's station. . . far back, near the tail, for visibility and to allow a bigger tank. The dart launcher is in front of the pilot and can be swiveled to any angle and all around. That's why we need a second man.

"Scale? The flier is big. The biggest thing I've ever built; except a boat. It's four times as big as your combat fliers, Baron. Four times.

"That's another reason for the flexible dart launchers. You can't chase Draks around the sky with this."

"You have flown this, loaded?" Amarson asked.

"Yes. Including dives and penetration of the thermocline. You can talk to the test pilots. They went up to Base XII with the first flier."

"Test pilots!" Amarson tore his eyes from the model. "How many more people are in on this secret? Did you tell the Draks?"

"That's all." Theiu worked his sprayer. "My factory people will stay at Base XII after they assemble the flier, like the Valley nutrient experts."

"Impossible!" Amarson almost shouted. "You are talking about fifty people. That's not a secret; it's a troop movement. I can't hide anything that big. Nobody could."

"We will have to try. If Domne hears of our work, he will stop it. He will not be out looking. He has heavy religious rites and duties during the riverfish hunting season. Paudre will see that he is kept virtually in seclusion for most of the time we need.

"If questions are asked, we can say we don't know what is happening; *if* you can hide the fliers."

59

"I can't hide them in the air! Four times as big as a combat.
. . . Be realistic!"

"Can't you fly them just at the rise of the Father Sun?"
Scientist Lewyll's voice was slow and calming. "Once in the
air, these fliers are designed to fly high. You could train at
altitude, where none could see."

"Landing. . . ?" Amarson considered. "Accepting a
takeoff at first light, I'd have to land in bright light. Especially with a new flier; a new, big flier. I'd want both suns in the
sky; not even risk a chance on one of the periods when the
Younger Sun is setting. The light is too uncertain. . . .

"A low apppoach from the jungle. . . perhaps."

"Exactly," Lewyll said. "Your Base XII is ideally suited
for that. You are far out on the perimeter. Visits are not
common. We could even undertake to see that they stopped
altogether, for a time, heh, *Ambassador* Theiu.

"Your Jungle Patrol could help with that, Baron. Also, the
rest of your flight commanders and your headquarters have
already a|greed to help—without knowing about this nutrient
weapon, of course."

"It will take some massive planning," Amarson
said. "And I don't really believe it will work, but I will do
it."

"I tell you it must work," Theiu said. He worked his
sprayer in emphasis with his words. "The secret must be
kept.

"Don't underestimate Domne. Remember, he almost had
you killed by simply playing on an obscure regulation and
your own warrior superstition."

"I am not likely to forget." Amarson put a finger on the
wing of the little model. "When will *I* get to see these
fliers?"

"The first will be at your base when you return tomorrow," Theiu answered. "All six by the end of the week. If I
moved them all at once, the size of the convoy would be
suspicious."

"And I will begin today," Scientist Lewyll put in. "And
calculate the precise hour of first light for you at Base XII. A
table for every day, from now, for a month, should do it."

"More than enough," Amarson said. "The secret won't hang together that long. There will be a leak.

"How long will your men need to assemble the fliers, Ambassador?"

"One day, each. A week."

"Then I train in a week. No, I begin training as soon as a single flier is ready, and rotate pilots. I can't have all six in the air at once until mission day. I couldn't hide that.

"And the Draks swarm. . . . By the two Suns! They could have picked any other place in the world to swarm." He smashed a fist into his open hand. "This particular swarm won't last long. They will go somewhere else, land, rest and mate. They may swarm once again, or they may not, and then it's all over till next season. But the time; now. . . .

"The time is bad for us. I will have to hold my training while the Draks are gone. I can't use my field for take-off, you see. Not while they are swarming. The Draks dive on the fliers on the ground.

"I can catapult my combat fliers out of the hangars; we are set to do that. . . but these new fliers. . . ."

"They will need almost all of your field for a take-off run," Theiu put in. "You will undoubtedly need clear skies."

"I hope they are easy to fly, these toys of yours. We will still be learning about them on the mission. I wouldn't like surprises, especially unpleasant ones."

"You will fly them," Lewyll said. "We know the skill of your pilots. That is why we picked Base XII for this job.

"Now, if you'll come over to the map I will show you the mission and tell you what we think you will find on top of the alps."

Amarson followed him to the map, and the planning went on in detail, as it was to go on in greater and greater detail for a week to come.

5

Amarson held the flier in a wide spiral climb through the blood-red light of the rising Father Sun and let the other five form on him. He kept the heavy flier circling for altitude while he began the ritual chant to take him through the thermocline. His timing was off and the chant was completed well short of the required height. There was no indication of the rough turbulence where the heavy air and the lighter air met at the barrier. The flier climbed slower with the liquid tanks full, and Amarson was rushing the ritual. The newness of the unfamiliar flier, its visual shape in the air, all added to change his sense of timing. The flier was bigger than the ones he usually flew in combat. Also he missed the lower wing. Flying with only the one large wing was still strange, uncomfortable, even though the wing was longer and wider than both wings on his combat flier.

The Riverman technician had lectured him about the thick wing and its skill at flying heavy weights, but the distrust of newness was still with him. He did not fully trust the idea of *hanging* a heavy engine, body-pod and pilot underneath a wing instead of sitting naturally on top of the wing. And the thought of the two liquid-filled tanks up in front of him, adding their weight to the whole. . . . Amarson's eyes kept scanning the curved pylon that covered the metal frame holding the wing and body-pod together.

The ritual was completed for the second time, Amarson's pulse speed and nerve response had quickened again to the rhythm of the chant, when the flier finally hit the thermocline and bulled its way through.

Amarson was totally surprised. The flier bucked and

pitched as it slid through the turbulent air at the barrier point. The fat wing waggled slightly, and then the flier was through. There was no violent maneuver of any kind and, with his senses heightened by the chant, Amarson had control throughout the penetration.

There was noise, however! The wing groaned, its covering screamed and crackled. The tank area up front made horrible pops and dings, as the slosh barriers dampened the liquid movement. The flier moaned and screamed. Then it was through into the thin air above the thermocline.

The silence, as the flier slid through the smooth air, was almost as distinct as the noise.

The noise brought Mardon, the Jungle Patrol bowman, up out of the firing port just in front of Amarson. His head was turning from left to right, in near panic. His hands gripped the dart-launcher frame around him and his claws were out. He had been briefed on the flier's rough movement during penetration, but not on the noise. He had been sitting down in the body-pod when it began. The racket must have been heart stopping.

Amarson pounded on the launcher strut that was part of his windscreen and, when the patrolman turned, made a combat gesture with his left hand. It was a signal that a Patrol leader always gives before a fight and it meant, "*Charge forward gloriously for home and hearth*," in the books, but had a more vulgar meaning in the Patrol. He got an equally obscene reply and a wide grin, that told him the bowman was still a fighting unit.

And so was the big flier. It had survived penetration with full tanks. . . the liquid in those tanks was a potent weapon aimed at the Draks. . . and Amarson's big flier was very much a fighting unit. It wasn't any combat spinner, but the speed went up in the thin air and the big wing was lifting the load higher and higher. Amarson began to feel better.

He had left his Base XII in a mess below him. The tightly organized training schedule of the last week had come apart on the last day. Too much had to be done, too fast.

The Valley tank trucks had arrived late and had to be driven right into the shelter tents with the fliers, in order to fill the

63

fluid tanks. Theiu's technicians and the Valley drivers had pumped all night to finish the job. Amarson had broken one of his own rules about working during the darkness hours.

Then there had been a Drak raid, a spin-off from the grounded, mating Drak-swarm in the foothills. The six Jungle Patrolmen—set up to fly with the dart launchers—had been pulled out to the jungle perimeter to fight. They'd missed their one and only training flight. So, now, those six men were riding up here in the air for the first time in their lives. Amarson hadn't had time to reschedule their flight experience.

They *had* spent the week shooting the twin-mount dart launchers from the back of a truck. Some of them could hit a moving target; some of them couldn't. If the Draks attacked the bug fliers. . . . Well, the bowmen would kill the Draks or somebody would get hurt. It was a weak link, but Patrolman Mardon said they were good. Mardon knew his men, and he, Mardon, was riding Amarson's dart launchers. . . . It might work. They all had listened to Lewyll's dry lectures on lead, relative motion, and judging distance. At least they had listened, like professionals, as if their lives depended on what they heard. . . the possibility existed.

If they soldiered in the air as they did on the ground. . . .

On the ground. . . . Amarson smiled a little at the thought of his Second Commander, coping with the mob and the mess.

The mess. . . . The mess was on the ground and he'd worry about it when he got back. The work was up here in the air. The job was killing Draks.

He looked behind him and saw the other five spread out, slightly below him. He waggled the wings—wing—to signal them into the flight pattern and watched the strange silhouettes form behind him. They looked even odder from another flier, but with a singular purposefulness that Amarson found he liked. One wing, long tank pods and all, they looked powerful, these new fliers.

Their pilots handled them well, too. The pilots were almost as loosely trained as the bowmen. The takeoff and fighting tactics, indeed all the flying pattern work, had been studied with blocks of wood on a table top. Now, and here, the flight was working in the air for the first time.

However, they could fly, these cubs. They were working out in the air. They'd be all right.

Amarson turned onto his course and increased his power settings to climb. The six fliers were aimed at the high mountains and they drove up the sky, higher and higher.

Amarson locked his controls for the climb and began to adjust his muscles to control the flier with the tiny relaxed movements of his flier's skill. He found, to his amazement, that the flier didn't seem to need this attention. The ritual words for his flying drill were thrown out of time as the movements prescribed by the words produced no effect on the flier.

Amarson broke off the ritual and studied this. He had been conscious on the test flights, and on takeoff and climbout, that the controls had to be moved farther and held longer, but he had expected that—because of the flier's size. This was no combat flier. He had expected to fly slowly. What he had missed, was the fact that the big, slow beast flew so smoothly from one maneuver to another. . . without a twitch, or hike, in the air. In fact, once the controls were moved, the flier seemed supremely indifferent to anything except a firm, positive movement in another direction. For awhile this worried Amarson. He was going to be doing some flying near the mountains at the end of this mission. The tanks would be empty then; the flier lighter. He didn't want to be overcontrolling and fighting a sluggish flier, then.

He began to experiment with his controls and soon found out that he wasn't overcontrolling—and probably couldn't overcontrol. The flier simply had an incredibly smooth ability to fly itself.

All this time, as Amarson had been learning the fine points of his controls, he had continued to climb. He had to top the alps ahead, if he could, and he had to get up high before the Draks sent scouts up to stop him.

The height gauge began to register in the shaded portion of its dial—time to use the breathing air.

Amarson reached out and slapped the launcher support

again. The bowman, Mardon, turned. Amarson unhooked his face mask from the breathing tank and held it up.

Mardon nodded.

Amarson pushed the mask up over his nose, as he had been taught, and slid the head band over his ears. He turned the valve on the air tank and felt the cool pressure inside the face mask. Just as the Rivermen needed these tanks under the river, so pressurized air was needed to breathe up here at this height. The Scientist, Lewyll, had said the pressure would help him breathe. Without the pressure, he would be able to breathe out, but the thin air would not be able to force itself back into his lungs. At this height, the pressure in his lungs and the outside pressure were equal. He could breathe out, not in; hence the pressure tanks.

Amarson lifted his head and sat up a little to check that the bowman was masked and then he glanced back at the fliers following him. He waggled the tail of the flier to signal them into their masks.

That is, he started a waggle. What he got was a slow, lazy tail-wave. This flier just wouldn't maneuver. He made wide hand motions at his own face mask. They caught that.

The pilot on his left blipped his engine and yawed out, so Amarson could see his signals. He was pointing down and forward. Draks!

Amarson tipped a wing down to locate them. They were far below. A large party, and they were rising, but they were too far below to worry about.

A shadow swooped over his head. What the. . . !

The bowman wal up; standing in his harness. The two dart launchers slid around on their firing rail, the curving tubes of the engine-powered, air-pump system standing out in rigid loops around the Patrolman. Mardon had seen the sign from the other flier and located the Draks. Then he had switched on the air pumps, armed his launchers, and was ready for a fight. All this without orders and on his first time in the air. The Jungle Patrol certainly made tigers!

The shadow that Amarson had ducked was the dart launcher riding across the protective stop-bar over his head. This kept the bowman from stitching darts through the flier's tail by accident. There were two more such bars protecting the wings. The pneumatic pressure generated to launch these darts gave them enough energy to shatter timber at two hundred meters. The damage they could do up close was unthinkable. Amarson was fully in accord with those protective stop-bars.

The bowman relaxed behind his launcher. He pointed to the Draks and shook his head. The Draks weren't going to attack.

Amarson gave him a break-off signal. The bowman was right. The Draks were out of range and falling behind. They were no problem.

It was the Draks ahead that they had to worry about.

A quick automatic check of his instruments showed Amarson that the flier was high enough to clear the alps. He leveled off and studied the peaks ahead. They were only minutes away and already he could see beyond them. Lewyll was right; there was a high valley.

The flight swept over the peaks and the wide valley became visible. Amarson signaled the flight into the pattern they had planned for the spraying. It was like a combat line, but with the big fliers grouped in units of two; wingman and leader. Another difference was the space between fliers. Amarson was going to take them down close to the ground. He wanted to give them plenty of air room.

He checked the pattern as it formed and started to pound on the launcher frame to alert Mardon. The bowman, however, was up, standing in his harness, and the tubes to the dart launchers were still rigid with pressure. The Patrolman was ready.

So was Amarson. He dropped the nose of the flier, pushed the speed control to full power, and took the flight pattern down over the Drak highland.

The instant the ship straightened in its dive, Amarson put his eye to a ranging bar. He pushed his face plate close to the bar and sighted at the ground. The image he saw was doubled, rocks, trees, a Drak berm; two of each. He had no way of knowing the height of the highland here and his height gauge was useless for telling the distance above the valley floor. The ranging bar was a Riverman device to gauge his distance above the ground. When the split image came together he would be low enough to pull out of his dive. There! Now!

He pulled up and flew level. The flight followed him. A quick reset of the bar and a little juggling with height gave him the range for dropping the liquid in his tanks. He noted it on his height gauge.

By this time the fight was far enough over the valley to start the spraying. Amarson found and pulled the wooden lever that had been added to the flier. The liquid began to stream backward, forming droplets as it fell. The spray stream glowed a frothy pink in the light of the Father Sun.

The other fliers made their drops as he did and the flight swept across the valley, trailing falling plumes of glistening fog.

Ahead of the flight was a Drak henge, a great circular mound of earth with wooden living camps inside. None of the camps had roofs of any kind—the Draks evidently flew in and out. Amarson was able to see into them as he flew across the henge. Most of the Draks crouched, startled by his engine noise, but some of them took wing. Ah, that was one point Scientist Lewyll had wrong. The Draks could fly at this height. The air on the valley floor must be thick enough.

Amarson could see the red sun glint on weapons, but the Draks were slow and heavy from their swarming and mating. Their wings beat in the thin air, but his flight flew on beyond them before they could climb to fighting height.

There was another henge off to the left. Amarson changed his course slightly to fly over it. This one was larger, about fifteen hundred meters across and crowded with inner structures. . . but not many Draks.

Amarson was puzzled. In the fleeting glimpses of the two henges, he had seen very few Draks. Those camps could hold hundreds. Only a small group had come back here from the swarm over Riverton. Where were the rest? Where would they swarm next?

The dart launchers rattled and shook, startling Amarson.

Draks! *Aiee*! Some of them were up here in the air at fighting height.

The bowman was shooting forward, over the wing. Three Draks! Only a single hunting flight?

The bowman fired again and missed again, as the Draks drifted above the flier and curved down to attack from above and behind. The yellow Younger Sun was almost below the peaks in that direction, but the Draks still curved to attack from the sun.

The bowman swung his dart launchers and fired again. The flier shook with the rattle of the dart belts moving up into the launchers.

Then the Draks were hit!

Amarson's wingman was firing, too. He saw the smoke trails from the launcher on his wingman's flier converge with the stream that Mardon was swinging through the sky. The two lines of darts seemed to touch the flying Draks and instantly two of them were rolling in the sky, stopped in the air by the dart impact, and falling.

The third came on, his beak open in a scream Amarson couldn't hear for the rattle of the darts. Mardon bounced the launcher over the deflector plates and across Amarson's head to pick up the Drak on the other side of the flier.

The Drak missed his dive and flashed by not more than ten meters out. At that range, Amarson saw the darts take the Drak. They tore into his body and an arm and a shoulder were literally ripped away and fell clear. The Drak's head and beak disappeared and then the body fell. The bowman stopped firing.

The lack of noise was so violent, Amarson thought the engine had stopped and jerked his eyes to the instrument panel. The engine was still running. The liquid level in the tanks was down one-half weight. Good, that finished the job here.

Amarson pulled back on the spray lever and cut off the valve. The spray stream stopped. The rest of the tank would be dumped on the watershed outside this valley.

Amarson controlled the flier into a wide climbing turn and fired a recall flare with his signal gun. Then he set his course south for the Jungle Patrol perimeter nearest the coast of the mud sea. He waited for the flight, scattered during the Drak pack fight, to form up on him.

The three Draks had been an isolated hunting party. There were no more Draks in the sky near Amarson's fliers, only the straggling group of six over the henges. The six that had first climbed to challenge Amarson's spray run.

The fliers closed in from their spread-out fighting pattern without hindrance, but one flier was in trouble. He was still spraying fluid. Amarson could see the pilot, his head down in the body pod, trying to free the controls. After a moment, he gave up, lifted both hands over his head to mean failure, and slid his flier across to join the tight flight pattern.

Amarson signaled, *follow me*, and altered course slightly to lead them back across the valley. He kept the flight climbing steadily to clear the mountains, but the new course took him back across the Drak henges. The falling spray from the one flier would not be wasted.

That spray was death for the Draks and he wanted to leave it falling on the henges and the Drak home camps; leave as much as possible, drifting down in ruby drops of death, as the Younger Sun neared the horizon in its mid-passage setting.

Mardon's dart launcher rattled across its frame, as he trained it forward and to the left. The Drak flight was close and he was tracking them.

Amarson signaled his flight to stay closed up, and continued to climb. He had seen two of the Draks waver on their wings and miss a beat. The height, their fatigue after swarming had cut into their endurance in the air. Amarson thought he could climb above them, avoid combat, or let Mardon get a shot as they flew by. He held his course.

He was right. The Draks began to drop. Their wings lost beat and stiffened to glide them to the ground. Four were left. . . then two. , . .

Mardon shifted his launcher mount to shoot under the wing, now tracking a single Drak, still coming at them.

The bowman in the flier on Amarson's left tracked his launcher to support Mardon.

The fliers swept by the Drak and it was still below them. Its raging cry screamed over the engines. . . then the straining wings collapsed, folded and the Drak fell. . . down, behind them, its fighting spear still clutched in both hands.

Mardon had not fired. The Drak had never reached the flight.

Amarson's flier cleared the mountain peaks and nosed over to lose height in a long slanting dive along the face of the alps. The rest of the pilots held station on him and followed him down. For twenty hundred-pulse counts, Amarson held a steady course and kept up the rate of descent that kept him close to the mountain slope. The Younger Sun slowed even more, in its mid-passage setting, and seemed to hang in the sky. The *Rite of Pausing*. . . and, as the sun stood still in its setting arc, Amarson turned the formation steeply and flew over the canyon junction. He headed back toward Base XII.

Now, they were flying parallel to the mountains, just about at the tree line. As the flight banked into the turn, the flier with the defective spray tank stopped spraying, his tanks empty.

A moment later, Amarson pulled the lever and began to dump his own tanks. The flight tucked in behind him in a wide arrowhead formation; his wing-man out to his right and the other four, two to the left and two to the right, behind and above him.

Amarson took a quick glance to check their positions, then brought his attention back to his flying. The ranging bar was no help here. He was flying along the sloping side of the mountains. This was contour flying by eye and instinct alone and it took concentration.

There was another danger, too, and Amarson kept a check on his height gauge. The thermocline was below him at about seven hundred meters. He didn't dare fly through that turbulent air, or the barrier, while he was so close to the mountainside.

So far, the flight and the mountain shoulder they were spraying were high above the thermocline, but Amarson was being careful. This contour flying could take them down a mountain curve and into lower altitudes.

Amarson's spray tanks ran dry and cut off. He signaled to

his wingman and a falling plume dropped from that flier. The formation would continue spraying, one flier at a time, to cover the maximum ground here on the mountain watershed. These were the places where the Draks rested on the way home from their hunts. The water draining from these foothills would carry Scientist Lewyll's deadly nutrient to every canyon and valley on the watershed. Death to the Draks! Death would go wherever the spray fell and spre₁d.

The rising, falling flight went on minute after minute as the mountainside swept by in a blur. The Younger Sun had set now, in the first of its three daily passages. The Father Sun dominated the sky, its giant disk filling the horizon and rising almost to the zenith. The Younger Sun would rise again about the end of this mission, or so the planning timetable noted. In the meantime, Amarson sprayed death by the light of the Father Sun; a symbolism he found highly appropriate. *Blood only stains the hands*, could become part of this killing ritual, if we needed one, he thought.

The spray plumes switched from one flier to another and fell down through the sky to snag on the forest tops below. The liquid fell on the forest floor, some fell in streams and water runs, but that didn't matter. In time the liquid would end up in the water as it had on the Delane. Then, wherever a Drak camped, or fed, or drank, the death liquid would find it. In the food it ate, in the water it drank, would be Scientist Lewyll's subtle death. The Draks would carry it back to the henges with them. That's where it would kill. In the mating of the Draks there would be death.

The liquid falling on the forest would be unnoticed, because it was timed to kill the sons of Draks; the next generation. Kill them like the *lenief*; forever. As the falling spray drifted down, Amarson was setting a trap; a trap in which no more Draks would be born—ever.

Amarson shuddered a little and took his mind away from the thought. The feathering tails behind his fliers were only a weapon to kill Draks. That was his job; kill Draks!

The tension of the contour-scraping flight brought back the uneasy feeling of worry. Something was wrong. Amarson hit the launcher frame to alert Mardon. The bowman nodded, stood up and began scanning the air around the flier. Amarson kept his attention on the ground ahead, except for a brief glance at his instruments, and over to the last flier on his left. His height was good and the flier was still spraying. It was the last one and its tanks ought to be almost empty.

The bowman signaled, *nothing*, but Amarson kept him at it; on watch. There was something. . . . Amarson trusted his combat instincts. Combat! That was it! *Draks*!

He tightened his hands on the controls and his claws ran out. A flight like this should have attracted a lot of Draks. That falling spray could be seen for. . . . By the Suns, they had been flying parallel to the Marches perimeter, for hours.

Where were the Draks?

Their swarming had been over for days. The mating and their ground period should be finished, too. There should be clutches of Draks in all the foothill ravines . . . Hunting parties should be out. . . .

A combat patrol would ordinarily be fighting Draks all over the sky by now.

The Younger Sun rose again. It climbed swiftly to *Point of Pausing* on its rising cycle. Amarson welcomed the added light. He wanted to be able to see the Draks. The yellow light helped.

Points of light flashed on the ground under the rising sun!

The Draks were ahead! He saw a long line of them first; eight or ten, flying just above the edge of the forest. Then another group, spiraling this time, and in the center of the spiral. . . Draks diving vertically. . . to attack. Their weapons glittered again in the light.

He searched the ground, although he didn't expect to see anything from this altitude. He found a road, then recognized a pattern of meadow and fields. His eye flashed west and he saw—*Base XII*.

Base XII—and above it, spiraling patterns of Draks; evil specks in the sky that grew larger as he watched.

There were three, four—no, five of the swirling attack patterns over the Base. He'd never seen so many Draks in a hunting attack.

They were as thick as when they swarmed, but this was no

swarm. The Draks were wheeling swiftly in the air. They were making hunting dives and beating quickly back into the spirals.

Aii-hee! He caught a flip and flash of color against the background of the jungle and recognized a flier. It banked high in a wing-tip turn, and slid back into the milling Draks. His cubs were up fighting! Of course they were. . . and we'll be there to help—starting now!

He drove the nose of his flier down and took the flight away from the mountainside. He signaled *Land in Pattern*, to them and throttled back to the penetration speed. His flier dropped faster, headed toward the thermocline.

The flight penetrated in good order and tightened up the pattern as close as they could fly. There was no need to signal *Draks sighted*. Everybody could see them. The sky ahead was filled. Wherever you looked. . . Draks!

Amarson saw columns of them flying toward Riverton. Theiu was in for. . . Riverton! They still had riverfish boats out hunting. They would be unloading cargoes at the docks. The covered docks wouldn't stop hunting Draks. The Rivermen would be caught. . . .

Yes, there was another column flying on—heading for Riverton.

By the Suns! The Draks *were* swarming! But not the lazy trance-like flight of their mating ritual. This was new. This was a combat swarm. The Draks flew to kill. All of them; every one that could get in the air. *Aargh*!

Now, the flight was getting close. The Draks would sight the big fliers any time, now. Amarson kept in his dive. He was headed directly at the landing field.

He couldn't fight with these big fliers; not even with their fluid tanks empty. He hoped the pilots behind him would remember the plan he'd worked out on the tactic table and stay in close pattern when the Draks struck. He had made the pattern so that the bowmen could help each other with their dart launchers. Those launchers, and staying together, were the only weapons these big fliers had.

Amarson looked at the fuel weight gauge. The tank was almost empty. The decision was no decision, really. He had to get these fliers out of the air—quick.

He shoved the engine control to full power and flattened his dive toward the end of the field. He took the flight straight in.

Now, the Draks were full size and their armor and weapons were clearly visible. They swirled and braked in frantic effort to fly out of the way of Amarson's flight. He saw a spiral scatter in front of him, as he flew right through it. The dart launchers began to fire. Mardon got a kill. The bowmen had plenty of targets.

A rackety roar distracted Amarson briefly, and he looked up in time to see a combat flier roll over the top of a turn and slide across the sky above the formation. Amarson let his teeth show in a fighting grin. He was proud of those cubs of his. . . . They could fly!

A Drak stalled in the air above his wing and was hit by a stream of darts. Amarson saw him die, in a flash, on the edge of his vision. The body hit the top of the wing and slid off. The flier put a wing down with the shock.

Amarson fought the controls and rocked the big flier into contact with the field. The wheels hit before the wing and the tail slammed on the ground—hard, but it stayed down. He pulled back the engine control to keep on the ground, but kept the speed up, because of the fliers landing behind him. He took the flier across the field, dragging its tail, just under lift off speed.

In front of him, Mardon swirled the dart launcher and fired. He was still fighting Draks. Amarson could hear his killing-yell over the engine.

Fighting Draks! These fliers with the swivel launchers could fight on the ground! Amarson couldn't fight them in the air, but here, on the ground, he had a new weapon.

He ran straight in, as close to the service tents as possible, but well out of line of the big hangar. The combat fliers in the air—when they ran low on fuel and darts—would have to try to land inside the hangar; just as they did during a swarming. That hangar had to stay empty for them. He couldn't take his big fliers in under cover; they'd take up too much precious room.

75

Besides, the grounded formation of fliers, their massed fire, seemed to be a powerful weapon. Draks were diving on the fliers but none were getting through. Mardon's bowmen were fighting. . . killing.

Amarson led the flight into position and controlled his engine to stop the flier. He left it running; didn't turn off Mardon's power. Those launchers had a lot of Drak killing to do and Mardon was firing as fast as he could find targets.

Amarson unfastened his straps and grabbed at Mardon to attract his attention.

"Keep at the launchers!" he yelled. "I'll get you help."

Mardon nodded and stabbed a hand at the dart storage bins. He needed a reload. Well, he'd get it.

Amarson rolled out of the flier in time to meet the chief groundsman jumping off a truck. It was the truck they had used to train the bowmen—its dart launcher was armed and joined in to support the flier's fire.

"We have fuel in the back, Baron," the chief shouted.

"Tie them down here, Chief!" Amarson ordered. "Refuel and keep those launchers armed and loaded. Don't turn off the motors. The bowmen need power. Understand?"

"Yes. We've been fighting the mount on the truck." The chief signaled his crew. They rolled a fuel drum out of the truck and went to work.

"We are refitting the combat fliers as fast as they come in, Baron," he went on. "They have been ordered out to defend Riverton."

"Good. They can't do much here. Keep them in the air."

Amarson ran out under the cover of a wing and over to his wingman. He slapped the body side and the pilot climbed out. They ducked back under the big wing.

Amarson fell over a thrown Drak spear and rolled forward. His hands grabbed the spear as he rolled and he came up defensively. There was no need. The Drak's body crashed onto the field, torn and broken by the steel darts from the flier's dart launchers.

Amarson turned and found a Jungle Patrolman beside him. It was the senior Patrolman who had met him in the meadow, so long ago.

"My thought is: I'm playing with cub's toys,"the Patrolman snarled, uncocking his dartbow. "That rattler has long claws."

"Senior, get your squad in around these fliers," Amarson ordered. "We've got a fighting fort here. Keep the bowmen armed—and replace them. . . if necessary."

"My thought," the senior Patrolman agreed. "The squad's on your fuel truck." He rolled off to collect them.

Amarson grabbed his wingman. "Get the pilots out!" he yelled. "Keep the engines running and the bowmen on the launchers. These fliers will stay on the ground.

"I want all the pilots at the fuel truck. I'll get them combat fliers, and get them in the air.

"Move!"

The pilot nodded and went off.

Amarson ducked under the body-pod of the flier and found the fuel truck rolling toward him. He waited for it.

A movement in the sky caught his eye. He looked at it directly and saw four columns of Draks, flying low over the forest. They were headed for Riverton. Riverton.

Riverton; the Rivermen, would be woefully unprepared for this massed Drak attack. They would expect the Draks to be swarming again, and slow; instead they would surface their boats under spirals of Draks flying with hunting speed and strength.

There would be dead men in that town by now. Amarson snarled. He needed a flier. He had to get into the air, over Riverton, to plan the fight. This new swarm of Draks called for tactics and team work, not single-flier, pack fights.

A yellow flier wobbled over the jungle and landed crossfield. It was out of line of the hangar, a sure target for a Drak attack. It flicked its tail up and rushed over toward the massed fliers. Amarson's groundsman was waving the pilot in under the protective fire of the Patrolmen and their deadly dart launchers. Amarson saw the flier and ran out to help unstrap the pilot and feed the new dart belts into the combat fliers' wing racks.

He had to get back in the air—quick!

6

Scientist Lewyll stared at the Draks through the slit windows in his tower wall. They swooped and swirled through the buildings of Riverton. He could see the diving attacks at the docks—and the kills. His hand clenched the top of the polished wooden box that he had hoped would save Riverton from the killing and death he now saw. Inside the box was his deadly nutrient. *Death of Draks*, the Baron Amarson had called it.

The whole plan was so futile.

Outside, in the sky, he was looking at. . . . Death for Rivermen. There was nothing he could do about it. His wide eyes closed wearily.

"Does that box hold your poison spray, Scientist?"

Lewyll whirled at the voice. The priest, Paudre, stood in the door.

"Paudre—Holiness. . . ."

"Yes, it is I. I'm no longer sure 'Holiness' is a word that applies to either of us. We have failed, Scientist.

"I walk through Riverton and let the people see the signs of the Two Suns." He crossed his arms over his chest, displaying the water sprayer he held and a sistrum with sun disks on its wires.

"But the people can't look into my heart and see my failure. All they can see are diving Draks.

"So, I came here, where I can share my sense of failure. . . . And I find you looking out at the black winged beasts. . . holding the weapon that failed. . . .

"Too bad Theiu and your Baron are not here. We could all share our failure."

Lewyll glanced at the map. "Amarson has finished his mission by now, Holiness. He is probably fighting Draks."

"No doubt. Your Baron has likely stirred them up onto this attack. . . angered them. He has driven them into Riverton." Paudre went over to the window slit and looked out.

"So many Draks—killing. Amarson wouldn't be driving them down on us, would he, Lewyll?"

"No. oh, no! You are wrong, Holiness. The Draks are swarming. That is all. Amarson had nothing to do with that. Neither did my spray."

"No, I suppose not. I can't blame him. The plan was mine as much as yours; or Theiu's. The failure. . . . more mine than yours, for I am supposed to be able to show you the Light of the Two Suns.

"Lewyll. Spray the Draks over Riverton. Kill them." Paudre's voice was low, pleading. "They are killing— feeding on our people. Oh, awful, Lewyll—the lesson Amarson said he could teach us. . . .

"Spray them, please! In the name of the holy Two Suns, spray them, and save Rivermen."

"I can't, Holiness. The spray doesn't work that way."

"*Aiee!*" Paudre's voice dropped even lower. He didn't seem to care whether Lewyll heard him or not.

" 'The spray doesn't work'. . . . I remember now. So, I was told. We made the plan to kill life, before it had a chance to live, didn't we?"

"The Draks must die!"

"And so we decided that the two suns will never shine on Drak life. We decided? Who? You, Scientist? By what right?

"And I? My doctrine says: All life has the right to the light of both Suns; Father and Younger. This is the law as The World turns. I? Less right than any."

Paudre turned from the window and walked to look at the big combat map. His voice when he next spoke was pitched in the half-singing mode he used for rituals.

"Tell me, Scientist . . . how would you change *your spray* . . . to make it a spray that denies sunlight to Rivermen? To Rivermen unborn? Heh? Then to the Valley People, perhaps?"

"You are sick! No one would think of such a thing!"

"You thought of it for Draks, Scientist! When there are no more Draks to fight, your Baron Amarson may think of spraying Death over Rivermen."

"Impossible. He has honor."

"I can't take that chance. I am the priest of Riverton. I cannot leave another mistake that will return to kill my people. It is the only way I know." The priest lifted his water sprayer. "By the Light of the Two Suns."

He covered the table and Lewyll with a heavy spray of water. His voice deepened to intone: "In the Light of the Father Sun, in the Light of the Younger Sun; I deliver the Darkness that Follows."

Lewyll watched him lift the sistrum and set it vibrating. He stared down at his damp clothes and arms in horror. The water was filled with tiny white specks. As he watched, the sistrum's sound went up the frequencies and the water began to boil and steam. The sound heated it.

The white specks settled on his clothes. The water dried away from them.

"Paudre!" Lewyll screamed. "Sun Fire! No!"

The white specks began to glow and burn. Lewyll screamed as they ate his skin.

Paudre turned his back. The rising glow and the flames of the table; the brilliance of the burning Sun Fire chemical lit his way down the tower stairs. Lewyll's screams followed him out onto the mole.

Outside, the screaming was suddenly louder. Paudre looked up at a diving Drak; screaming down at him. The priest folded his arms and began a prayer. The bright glow of the Sun Fire still spotted his sight. The sound of the scream was still the voice of Lewyll in his ears.

The Drak broke off its killing dive. It beat its wings for altitude.

A pulsing roar tore the scream from Paudre's ears.

A sun-yellow flier slid down the air, close to the water and pulled up into a climb; driving after the Drak.

The flier pilot fired his dart launchers as he lifted and chased the Drak above the mole. He missed his shot, but the spent darts, fired almost straight up, fell back on the mole.

One dart struck Paudre a glance on the side of the head and he fell: Four more pierced his body.

Paudre had a final vision, of the flier rolling into a tight curve, and of a dying Drak, falling from the sky; then the flier blurred into a tiny, yellow Younger Sun. A red glow, as of the Father Sun, swelled behind his eyes and the Darkness followed.

THREE

Ameera

1

The first ten-truck grouping had left with the rising light of the Father Sun with orders not to stop for *Point of Pausing*. They had a long way to go and the road through the jungle was still unfinished in spots. They would have to drive hard to make the two hundred-forty kilometers to the refueling camp, and hold an even tighter schedule to get them to the night-stop after the Younger Sun set for the last time.

Amarson had sent Heralds along with the trucks to chant the rites as they rolled, and he'd stationed an armed company of Jungle Patrol throughout the trucks to fight them through. There were mobile dart launchers at the fuel stop and the Jungle Patrol held perimeter defense around the night stop. But five hundred kilometers was still five hundred kilometers, and the trucks would be open to Drak attack all along the way. The second day's trip was equally long. It was possible that they might get through to Fort without a fight but nobody believed the odds.

Amarson walked back into the Lodge. Partly to avoid the confusion out in the Plain and partly because the Lodge was his home and his place as a Marchholder—Baron Rufus.

The confusion outside was the second group of trucks. The

83

truck drivers and group leaders were trying to get as many people loaded as they could before everything came to a halt for the *Point of Pausing* ceremony. Patrol troopers were trying to hold families and children close to the trucks they were assigned to ride and, of course, half of these families had pressing reasons for being on another truck entirely. The noise alone was enough to attract Drak hunters, if the movement didn't.

Amarson took himself out of sight so he wouldn't be drawn into any of the arguments. The leaders were all Jungle Patrol men and knew what they wanted to do. It would get done, and loud swearing, even a few heavy fists, wouldn't be noticed. Two days and a thousand kilometers in the trucks would give the Marchholders a lot of other things to complain about before they reached their new-built homes in Amarson's southland city of Fort.

The big main hall room of the Lodge was bare, empty of hangings and movable furniture. The state chairs and the long administration table of Amarson's baronial office were still there... and in use by Mitch and a battle staff. This furniture, like Amarson's huge bed in the Quarter's sections, was hewn from jungle timber and was too massive for the move. It would be destroyed in place when the last guard torched the buildings.

Amarson didn't want to involve himself with Mitch's operation either. The work and pressure of getting the first trucks away had left him feeling a little disgusted with People and he didn't want Mitch to feel the effects of his emotions.

But an armed scout came running in at the same time as Amarson entered. The trooper's hurry and obvious concern made Amarson stop and listen. That and the fact that the trooper was a girl, taller than most and a strikingly attractive, pale-furred beauty. A beauty that was still strongly visible even though her matted and ruffed fur was streaked and stained with her fast courier run through the jungle.

"The Sixteenth squad of the Third," she said. "We're getting relay signals in from the Riverton Road. A swarm spiral has something pinned down there. We can see the top of the swarm from our tree-top scouts." She handed Mitch a signal board that documented her verbal message.

"They'll find us here when they widen their fly-away spiral." Someone said the obvious and the room was silent for half-a-hundred heartbeats. The move of the People to city Fort was happening all across the Marchlands, from every base and lodge post. Mitch and Amarson had made their plans for the Move on the assumption that the Draks would catch them in one phase of it or the other. The silence was caused by everyone pausing a second to review his part of the operation. A coincidental stop in the activity.

The silence was reinforced by a quiet from outside, as *Point of Pausing* began and the crowd hushed itself for the Rite.

"My guess is they're harassing the trucks coming out of Riverton," Mitch said, speaking into the wordless sound of the Herald's chant. "They didn't come in last night, so if they camped on the road and started at first light. . . ."

"Show me where your squad is scouting, Patrolman." He shuffled a pile of charts and slid one flat across the table. Mitch always liked a map to focus his attention while he was planning. Wherever he set up a working headquarters you could always find a mixed assortment of charts.

"My group's here," the girl said, after locating familiar marks on the map. "The outer road guard would have been there. . . when they saw Draks."

"Would have been?" Fort's Food Administrator had been dealing with Jungle Patrol *hunting* parties for too long. He didn't remember how they *fought* Draks.

"They will have pulled back into the perimeter by now," Amarson said. "The Road Guard was only two men, probably. Not many more. . . and they didn't sight the Riverton trucks, or they would have gone out to help."

"As you say, Baron," the girl trooper recognized Amarson. "Two men. . . . And orders were to fall back on this position, anyway. My squad was coming in behind me."

"That's right. We're not going to hold anything, or attack Draks," Mitch said. "I just don't want to leave anybody behind."

"The Riverton trucks will be armed. Better fire-power

85

than a Jungle Patrol company. And they're running empty. They'll fight through, all right.''

"Thanks for the report," he said to the girl. "Get some food and you can check back with your unit.

"Now," he turned back to his staff. "Now, how much longer are you going to need with this second group, Da'anald?"

"They're loading. They're loading." Da'anald was fidgeting. He had heard the instant hullabaloo from outside, that signaled the end of the *Point of Pausing* ritual. Like Amarson, he had shed most of his patience loading out the first contingent and he had little left for standing through Mitch's operational meeting. "Loan me the Trooper. I'll send her back when the first truck leaves.

"Come on, Corporal!" He grabbed her by one arm and hurried out the door.

"Let him go," Amarson said as Mitch bristled to stop him. "You'll be able to hear his swearing from in here. Your timetable will go faster, the louder he yells."

"Grmmm. You may be right. I hope he gets them out of here before that Drak swarm finds us.''

"Our trucks all have dart launcher mounts," Amarson said. "How will you be fixed when they leave?" All of the trucks, both ten-groups, were being sent out with Jungle Patrol guard. That was a weapons drain on the Patrol guard around the lodge. Mitch and his staff, and the tag end units of the guard, would stay on to burn out the buildings and go to ground until Amarson could send trucks back along the road to pick them up. The plan was to bring everybody out—not leave anyone behind—but Mitch had to have a strong enough group to stay alive until the trucks came back.

"Mardon tells me he has them already picked out," Mitch said. "There will be about a company. I wanted to leave a dart-launcher, so he'd have some fire power, but he didn't want it."

"Those work better for us as truck mounts. A ground squad can't carry enough darts to keep one in action, if they're moving. Mardon can fight better from the jungle. A company, heh? I'll be sending back three trucks for fire support, so that'll handle a company plus any extras. Make sure they all come out on the trucks. I don't want any hero types trying to march out. This is no training-drill hike, even if there is a good road."

"Have you heard anything from the other bases?"

"No. They were supposed to start moving the same time that we did. But we're isolated here, unless they send a flier down to tell us news."

"They will be using the big fliers to shuttle people and flying combat over for them. I don't expect they would spare anything for a message drop. We'll meet them at Fort. They'll still be at it when we get there. Air shuttle covers the ground faster, but they can't carry the volume of personnel that we can move in the trucks. And we're right out on the edge of their fuel range—from Base One and Two. Base Nine was all assigned to air cover missions around Fort and they are based there now. Our trucks will come under their fliers about mid-passage of the second day."

"Well, then, no messages, means no hitches in the plans," Mitch said. "Your flier is the only one into this field since we started the operation. The field isn't big enough for many more, anyway."

"It was hardly big enough for me," Amarson said, remembering the landing. The landing strip was not a proper base field at all, just a flat strip of grass in the jungle. It had been built to take his own personal flier and to take courier fliers. It was very small and very short when you tried to come into it with one of the big single-winged fliers.

"Baron, will the trucks you send back for the last of the Jungle Patrol. . . ?" The food administrator, Almann had something to say and this looked like a good place to interrupt. "Will they be able to carry back any material—food, supplies. . . ?"

"No, Almann. Just patrolmen. . . and a little loot. But we won't see any of that. Anybody that Mardon picks to stay with him will earn his pay. . . and anything else he wants to pick up. Warrior's Right. Why did you ask? Do you have something vital that we'll have to leave behind?"

"Noooo. Not really. Nothing that I can't replace from the

jungle around Fort. Certainly nothing traded out of Riverton. Lots of perishables, of course,'' he flattened his ears and spread his hands. "I'm leaving behind so much.''

"We all are, Almann. The People are moving with what they can carry. There will be homes for them at Fort and you'll have hunters up there to build back to comfortable food stocks. We'll still have trade with Riverton and the Valley and your perishables are replaceable. The People aren't.''

"We're leaving Draks behind, too, Almann. Remember that!''

A rising siren-warble cut across his words. The alarm signal.

"Draks!'' Mitch said. "They caught us!''

There was a general rush for the door. Mitch rolled his maps with quick scrabbling motions. The conference was over and his maps were going out with the trucks. . . . Then he gave up the task, found his own bundle of non-essentials to leave behind, and walked away from the crumpled bundle to go out and fight. By the time he reached the door he was running.

Amarson paused near the door and reached for. . . . His hand came away empty. The weapon rack had long ago been packed and taken away.

"Almann!'' he called as the Administrator passed him. "Get those trucks loaded. Don't let the People scatter!''

"Aii-ee, Baron!'' Almann acknowledged.

2

Outside, the confusion around the trucks was even more frantic than it had been before Amarson went into the Lodge. The warble of the alarm siren had started everyone moving frantically, but Amarson could pick out the Jungle Patrol uniforms holding firm positions around the trucks and lifting people and bundles aboard. Their discipline was holding; they were trusting the perimeter guard to fight the Draks while they loaded the trucks.

A heavy winged figure curved over the open plain and Amarson crouched in defensive reflex. Another body plunged down over the jungle tree tops and crashed into the ground. A Drak stooping to kill? No. The body was writhing in death agony, the wings beating futilely at the ground as a dozen metal quarrels killed it.

A patrol dashed to the body and tugged away the fighting spear—souvenir trophy or weapon, the Patrol had a tradition of scavenging both from their Drak kills.

Amarson still had to find a weapon for himself. He couldn't fight Draks with his claws. Not in a melee like the one this was liable to become. He risked a glance at the flier field. His yellow-painted flier was pulled well back under the protection of two big trees. It wouldn't get damaged, but it wasn't available as a weapon for Amarson. The People here in the plain were Amarson's own Marchholders. They lived on and around his Lodge and the title he carried, Baron Rufus, was a direct responsibility to them. He couldn't take his flier into the air, even to fight, as long as there were Marchholders on the ground, leaving their homes to make the move to Fort. They were making that move, because he had told them that it was necessary to stop the constant Drak hunting raids on their persons. For Amarson to fly away, while they couldn't. . . . That was an act so close to running away that Amarson wouldn't permit himself to use his flier at all. He had ordered a pilot up from Base XII to ferry the single-winged flier back to operational duty.

He hadn't looked to see if the flier could be flown, but to see if it had a field of fire for the twin dart launchers mounted on the body-pod. It didn't. The trees blocked any use of that weapon.

But there was a truck. . . the last truck still loading. Its mobile dart-launcher was unmanned. Where was the patrolman?

He saw the uniforms struggling to shove people onto the back of the truck. Probably back there. . . . Well, that was important. And it gave Amarson a weapon to use. A way to fight Draks.

He started off toward the truck.

A Drak dived. He caught the move on the edge of his vision and saw that this was a fighting dive, not a death plunge. The Drak came down.

A scream tore its way above the hysterical noise of the crowd. . . and cut off. The Drak had hit its target, made a kill and was on the ground. The flash of its fighting knife was a white-yellow flare in the sunlight, turning fire crimson as blood stained it. There were People being killed, there.

The Drak took to the air again. Amarson could see the dark streaks of dartbow quarrels following it and the hesitant wing-flap that told of some hits. Then he was at the truck.

One of the Holders, wearing a merchant's hood, was fumbling at a pack of his belongings on the ground by the front wheel. He was tugging to free a hunt-bow from its straps. Amarson knelt beside him, grabbed his shoulder for attention and nearly got a fighting knife in the stomach. The merchant carried white hair around his mouth and ears, but age hadn't slowed his knife hand much. The knife was Jungle Patrol issue.

"Up in the truck!" Amarson ordered. "Roll up the canvas! You can fire over people's heads. Any more bows packed?"

"Plenty. I'll find them." The veteran recognized his Baron the instant he'd held the focus of his knife thrust. He turned away and climbed the side of the truck to shove up the canvas. Amarson tossed the bundle up to him and saw the fighting knife slash the pack ties, as the veteran stopped being a merchant and went back to war again.

Amarson jerked the door open and climbed into the trucks' gun mount. The dart belts were loaded and he knocked off the safeties and swung the mount to look for targets.

He found them. From this position, above the ground by five meters, he could see out across the trees that ringed the Plain. He could see a line of six Draks beginning a swoop into one of their spirals. They would wing up that tightening curve until they had fighting height over the Plain. He swung the launcher frantically, to track this nearer target. Swung up to and past, to lead the heavy beak and glaring eyes. He saw the beak open to scream and noticed the color-smear of tree foliage behind his target. His over-fire wouldn't hit anybody. He held the triggers back and let the Draks fly into the sight's deflection ring. One Drak tumbled in the air. At that distance the dart-launcher threw a meter-wide grouping of darts. Amarson saw their smoke trails planing flatly into the wings and body. The Drak dropped his fighting lance and half rolled, jerking out of the tumble with the impact of his death. Amarson let off the triggers and swung the launcher up the spiraling figures. He didn't have to follow the falling body down to its impact with the ground. He knew a kill when he saw it in his sights.

The swarm was closer now. He triggered a four-dart burst at the maximum elevation ring to see if he could reach them. One of the Draks locked his wings and swooped to dodge. The quarrels could reach that far. These launchers had claws as long as the ones on his fighters.

The smoke trails arced high, but he found the proper lead and the smooth curve of the spiral was broken as the Draks were forced to rise and fall to dodge his fire. Some were taking hits, but at this distance the darts were wounding, not fatal. In a moment, the flight had risen beyond the smoking quarrels, and Amarson stopped shooting and dropped his aiming point down the sky. He'd wait for their fighting dive, time the drop, and see if he could make some kills.

At last he could help. Mardon could have his perimeter guard firing from the jungle as the Draks dropped in their deadly dive. The Draks would fly through this cross-fire coming down, and in their slower, more vulnerable climb back up to the spiral. Oh, yes the Patrol would make kills. They had fought this way before.

A dropping shape crossed his sights. He raised the trigger handles as he fired to lead its fall, then brought the sights back up to catch the next Drak's swoop. Two more like that and the Draks were all down, on the ground, or flying so low that Amarson couldn't use his fire. There were Jungle Patrolmen in the trees rimming the clearing. From the top of this truck a depressed angle of fire would overshoot into them.

Amarson swung his sights up and began to find and lead the Draks circling the Plain or those climbing back up to form another spiral. He fired in short bursts whenever his sight ring caught something. He got some hits, saw at least one clean, wing-fold kill. But the angles were tricky, usually coming toward him or flying away on a curve, and other times he couldn't be sure, despite the marking traces of the smoke trails. He fired in short groups of four or six darts so that his misses wouldn't cost too many quarrels and he kept shifting to find a new target. He couldn't manuever this truck through the sky to follow one Drak for a kill, so he let the Draks do the flying and didn't make the cub-mistake of trying to shoot at one target until all his darts were gone. There were plenty of Draks in the sky, and plenty of other dart-bows shooting at them. He concentrated on adding to the dart stream in the sky over the plain and let the Draks fly into the deadly quarrels.

The dart-launchers clattered to a stop. They were working on empty belts.

Amarson reached down to unclip the extra belt cans and reload. A hand slapped him on the leg three times.

"Baron! The truck is ready to go." A Jungle Patrolman was crouched below him in the cab. The bowman assigned to these guns, for a guess. "I'll take back my launchers."

Amarson nodded and climbed down beside him. "Empty belt," he said, reporting on the gun's status. "I didn't reload. Good hunting on the trip."

"*Blood only stains the hands*," the bowman replied, and handed Amarson his fighting bow and a belt of quarrels. "Take this, Baron. It's wild out there."

Amarson folded his hand around the bow and slid out of the cab. The driver was waiting for him to come down and climbed in as soon as there was room.

The engine started right away, and Amarson had time for a glimpse of three or four bowmen firing out of the side of the truck. The veteran had found himself a fighting squad.

"Baron! Eyes up!" A voice called and a hand jerked his leg out from under him, pulling him to the ground. The rattle of firing dartbows was loud in his ears. He rolled sideways to look up and straight into the gaping beak of a dropping Drak, its wings spread wide in hooking brakes against the air as it stooped to kill.

He jerked his own dartbow up and fired off two quarrels, then continued his roll over to the right. Over on top of the patrolman who'd jerked him down. They twisted together, trying to get out of the way of the Drak's dive. Amarson just grabbed onto the patrolman and continued his roll—over and over.

He heard the angry rattle of dartbows again, the scream of the diving Drak, and then the grinding roar of the trucks' engines as they accelerated and headed for the road out of the Plain. He also discovered, in his rolling tangle with the patrolman, that he was holding a girl. A very full-formed, roughly-muscled girl who was fighting to get clear and get another shot at the Drak. She did. Pulling loose from Amarson's entangling arms and legs and shooting from a half-prone position, lying on her back.

The final shot hadn't been necessary. The Drak's braking wings had lost their beat, and it hit the ground head first. It would have died of a broken neck, except for the fact that four quarrels were impaled in its skull and one had torn a gaping fountain in its neck. Somebody, close by, was a very good shot.

Somebody jerked the girl trooper to her feet and Amarson could see the really beautiful lines of her face and ears. She had a tawny-pale fur that was unusual even when spotted with the dust of their rolling encounter. The patrolman who had helped her up was shorter and square, also female, Amarson realized, but as tough looking as Mitch. Three more Patrolmen gathered around, one pulling Amarson off the ground, but they were men. A squad. And the girl wore the chevrons. Amarson found the rank badges as she dusted her shoulders.

A flash of uniform near the Drak. . . . Another girl trooper was darting in to stand on the beating wings. She swung a fighting knife and hacked off a trophy wing tip.

"*Hoo—eee! Heet!*" The squad leader's pale arm flashed up and over in combat signal. The trucks' motors, the Draks' fighting cries and the noise level in the plain forced her to use hand-speech. One of the troopers slapped Amarson's back to urge him to come with them, but he was already moving. Amarson could read the girl's signals and she was right. "*Get to cover*!" was a wholly sensible thing to do right now. Right now! Amarson was a seventh member of the squad as he crouched and followed those tawny legs toward the trees. The squad closed in around him and concentrated on sprinting.

They ran in under the tree-line and someone grabbed Amarson and pulled him down. He took the fall and scrabbled to the left on his hands and knees. He'd seen the banked earth revetment as he ran by it.

He slid over the earth wall and down on top of the girl squad leader.

"Gruu—mmph! Get off!" she snarled. "Saving your neck doesn't entitle you to sit on me. What's the matter, don't you like to get dirty?"

Amarson slid sideways and up onto the dirt bank. She didn't need an answer; didn't want one. And he wanted to get in a position to shoot. There were still Draks to kill. He shoved his dartbow out to find a target.

But the fight was over.

Her voice had been loud in a silence that had echoes. The sky over the plain was free of flying Draks and the trucks had all left. The plain was empty except for the silent mounds of bodies humping its flatness.

Amarson's ears were still ringing from the clatter of the mobile dart-launcher and the roar of the truck's engine. But he didn't hear the sound of any more firing. The dartbows were quiet.

Across the plain a Jungle Patrolman came cautiously out of the tree-line and walked out into the open. It was Mardon, his wide shoulders and alert head easily recognizable from this distance. Amarson got to his knees to go out to meet him.

"Better hold on, Baron," the girl's hand was on his leg. "Let him blow the all clear. There's a lot of trigger-happy troopers out there right now."

Amarson sagged back to the ground. She was right. Mardon's troops would shoot at anything that moved, until they calmed out of their fighting focus. He safetied his dartbow and half-rolled to look at the girl.

She'd collected another smear of dirt across one ear and the side of her face, but it made her grin look young and delightfully fierce. Amarson realized she was laughing at him.

"Sorry about the crack, Baron. You are dirty enough to make a drill-master happy."

"I expect so. This plain wasn't made for cub-crawling. The trucks have cut it up. Your ear's got combat-dust on it, too. My fault, I expect. Thanks for taking that Drak off my head, Corporal."

"Ameera," she said by way of introduction, then proceeded to name the rest of her squad in a loud voice as introduction and roll call."

"Dragna. Leeash. Kreak, Maroni, Mithee."

"Hey yoh!"

"Ay Corp."

"Meera."

"Ho!"

"Trophy, Ameera!"

"Yes, I saw that, Mithee!" Ameera said. "One bloody stupid stunt. And you're going to have to carry the stinking thing, too. Herald only knows where our baggage packs are." She was grinning at Amarson as she called out the reprimand. Good noncoms didn't try to stop trophy taking, they just grumped at it on principle.

"My squad, Baron. A bunch of rough-ears, but they shoot straighter than most."

"They do that." Amarson was remembering the four center head-shots he'd seen as the Drak crashed in. "Glad of it, too. But what were you cubs doing out on the plain?"

"That Truck Boss, Almann, commandeered me and the squad just caught up. I knew they'd find me when the perimeter rolled back. They generally do."

"Ah, you were the courier," Amarson said. "Didn't recognize you."

"My face must be muddy," she said. "I wonder where I can function a liter of water."

"There's a bath in the Lodge," Amarson said absently,

95

then, "How far out were those trucks from Riverton? Did you see? . . . or anyone tell you?"

"Oh, no. Get me near a bath and I'll get shot for desertion. Capt. Mardon will have water-points and cook-fires going, right off. He plans those like he plans a fight.

"The trucks?" She thought about his question. "I didn't see. About two hours out, for a guess. Trail-rumor. I don't know."

Mardon's whistle cut the air.

"There's the all clear, sir. You can get a better answer from Mardon." Ameera sat up and got to her feet. Amarson stood up with her to discover that she was almost as tall as he was. Her Patrol grip—hand on his forearm—was as firm as his own return salute. "That was a good fight, sir. Short. But a good kill."

"Hi-ya, Baron. Do you want a trophy quarrel from the Draks?" Mithee bounced up out of the bush.

Amarson took one look at her and doubled over in laughter. Ameera swung around, frowning, then began laughing in her own turn. Mithee was evidently the squad clown for she seemed fully conscious of her appearance, even strutted a little.

She was wearing the trophy wing-tip, hooked by its tip-claw into the back of her belt and flapping behind her like a skirt-cape. The torn, knife-cut, edge of the wing-flesh had spattered blood all over her legs from the back of her knees down to her ankles.

"Trooper. . . you're. . . a mess." Ameera said between laughs. "Blood. . . only . . . stains. . .the. . . hands." The Patrol battle phrase, corrupted into absurdity by the parts of Mithee that were actually stained, sent Ameera into laughing so hard she could barely talk.

"Dragna, put this. . . on water detail. They'll take. . . one look and give us double rations. . . triple." She turned back to Amarson, not even trying to apologize for her messy trooper. Amarson was Baron Rufus of the Lodge, but he'd fought with her squad. And her troops had killed a Drak. There was nothing to apologize for.

"They shoot well," Amarson said still laughing. "Find

that bath, before they burn the building. Good hunting.'' He left the revetment without any sort of goodby, as was Jungle Patrol custom.

He went out to find Mardon and get a briefing on when the next group of trucks would arrive. He walked slowly out across the plain, knowing that Mardon would see him, recognize him and meet him, long before Amarson could begin to search out the Patrol Captain.

He moved slowly across the plain. The laughter he'd shared with Ameera's squad in their after-combat boisterousness died away from his heart. The plain was broken with mounded bundles of cloth that had been living People. He saw the jungle-colored Patrol uniform, usually in small clumps of three or four near the winged and broken body of a Drak kill, but there were the bright, colored-cloth bundles too. Not all of his People had been carried safely away on the trucks.

He measured the distance from where the truck had loaded to a fighting stand where uniforms and color-cloth were tumbled together near a Drak. There were some of his People who had come out to fight. A long way from the trucks. *. . . And that wasn't a Jungle Patrolman's body fastened to the fighting knife in that Drak's throat*!

"The Jungle Patrol has recuited some valiant fighters today,'' Mardon had found him. ''They will get full honors in burial, at the least. The Draks did no butchering and we gave them no time to feed.''

"Some of them were veterans,'' Amarson said, meaning the Marchholder corpses. ''The Warrior's Code runs deep.''

"There are women over there, '' Mardon pointed. ''Your Lodge Marchholders breed courage.''

"They know how to fight Draks, Mardon. They've been doing it long enough. That's why I'm moving us all to city Fort. You and I spend all our time flying and fighting to keep the Draks out of Riverton's skies, away from the Valley Harvest. But the Marchland skies always have Draks. . . . and this. . . '' he swept his arm across the Plain, ''. . . is our harvest.'' He counted the Drak corpses. ''Seven Draks. Aargh! What a victory. Have you counted our losses?''

"It's being done. More than seven." Mardon was not proud of the figures. "I couldn't keep my squads in the jungle. They kept attacking out into the open. Most of them have never fought an action where they could see the Draks killing our people. I lost men who should have known better. Those that stayed at their fields of fire will be steadier next time, but I lost good men." Mardon's warrior mind balanced accounts and didn't waste time fighting old battles.

"I don't want a *next time*," Amarson growled. "I will see to it that city Fort has fliers over it. Our skies will be free of Draks too. That will be a promise I can keep.

"When will the trucks from Riverton get here?" He changed the subject. "You sent a message that they were fighting Draks. Was that the swarm that hit us here?"

"Maybe," Mardon said. "But there could have been two swarms. I've only got two squads out of the five positions. Just enough to check for survivors. The Riverton trucks should be here by now. . . .And they may bring more Draks. That's what I meant by next time. My cubs will be steadier. And we did get your people out.

"Some of the Draks followed them, though, Baron. They'll be doing a little fighting."

"It was expected. Nothing we can do about it now, old friend. And these Riverton trucks will get *your* men out. Then I'll be back for you. Depend on it!"

"I'll be here when you come back," Mardon said. "But I hate the idea of burning your Lodge. Sure you don't want to change your mind?"

The grinding of engine noises and the warble of the alarm cut off any reply Amarson might have made.

"The trucks are here," Mardon said. "And here we go again!" He was pointing up to the left. His whistle began sounding the three-blast, *Take Cover*, followed by his signature code.

"Amarson! Take the drivers and everybody into the lodge for cover," Mardon said. "They won't have enough quarrels left to help us. Their belts will be empty if they had to fight their way in here."

Amarson nodded and headed for the Lodge. He kept a sky

check on the Draks' but he didn't expect to have to fight. Mardon's troops had their ranges and timing. One more huntbow wasn't important.

The Riverton trucks rolled into the Plain, still moving fast. The lead driver picked up Amarson's arm signals and headed in close to the Lodge. He pulled on by and stopped. Three more trucks followed him in to stop at close intervals. The next swung out and doubled the rank. Amarson discovered he had a squad of assistant traffic directors. He caught a glimpse of a pale-furred figure through the swirling dust of the trucks. Corporal Ameera's squad. Well, he could use the help.

"Heh ho, Corporal!" he called as she dodged a truck and ran close to him. "Are you following me?"

"Yes, Baron. Want to hire a bodyguard?"

"Do I have a choice? Keep Mithee away from my trucks. They need their wheels more than she needs trophies."

"As you say, my Baron." She laughed. "Shall we start another row?" She pointed at the still rolling trucks.

"Yes," he said. Then, "Ameera, the bodyguard? Mardon's orders?"

"No. Mine." And she sprinted away into the dust.

The trucks showed that they'd had some trouble. Torn canvas, some bent support bars, and the second truck had a shattered windscreen and dented cab. Most of the windscreens he could see were cracked in one way or another. And there, in the second rank. . . *Aiiee*, the whole dart-launcher mount was smashed and bent against the cab roof.

The Draks must have been using the same dive and smash tactics they used against a flier. But the trucks were thicker metal, moving with more mass. A Drak diving to hit the side of a truck—to hit and grab, and kill with fighting knife— would be smashed and broken against the metal.

"Get out! Inside the Lodge!" Amarson jerked open a cab door and called up his orders, as soon as the motors died, so he could be heard. "Leave the trucks. Get inside!"

He moved rapidly down the line of trucks opening doors and repeating the orders to the drivers. The truck crews were shocked, exhausted from their running fight and they just sat slumped in position. They moved readily when Amarson jarred them and no one was hurt badly. There were glass-cut wounds and one broken arm. The bowman in the smashed launcher-mount was dead, but everybody else was walking to the Lodge.

Amarson was between the rows of trucks, calling the crews out, when he heard the dartbow fire start up from the jungle perimeter. The Draks had decided to come down.

He jerked open another door. "Get out!" he called. "Come on out of it. Fast! Move! Move!"

He had found his pilot in this truck. The man's uniform was bloody, but recognizable. His arms and chest were caked with dried blood, but his face and eyes were marked. The windscreen had shattered on this truck and Amarson expected glass had cut him badly. But he wasn't blinded. He could still fly if the medics patched him.

"Come on, Flier, *move*!" The truck's bowman was trying to get room to climb down from the mount. "I'll push him, Baron. That blood isn't his. It's all Drak. Flew right down my dart. . . ripped its head off and then hit right on our front. Sprayed everything."

The deeper rattle of a dart-launcher started up close by, the next truck over, then stopped short. A voice began swearing and calling for more darts. . . . A high, frustrated screaming, futilely repeating itself.

"Get to cover. In the Lodge!" Amarson snapped at the bowman and the pilot. He crouched to run around the front of the truck and through the third line to where he could see the Plain and the sky above it. He stayed close to the bulk of the trucks. His dartbow had only a half-a-clip. That, and his fighting knife didn't give him any edge in a Drak fight. But he had to see.

And he saw.

The Drak was not ten meters away, on the ground and whirling in its wing-high flighting stance. There were two patrol troopers facing its attack. No, one down on the ground, the other. . . .

Amarson saw the flapping, torn-skin skirt and recognized the trooper Mithee.

Ameera's squad!

Then he saw the flash of white-yellow fur against the Drak's swirling legs. *Ameera*!

The girl was close against the Drak, inside the reach of its fighting spear, clutching at its body to hold herself in front, away from the beating wings. Her fighting knife flashed once, twice. The Drak had not grabbed her. She'd gone inside its weapons and was fighting to stay there.

Amarson broke into a run. He was yelling, but he didn't hear the sounds. The girl had seconds in that fighting grip. The Drak would throw her off and into the reach of its spear, or grab her up to tear with its beak. . . .

He hit the Drak's side with his shoulder and full weight. He grabbed the lance shaft with one hand and slashed over and back with his knife. The blade cut tendons and muscles in the Drak's arm and the spear came away into Amarson's hands. He took the downward blow of the wing across his back and shoulders, rolled forward with it. . . and around. The lance jabbed up and caught the Drak at the base of the throat.

"Graa-aagh!" Amarson growled deep and thrust it up until the skull-shock jarred his hand off the lance shaft.

Then he grabbed the girl's hands, crushing them roughly to break her grip and pulled away from the Drak in a twisting, rolling dive.

He fought to get his feet under him and lift the girl's body away, but found somebody's legs blocking him.

A dartbow clattered. A whole clip. Somebody was standing over him and wasting darts on the Drak. A dead Drak: Amarson knew where he'd put that lance-point.

"That's enough, Leeash," a voice said. "It won't be any deader. Let the Baron up."

Amarson got to his knees, then to his feet. He still had his arms around the limp girl. And he lifted her into a carry as he got up.

"Sky's not clear, Baron," Dragna was close beside him. She and the other trooper had picked up the fallen patrolman, Meroni—their arms locked under his armpits—in a walking carry and she was crowding Amarson with her free shoulder to get him moving. "Draks up high. Head for the Lodge! Get her under cover! Get inside!"

Amarson broke into a jog. He was hearing his own words thrown back at him, but Dragna was right. They had to take cover.

"Mithee!" Dragna's yell was parade-ground loud. "That's the Baron's kill! He'll cut his own trophies! Rearguard us, damn it. And stay up."

Amarson didn't care about trophies. He tightened his grip on Ameera and dodged between two trucks. He carried her through the truck-park and in under the roof of the Lodge's entry. He moved fast, purposefully, but he ignored the fighting noises behind him. Ameera's squad closed in behind— the two troopers carrying Meroni between them and Mithee and the odd man bringing up an airguard watch behind. Mardon's troops would fight the Draks as they were positioned to do. Mardon would also have a medic on his way to the Lodge—the truck damage would tell him one was needed. Amarson was carrying the girl to cover and to that medic. He hadn't taken the time to look for wounds and he felt her heart beating rapidly and strongly against his chest. She was alive, a marvelous thing in itself after that fight, but he wanted the medic to make sure.

He carried her into the main hall, looking for Mardon's medic and came to a jarring halt.

The main hall was crowded with the ten or twenty crewmen of the Riverton truck convoy. They were sitting and lying on the floor, and leaning haphazardly against the walls. Some were lined up along the conference table where two of Mardon's medics had set up an aid station. Despite its size, the main hall was a disorganized barrack of exhausted men.

And standing in the middle of this disorder was a sleek grey-skinned Riverman, the Ambassador Theiu. He stood isolated by the fact that he was the only Riverman in the room, and by his hand-sprayer which was filling the air around him with a damp fog.

"Theiu!" Amarson said. "Ambassador Theiu. By the Two Suns! What are you doing here?"

"Put me down." Ameera said weakly. "I'm dizzy, but all right. Put me down." She stirred a little in his arms, but didn't really struggle. Her voice was protesting, but her head

102

didn't move from where it lay against his shoulder.

Amarson ignored her, and put aside the amazing fact of the Riverton Ambassador's appearance for a moment. He went across the room and through into the sleeping quarters. The bed in there was empty and he put the girl down on it.

"Him, too," he said, indicating the more than ample room. Dragna had followed him in with the other wounded squad member. She was going to keep the group together.

"What's wrong with him?" A medic—Mardon had sent three—had followed Amarson into the room. "That shoulder all?" He pressed a drug-bulb's needle into the man's arm and said, "Shock. The Drak hit him from the air—or on the ground?"

"Ground," Dragna said shortly.

"Then he'll live. Get him cleaned up and I'll look at it again." The impact shock of a diving Drak, hitting out of the sky, would have made even a shoulder wound fatal. As it was. . . just messy, if the bone wasn't torn away.

"What about the Corporal?"

"My head," Ameera said. "Something hit. . ."

"Keep your hand down. I see it. A nice clean scratch. Missed the ear?" He was probing the side of her skull, feeling for any softness that would indicate a bone-break.

Amarson touched Dragna on the shoulder and indicated the door to the bath area. That old campaigner would know what to do with the hot water still in the storage tanks.

He looked at the girl lying on the bed. He couldn't see her face, the medic was still working on the cut, and the room was crowded—the bed was crowded. But somehow Ameera seemed to take possession of the room. The medic was there because Ameera was hurt. Dragna had brought the rest of the squad in because Ameera was their leader. The other wounded trooper was there because Ameera's squad didn't leave their wounded behind. The dark wood and forest colors of the room were accents to the pale luster of her fur. The bedroom, for the moment, and because she was in it, became Ameera's room.

Part of the feeling, of course, was that Amarson had left

this room. He'd moved all his personal equipment and resettled his household at Fort. In fact, he had been living at Base XII for most of the last year, flying and fighting. The big oversized bedroom was no longer a part of him. He felt more at home in Flight Base quarters.

But Ameera lay in state in the room, surrounded by the people who depended on her, worried about her. The solid, timbered room was alive again.

Amarson began to regret the orders he'd given to burn the building. He turned and went out, back into the main hall to face a more pragmatic problem.

Ambassador Theiu. What did he want and how in the name of the Two Suns was he, Amarson, going to get him back to Riverton?

Mitch and Captain Mardon were with the Riverton Ambassador. That is, they were standing together in a group. Mitch was talking to Theiu. Mardon was standing with one hand hooked in the sling of his dartbow and the other behind his back. He was pushing the bow stock out and back in little nervous twitches. He obviously wanted to be out in the jungle with his men, not here in the Lodge. He must have come in to get a policy decision from Mitch—something he didn't want to talk about in front of the Riverton Ambassador, for a guess.

Mardon was the first to see Amarson and he went single-mindedly to the thing that was bothering him.

"Baron, will your timetable for the move be disrupted if I hold my men here until tomorrow? There are dead to bury and by then we will be past mid-passage. My thought is: the trucks wouldn't make the fuel dump by Dark."

"I don't think the truck drivers are going anywhere," Amarson said. He had thought about this when he first saw the main hall. "They'll drive if ordered, but we'll have wrecked trucks.

"Do as you plan, for the rest of today. We'll take the trucks out at first-light tomorrow, Mardon. We've got the early group off today before the Draks showed up. You can do the same tomorrow and be hidden in the jungle if they decided to attack you again.

"Read the Warrior's Rites for the dead when the Father

Sun sets. That will be a fitting ceremony for our leaving Lodge."

"Food and rest will help too," Mardon said. "Hot rations and cook fires after a fight are better for morale than ration-packs on the run."

"Get some rations in here too, will you?" Amarson gestured to the main hall. "They can cook for themselves, but why should they? We'll need alert drivers tomorrow."

"Already laid on," Mardon answered. "I've got a crew checking the trucks for damage, too. Nothing we can do to fix them here, but I don't want to roll anything that won't go all the way."

Amarson nodded. The trucks didn't have to be pretty, as long as they would roll.

"Ambassador Theiu," Amarson greeted the Riverman formally for the first time. "Have they given you water? You came out here at a poor time for official hospitality."

The Ambassador gazed around at the Marchholders standing around him. He lifted a sprayer and wetted the smooth skin of his face. The dust of the truck trip had dried his skin and eyes painfully.

"Word came that you were leaving Riverton," he said. And I came myself to see why the March People are abandoning the Compact." Theiu's words were blunt and, considering that he was surrounded by armed Jungle Patrolmen, fairly courageous. He sprayed his head and face again, but that was the only sign he gave of any nervousness.

"Did you see the reasons out there on the Plain?" Mitch said. "Did you see the body-count?"

"Mitch!" Amarson stopped him. There was no need for anger at the Riverman. Of all the River people, Theiu had been a consistent ally and friend. Other supplies came from the Valley grudgingly or only on demand, but Theiu's factory sheds continued to build and deliver the fliers and the dart-launchers that Amarson's squadrons and the Jungle Patrol needed so badly. That job of vital supply and the thankless position of Ambassador to the Marchlands were two jobs that Thieu took very seriously indeed. And Amarson honored him for it. Over the years he'd come to like the Riverman as well as he liked Mardon, or Mitch, or any of the Marchholders.

"I haven't left Riverton, Ambassador," he said. "I still have full flier squadrons at Base XXI and at Base II and III. Commander Mardon has only half a battalion here helping to move my Lodge People and the other bases have supplied half-strength detachments for their moves. None of the mountain battalion has left the highlands above the Valley. Riverton has just as much protection from any Drak hunting party as it had at the beginning of the year." Amarson was speaking slowly. He was tired, and the tones of his voice were beginning to show it. The adrenalin surge of two short, violent combat actions in the last five hundred heart beats was beginning to drain away, leaving his body dehydrated and his muscles overworked and needing rest.

"Baron, I know the way you are being treated by some of my people, but that will not last."

"I know a way to stop it," Mitch growled, lifting a hand and running his claws out.

"You also say, 'There is no honor in killing a River-man,' " Theiu said. "My people don't like either alternative, Commander. But most of them do like the way you kill Draks. I like the way you kill Draks and surprisingly there are some of you I like personally." He stopped and sprayed his eyes as he blinked them slowly. "Also, surprisingly, I don't know any of the people of the Marches that I hate personally. Do you, any of you, hate a Riverman—personally? Or have we begun to hate each other the way we hate the Draks?"

"The Draks are enough for all our hates," Amarson said. "I repeat, Ambassador. We are not leaving Riverton. My fliers will continue to attack the Draks in the air over Riverton. But at the same time that I fight to keep Rivermen from being hunted and eaten by Draks, I must fight for my Marchholders. There are Draks in our skies, too, Theiu.

"That is why I am moving my people. I have found a place south of here, down the coastal plain. The high mountains are one side and the mud sea is on the other. With a narrow sky space in which to fly patrols, I can keep Draks from hunting my people, while at the same time fighting their swarms and henge camps on the River and Valley marches.

"Look, Theiu," Amarson shook his head to clear his sight. "You have a long trip. But I will show you all I plan to do. That is all I can show you with what we have here. All of our records and plans have been sent south to city Fort.

"Ambassador, get something to eat and let Mitch show you on his maps the way our patrols will protect—will continue to protect—the Valley and Riverton." Mitch would still have a map around that would serve for a briefing.

"Mitch, sheathe your claws and talk for me in this, will you? Mardon can't stay. He has his troopers to get ready for the move tomorrow."

"As you order, Baron," Mitch said stiffly. He didn't like Rivermen, but he liked the new patrol plans and he could explain them.

"And I'll have to think of some way of getting you back to Riverton," Amarson said absently. He couldn't bring his mind to focus on that problem. . . . He certainly didn't want to carry Theiu all the way to Fort. . . .

"I had planned to go back with your flier," Theiu said. "The pilot told me he was coming out here to bring back a flier to Base XII."

That statement alone was evidence of the importance Theiu put on his trip out to Lodge. He almost never flew. His factory made the fliers, and Theiu had helped design the improved versions, but he didn't like the air. And to deliberately plan a trip by . . . flier. . . .

"Heh. Yes, that would be one way. . . " Amarson was very tired. "Mitch, please show the Ambassador what he wants to know. And send someone to call me before sunset. I want to stand the Warrior's Rites."

"As you order, Baron."

Amarson turned away and walked toward his bedroom. He was actually going through the door before he remembered that that room was crowded too—filled with Ameera's squad.

But it wasn't crowded.

The big bedroom was empty. Emptier because Amarson half-wanted to see Corporal Ameera again.

He went to a cupboard where they'd left his kit bag for the

truck trip, and pulled out a robe. He struggled out of his dusty uniform shirt and wrapped the robe around his shoulders. Dragna and the combat squad probably found the room too uncomfortable to stay in it long. Jungle Patrol troops don't like to be inside walls, or under roofs.

They'd probably gotten away from the medic and back out into the jungle. That squad was a fighting unit, they wouldn't let wounds keep them out of Mardon's Drak killing. Ameera hadn't been hurt and a field dressing would have taken care of the other spear wound. That trooper Dragna probably trusted her own remedies more that the medic's anyway.

Well, he'd meet them again on the trucks. . . . No. He probably wouldn't. Mardon would be sure to keep a tight squad like that as part of his rearguard.

Amarson lay down across the bed, letting the strain in his back and shoulders melt into the firm support under him. In a few hours he would have to go back out on the Plain for the Warrior's Rites. The Patrolmen out there were his People too, as much so as the Marchholders who'd lived near the Lodge.

He would stand the Warrior's Rite and then ride out with Mitch and the Patrolmen Mardon was sending to Fort at dawn. But the trucks would come back for the rearguard—for Ameera's squad. . . . For Ameera.

The door to the bath-area opened.

Ameera walked in, toweling her head and ears.

Her uniform was still jungle-stained, but she'd brushed it clean. The most startling change was her own fur. It shone and glowed an ivory-white with a delicate pattern of gold. She had seemed striking against the room's dark coloring when Amarson had first brought her into it. Now she was blindingly magnificent.

Amarson had turned his head to look at her, but he made no other move. He had been nearly asleep when she walked in, but he saw her clearly. So clearly—every detail of her face and form was sharp and bright—that he knew he was wide awake. He also felt his pulses begin to hammer.

Ameera was in uniform, but she had left her weapons somewhere—in the bath-area? She wasn't even wearing her

108

fighting knife. She certainly didn't plan on going back to combat.

"Baron Amarson." Her use of his name was a simple salutation. She didn't show any surprise at finding him on the bed. "I changed my mind and decided to use the bath."

"Is the rest of your squad still in there?"

"They will come back later. They're out locating our cook fire. The fighting's over. . . for today."

"The water will still be here. We won't take it with us tomorrow. Your troops deserve it. You got two Draks today."

"One Drak was yours, Baron. You pulled him off my back."

"I pulled him off your knife. *Blood only stains the hands.*" Amarson used the Jungle Patrol phrase routinely. He had been deliberately keeping the conversation on a trooper-to-trooper basis. He was deeply conscious that he was talking to a beautiful woman. A woman who was becoming more desirable every half-hundred heartbeats. He could smell the damp-fur wetness of her.

She pulled the towel into a scarf around her neck and walked forward one step at a time until she stood close to the bed.

"Baron Amarson, you and I have fought Draks together. In that last fight your knife protected my life." Her voice was deeply formal and her eyes were wide and dark, expressing her emotion.

"I stayed behind. . . . " she faltered. "I sent the squad away. . . because I. . . . " She hesitated again and Amarson saw her claws slide out, then in again. She went on firmly.

"Baron Amarson, I have come to take your name."

FOUR

Huntbow Quarry

1

Oz pointed, extending his arm slowly, his tail tip twitching for attention. Lady Ameera didn't acknowledge the point. Her huntbow was already leveled, sighting at the *hourn*. She let her ears flatten in annoyance. The guide shouldn't have risked the movement. *Hourn* had very good eyesight.

Also, Ameera was annoyed that he should have felt the need to point out the game. She could see it quite well. It was the only *hourn* on the entire stone ridge.

Three years of continuous attack against Draks had brought the Marchlands to a point where their supply lines were stretched away from Riverton and the Valley harvests. The Marchholders had long ago begun hunting the jungles of the upland ranges. Lady Ameera had organized hunt schedules for regular supply of Fort and had gone out herself on the formal sporting hunts that the Heralds had brought back into Marchland tradition. She was a capable stalker and the *hourn* was a clear target.

Ameera and Amarson had been hunting for three days now, and this single animal was the first they had seen. Amarson had been about to give up and call off the hunt. This trip was supposed to be relaxing; a semi-therapeutic vacation for him. Climbing endlessly, up one ridge after another, with no shooting—not even the smell of game—was bringing back all of his old tensions and frustrations. A day in the sky, in a combat flier, was more therapeutic, even though it left him physically exhausted. This hunt was supposed to be a relaxing vacation, but a hunt meant that the hunters were supposed to make an occasional satisfying kill; not just walk through endless mountains. Ameera was conscious of the Baron, behind her on the scree, kneeling and ready, but honoring her right to the first shot.

The bead sight of her huntbow held steady on the *hourn's* chest. Lady Ameera was waiting for the animal to turn away from the cliff face. A shot now, and the *hourn* might bound, dying, out and down the cliff drop; making a long dangerous climb necessary to recover a battered trophy. In a few seconds the *hourn* would turn, go back the way it had come, or curve left across the scree. She held her aim.

There! The *hourn* turned.

She drifted her sight slightly to the shoulder target and squeezed in her trigger.

Tweet-anng! The huntbow loosed with its whistling rattle and recocked itself. Ameera shifted her aim to lead the *hourn*, anticipating its leap when the quarrel struck, and fired again. The shock-startled *hourn* dove forward. Its forelegs buckled from the impact of two quarrels and it rolled, head forward, shoulder down, across the scree slope. Then it struggled to its feet and lurched uphill, over the ridge-line.

"Great shot!" Amarson called. "A kill shot! Both times!"

Lady Ameera stood and safetied the huntbow. She laughed lightly. They still insisted on telling her things she knew.

The *hourn's* tremendous vitality had taken it up the crest, running raggedly; but it was dying as it ran. Both the quarrels *had been* good kill shots. Lady Ameera's hunting experience was skilled enough to tell her that. Now, the job was a chase until the *hourn* dropped. Hunter's Obligation. She loaded a new quarrel-clip into the huntbow and started to climb around the rock-fall.

The guide, Oz, was already up the scree, checking the

blood spill. He'd pumped his climb-pack light to cross the distance in two great leaps, his tail floating to balance his mass. Now, he was bending over the blood spoor, the swollen balloonets of his climb-pack hunching over his shoulders like two extra heads. He pointed up the scree and hooted his high hunting-call.

Amarson safetied his huntbow and levered his own climb-pack. He had held his eyes on the rock saddle where the *hourn* went out of sight, and now he began climbing directly up to that point. He moved in controlled jumps, his weight lifted and lessened by the buoyancy of the climb-pack. He jumped, balanced against the pack's lift and landed, then jumped again. He didn't have the guide's sure skill, to run with the long bouncing stride Oz used, but he'd picked the shorter distance. He arrived below the saddle in nearly the same time as the guide who had tracked the *hourn's* spoor that far.

Oz went over the ridge first, walking light because he expected to have to follow the *hourn*. He gave a great, surprised hoot, and quick-called, "Bahr*oon*!"

Amarson hurried over the ridge. . . .

. . . And dove flat; scrambling on hands and knees down the reverse slope. His move was a combat reflex. He would have rolled to the right in his dive, but the fragile climb-balloons forced him into a sliding scrabble. He was trying to clear Oz out of his sights; to get a right-side vector so he could shoot without hitting the guide. He scrabbled frantically

Lady Ameera began to run up the turf verge of the scree. She reached the ridge line and went to earth, her head and huntbow topping the ridge at the same time.

Down-slope, less than five meters from Oz, a Drak crouched over the *hourn* carcass. A Drak! On the ground. . . furring and beating his wings in threatening arcs toward Oz. . . . A Drak! What was it doing *here*?

Amarson triggered off a shot. It missed! Expecting the Drak to fly, he'd held too high. The second quarrel snapped across the front of the Drak's gaping beak. Another miss. He wasn't used to shooting at Draks from the ground. His eye automatically adjusted for deflection shooting.

113

Oz was back-peddling away from the Drak, up a slope-tier of rock. The Drak moved after him, carrying the *hourn*, and jabbing at the guide with a short pole.

Amarson held his fire. The huntbow clip held four quarrels. He had only two more shots and he needed a kill-shot or a good disable that would give him time to reclip the huntbow.

He saw Ameera crouched on the ridge-line, her huntbow raised. He chopped an arm-signal at her to hold her fire. The Drak was too close to Oz to risk wounding it. A wounded Drak would kill the guide instantly. The little guide was only alive this long because the Drak didn't have a fighting spear. The pole it was using wasn't a spear—or the spear-point had broken off. In any case, the Drak was just jabbing the shattered end at Oz in defense of the *hourn* carcass.

Amarson held his sight on the Drak's chest, but the flapping, swirling wings wouldn't give him a clear shot. He wanted a kill-shot, not a wing-shot.

Oz kept moving away. It was all he could do. His huntbow was still clutched in one waving hand. He hadn't even tried to bring it into firing position. He was too busy trying to stay away from that splintered pole.

"Oz! Behind you! Look out!" Lady Ameera's yell came clear and quick, but pulsebeats late.

The Drak charged, flapping clumsily.

Oz jumped back from a rock ledge. . . and there was nothing under his feet. The ledge rimmed the cliff-faced canyon.

The Drak rushed the cliff, its scream mixing with Oz's startled yell. The Drak took wing, flying heavily with the load of the *hourn* carcass. It veered to the left, flew down the ridge-line, never climbing more than a few meters above the rocky ground, then went out of sight beyond a nose formation.

Oz was falling. Not fast, his climb-pack had cut his weight, but falling out of control. He had hurled himself backward to escape the Drak and gone over the cliff-edge. His backward, panic-lunge had thrown his feet up in the air and he was tumbling awkwardly, feet over shoulders. The tumbling kept turning him upside down and away from the cliffside.

By the time Amarson could scramble over to the cliff edge the little guide was five meters down and still sinking. He was still tumbling, too, and seemed to be further away from the cliff. . . . No, closer! There! His foot had touched the rock.

His tail was swirling visibly, cutting circles in the air as Oz fought to gain his balance in the fall. He had to straighten out, fall feet first, facing the cliff, so that the balloonets of his climb-pack could help his fall. Oz was twisting to keep those balloonets away from the rocks of the cliff. That's why he kept jabbing and kicking at the cliff instead of grabbing for a hand-hold. The climb-pack would break his fall to the point where it would be no more dangerous than a dekameter jump. But. if the balloonets were ripped. . . . The cliff was not large, about three hundred meters, down to a sloping bench and the bottom of a water-erosion canyon, but Oz had already dropped half-way down the face. If the balloonets ripped. . . an unsupported fall of a hundred-fifty meters could break legs or ribs. The fall could kill the little guide.

Kill! Amarson came back to combat awareness with a shock. He rocked to his knees and backed hurriedly away from the cliff edge. Draks! The Drak. It would be back to attack.

He spun around to signal Ameera: arm in the air, his fist circling. He saw her glance at the sky, crouched in startled reflex and break for cover.

He sprinted back to the plinth-pile of boulders on the ridge-line and backed against it. He pumped down his climb-pack, transferring the buoyant gas back into its tanks. He wanted to be full-weight if he had to fight; wanted to be able to trust his muscles and fighting reflexes for full, familiar responses.

He anxiously scanned the sky, up and around, as he re-loaded his huntbow; ejecting the single quarrel and putting in a new clip. He rearmed the guide's bow too. He'd picked that off the cliff-edge on the run, as he scrambled for the rocks. That fighting instinct was normal, anyway; a Jungle Patrol trained habit of collecting weapons. His eyes swept the skies.

Other Draks? There should be a hunting pack—three or four at least. Amarson's flier squadrons had driven the Drak to that point in the last three years. They no longer hunted alone.

He kept on sweeping the sky, using a flier's swing of his head—front, left, right, and front again—letting the overlap of his peripheral vision cover his back. He would see flying Draks as they moved on the edge of his vision more easily than by looking for them directly. But the sky seemed clear and gradually he relaxed.

Their Drak had been a lone hunter after all. It could still come back, and Amarson would stay alert for that hazard, but the Drak had taken the *hourn* carcass. It wouldn't have food-need to come back, and it *had* flown away from combat. . . .

Amarson came up out of his crouch, signaled; *clear*, to Ameera, and waited for her to come up to him.

"The Drak, Leon?" she asked. "They don't hunt alone, anymore. Where do you suppose the rest of the pack is?"

"I don't know. They aren't in our sky. We were certainly targets for long enough. Mitch and Mardon are right, I guess. I don't have any business flying combat."

They climbed slowly back to the cliff edge. When he ducked away from the cliff to check for Draks he had no intention of deserting his guide. He actually hadn't been able to do anything at all to help Oz while he was falling, and the move back to the rocks was a means of providing covering fire for all of them in case the Drak hunters had dived in to attack. In any event, he was a little disgusted with himself for wasting precious pulsebeats watching the guide fall. If the Draks had been in the sky. . . . He had let himself lie exposed on the edge of the cliff. . . . Ameera had been on the ridge in a completely vulnerable position. . . . Diving Draks could have caught them easily. He'd been a long way away from the scant protection of the rocks. His commanders had been right. He had lost his combat edge. This vacation hunt had been necessary after all. If there was any vacation left. If the guide was unhurt. . . unhurt. . . .

"*Har-aroo*!" Amarson called down.

Oz looked up and waved. He was sitting on the shelf at the

bottom of the canyon. Sitting, rubbing his right ankle.

"*Hoy! Hoy!*" Amarson hooted to attract Oz's attention. He stuck his arms out and broke an invisible stick between his two hands in query. The guide was too far away for shouted conversation. A lot of noise might bring the Drak back. Amarson repeated his broken-stick sign, asking about the ankle.

Oz made negative waves with his hands, got stiffly to his feet and took a few limping steps. The limp looked bad even from this distance, but his ankle obviously wasn't broken.

Amarson took another look around the ridge line. The sky was still Drak free. There was time to think about how to get the guide back up the cliff.

"Rope?" Ameera asked, reading his expression.

"Oz has some back at the camp. Pack lashings, tent ties and the like. Perhaps enough could be knotted together. The trouble is. . . ." He looked toward the Father Sun arc. "The camp is back down-ridge. . . at the tree line. A good half-day down and back."

The Younger Sun was in mid-passage, due to rise soon for its Second Pausing. It would cross the sky and be near setting again before Amarson could complete the trip. A rescue during the final hours of daylight, as the Father Sun set, would be difficult. Amarson didn't find the idea of climbing around this rocky cliff near the dark-period appealing. He didn't much like the thought of leaving the guide alone, and unarmed, for all that period.

"I won't go," Ameera said. "With Draks in the sky the Jungle Patrol must stay to fight. I've earned the right long ago. . . under arms."

"Huh-ayah? A one Drak pack-fight? What do you want? Medals? There are no trophies, remember.

"What right? You'll go if I tell you!"

"Weapons fired." She shook her huntbow, then pointed down into the canyon. "Battle wounded. Warrior's Code, Leon.

"I'll claim my reward later when we are safe in camp." Her voice was soft on this, leaving little doubt what the reward would be.

117

Her body was tense and alert from the fighting stress, and the smooth leather of her huntdress revealed and accentuated her form. His desire hurried his pulse.

"Warrior's Code?" he laughed. "What will you claim, Lady? Warrior's right or Lady's Waiting?"

"Perhaps both, Baron. I fought as rear-guard just now. And I am greedy. I've seldom been with you smelling of fighting like this." Her nose widened and her ears flattened delightfully. "Never without the smell of flier's leather and fuel."

"There's time, Lady," Amarson's voice was teasing, half-serious. "If we hurry back to camp. We can come back after the dark-cycle. . . and pull Oz out."

"Leon!" Her indignation flared up as quickly as her desire. "Get him up out of there. Or he'll be Drak food before dark."

Oz was waving him down the canyon. Telling him to go get ropes? Well, the decision couldn't be delayed too much longer. Amarson measured the height of the Father Sun's great horizon-spanning arc. No, if he was going to hike to the camp he would have to leave now.

"He seems to be in a hurry, too," Amarson said.

The guide was still motioning down the canyon. He was pointing at the cliff, the side of the gorge, further along. Oz waved, beckoned and pointed, then started limping slowly along the bench, down the canyon, away from Amarson.

Amarson slung the guide's huntbow under his arm, but kept his own at the ready. He went back over the saddle-ridge and started down the scree slope. Lady Ameera followed him, ten meters back and guarding a sky-watch to the rear. Working as Amarson's rear-guard wasn't hard, cub tactics really, but she took the job seriously. The Jungle Patrol always took Draks seriously.

They worked their way back to the left, moving across a sloping meadow-patch. The morning's hunt had been well above the tree-line, but this section of the scree slope was level enough to hold soil and water; was covered with a short, mossy grass and bunched with twisted, thorn bush. The vegetation glowed fire-orange in the mid-passage light of the

Father Sun and each bush clump cast a single, deep-black shadow.

Amarson twisted his way through the brush and found the edge of the gorge again. In all, he'd moved about a kilometer downhill and, when he looked over the edge, he grinned and quickly waved Lady Ameera in beside him.

At this point the walls of the canyon had changed character. The cliff wall was broken and checked with cracks. The rock, as he looked down on it, appeared layered and folded. Also, it slanted away from him. It wasn't a sheer, straight up-and-down rock face anymore.

"So, that's what he was so excited about," Ameera said. "Oz can climb up this section of rock and get out of the canyon."

"I'm not so sure," Amarson said. "He should have been here by now. We came the long way around."

"Look!"

Oz was working his way down the bottom of the canyon. The sloping bench he'd landed on had slanted down and flattened into the canyon bottom proper, but the guide had been forced to move slowly. When he finally came into sight, his limp was pronounced and he didn't walk around the boulders in his way, but sat on them and swung his feet around. His stops for rest were frequent. Amarson watched him stop three times in the last fifty meters. Evidently his ankle-sprain was hurting him a great deal.

Amarson also noticed that Oz's climbpack was pumped down. He narrowed his eyes, flattened his ears, at that. The pack must have been damaged, or the guide would be using it to ease the pain in his ankle.

Amarson made another combat scan of the sky, narrowing his eyes on the eastern arc where the Father Sun's half-disc covered half the horizon. He could see Draks against the red glow of the sun, if he did not look too long, and the sun-angle was an habitual attack position for Draks. But there were no winged spots drifting against the Father's background. . . . Or in the rest of the clear, mountain sky. Still no sign of Draks.

Except for the single hunter that had attacked them, he

could almost believe there were no Draks anywhere. The quiet of the hills; the deep shadows of the rocks; brush tops and grass beards shining a transparent carmine in the calm light of the Father Sun; all gave him a feeling of being isolated, on the mountainside. . . in some place where time had slowed far down. He knew about the guide's struggle; was aware of the far-off threat of the hunting Drak, and felt the faint tug of duty from the Marchlands, where daily combat with the Draks had been, and was, his responsibility. But none of these things called him strongly.

There was time for all of these things, seemingly endless time, up here on the shoulder of the alps. The only vital thread of reason he could carry was wrapped in the slowly limping figure of Oz.

"That limp makes him look like a clown," Ameera said, "but it must be painful. . . .

"Leon, he will never be able to climb up. . . without help." She reversed her own previous opinion.

"That's becoming obvious, Lady," Amarson said absently. He was studying the broken cliff wall below him.

"Have you ever climbed a mountain cliff, Leon?" Ameera was studying the Baron's face. Oz couldn't climb out, so it followed that Amarson was planning to climb down and get him out.

"What? Oh, yes. Three times. . . Jungle Patrol drills."

"*When*?"

"Oh, back when I was a cub." Amarson was deliberately casual. He had decided to make the climb. "It's not something you forget." The time was past when he could try to reach the camp and bring back what rope he could find. He would have to climb down and help Oz out directly.

He made one more sweeping survey of the sky and ridges. When he went down there with the guide, both of them would be trapped in the tiny canyon. As he climbed, he would be doubly vulnerable: unable to fire a huntbow. Ameera, alone on the cliff rim, would have the only weapon. A single attacking Drak would be a prime hazard.

These thoughts—as much as the red-lit peace of the mountain meadow—made the time run slowly. But they did provide him with a single line of action; a comfortable lack of alternatives.

He took the guide's huntbow and extended it to Ameera.

"Take it down to him," she said. "I can only fire one at a time. I'll be safer if I hide. If we are attacked, three bows are better than one and a half."

Amarson nodded. "Stay off the skyline," he said. He didn't add anything in the way of farewells. He intended to come back.

Ameera slid under a thorn bush near the edge, where she could see. Her eyes widened and took on a deeper color in her concern, but her huntbow was out and ready. She was out of sight, but she could see the sky. . . if need be.

Amarson rehung the huntbow, pulling the straps tight so it wouldn't swing and hinder him. A pocket in his pack yielded two climb-hooks. He carried four; these and two spares. They were part of what Oz called *safety equipment*; items that Oz included in Amarson's pack each time they left the camp to hunt above the timber-line. Until now they had been dead weight. Suddenly, like any safety device, the hooks had become vitally indispensable.

He searched for a starting foot-hold and lowered himself over the cliff edge. The climb-hooks unfolded and he fitted his hand into the thong and finger-grips. He set one hook in a rock crack and put his weight on the foot-hold. A brief touch at the levers of his climb-pack and the balloonets swelled up behind his shoulders. He didn't inflate them fully. He needed his body-weight to hold him on the foot-holds and for a drag at the climb-hooks to keep them seated. That much of the drill he remembered. He had no intention of trying to jump down this broken cliff. Even with the pack at full inflation the risk was too great. Two twisted legs or a single broken bone and a simple rescue would become tragic. Ameera would be alone on the mountain. Her signal fires would bring help and she would burn them high, but help was a long way from here and now. He and the guide could die in that canyon. . . without the attack of a single Drak.

Amarson was not a skilled rock climber, so he went slowly, placing his feet and climb-hooks firmly and with much feeling around for the right place. He went slowly, but eventually he reached the bottom.

"Five meters yet, Bahrun," came Oz's voice, surprising Amarson into a startled jerk. He'd become so used to the silence, with only his own hoarse breathing and the scrape of the hooks filling it, that the voice, coming out of nowhere, stung his nerves.

"Two more steps," Oz advised again, after a time that seemed fully as long as the rest of the climb—five meters, indeed. Then: "Your next step down will put you on th' groun' . There you be!"

Amarson grunted, brought his right foot down to meet the left and looked down to check that he was indeed on solid ground. He released his climb-hooks, one at a time, and pumped his climb-pack back to its tanks. Then he took two steps away from the cliff toward the guide and all his leg muscles began quivering and shaking with the strain. He swayed and sat down quickly.

Oz found a rock that was just the right size and sat on it, easing his leg out to one side.

"When we go to tell this tale," he said, beginning to stroke and groom the dust out of his shoulder and chest fur, "we might put in five or six Draks. An entire hunting flight, perhaps." He flipped his hands up the back of his mane and rattled his ears to settle the fur. "No man'll trade us *frooge* for a tale about gettin' chased into a hole by one Drak."

Amarson flung up his head, scanning the sky above the canyon. He was startled by the thought behind Oz's words. He *had* been chased off the ridge by his fear of a hunting flight. No other Draks had appeared, but he had run as if they were in the sky. And that exposed climb down the cliff. .. he had been running scared like a Jungle Patrol cub.

Amarson dropped his eyes back to look around the canyon. He was measuring the height of the cliff, and the amount of room a Drak might have to fly in this narrow space. He saw the look on Oz's face in passing. A wide-eyed transition from amazement to fear as the guide realized that Amarson *was* expecting more Drak.

The play of emotions, so extreme as to make the short fur

dance across Oz's face, produced a comic effect on the guide's otherwise solemn face. Amarson found himself laughing. First at the guide, then continuing, half hysterically, as a release of his combat tensions. He had a hard time stopping.

Finally, he said, "One Drak. You're right. The story will have to be better to be told at all. And we'd better forget the sprained ankle and my wobbly legs. Think up some better fighting wounds, perhaps. . ."

"You were waitin' for more Draks," Oz said, refusing to pick up on the joke.

"It seemed likely. They rarely fly alone anymore."

"Be there danger, still?" Oz was searching the strip of sky above the canyon.

"Not from that. A hunt pack would have been here by now. But one Drak, alone in the mountains. . . I don't know what it will do. What do you think? These are your mountains."

"I? I no track Drak; I hide from them." The guide got up and tested his ankle. "And I want to hide now. Let us go out o' here. . . I like trees around me.

"I know one thing," he changed thought. ". . . Why the hunting was so bad. . . why we did not find any *hourn.*"

"That one Drak," Amarson said. "It's been hunting this ridge? Then, that argues for it being alone. A hunt pack would have ranged further."

"Mayhap. But they would have killed off everything. The life rhythms of this land are balanced, do you see? There's a great bit of life around the camp, burrowers, creep things, flyers-in-the-bush. . . And we did find one *hourn.*

"Nooo, Bahrun. I say one Drak. In the rocks above us, beyond the ridges, else I would have noticed signs below as we came up through the trees. More hunting Drak in the edge of the forest would destroy the balance of life."

"One Drak, Amarson agreed. Do you think it will come back? Hunting us?"

"How do I know, Bahrun? You be the one who fights Drak. I hide from them. Can't we get out from this canyon?"

"I usually fight them in groups. . . and in the air."

Amarson stood up, testing his muscles. "This is new, being on the ground with a single hunter. I guess we are both beyond our experience, heh?

"But, about this canyon. I don't know. It's narrow. A Drak couldn't fly too well down here. We might be safer staying here. Do you know? Where does it lead? Can we follow it down, closer to our camp? Can Lady Ameera safely walk the top rim?"

"I think not. It has no water, yet for all, it be a water canyon—made by rushing water—not a split in the rock. As nature is balanced, that means the run-off be swift and fast. We will meet rock-drops and rough canyon floor lower down. In the water season, you might find tall falls and angry rapids. You can travel that trail, Bahrun, I cannot, for some days."

"I have it in my head the Drak be off to eat the Lady Ameera's *hourn*. Would their balance pattern mean they kill with no hunger? The meadow trail will be softer and swifter even if the Drak horrors us. Will the danger be so great, up on the meadow, with you and the Lady to guard us?"

"Not too dangerous," Amarson said. "We can see more sky up there. . . and anything that flies at us. I was thinking of an alternative to climbing that cliff."

"I see not one. We have hunt-rations, but scarce water."

"Then we climb," Amarson said. "What is wrong with your climb-pack? You didn't inflate it for the walk down here—to ease your ankle—so the fall must have damaged it. Heh?

"One cell may be enough." Amarson unstrapped his ration bag and started to unpack it. "Let's get these bags unpacked. We'll put the rations and the huntbows in your pack. Leave all the rest. I can cut up this pack for straps."

"Straps?"

"You'll have to ride my back, so I can carry you up the cliff. If I can get enough straps out of this. You can tie onto my climb-pack and we'll get lift out of both sets of balloonets."

"*Aye ha*, that'll work," Oz said, nodding brightly. He

began pulling his pack open. "My pack will hold gas long enough for that."

"It had better. Mine will barely have enough lift for both of us. Equipment made for you Valley People is just barely sized for by body weight. But it'll be enough, I think. I'll be climbing, not trying to jump."

"Aye. It will serve. Cut the straps from this game-bag." Oz handed him a tightly-folded package. "It opens out to a sack big enough for *hourn*; meat and trophy. A great lot of straps."

"Good!" Amarson's knife slashed the sack into wide ribbons. Oz quickly repacked his ration bag and clipped it back on his pack.

"Can you rig a harness for yourself?" Amarson asked, sitting down on the guide's rock and shifting so that his back and the pack were close to Oz. "I'd rather not take this off."

"Aye. I will not need much." Oz took the strips of bag and began knotting them to the pack-rack. Eventually he said, "That'll do till I climb on, Bahrun."

"Hold a bit. Let me clear this huntbow." Amarson unhooked the sling. "You should have one of these on sling," he said. "When I start to climb, you're the only one who could use them anyway.

"Now, you can climb on."

Oz took the huntbow, tied Amarson's bow into his pack and crossed the other one behind his back. Then he lifted himself into the loops he'd tied on Amarson's pack.

"Tie this around," he said. "Up under the arms. It be tight across my back and will hold."

Amarson took the strap. "Comfortable? Ready to climb?"

"No comfort, but I can grip you."

Amarson valved a little gas into his balloonets and stood up. The guide's stocky, two-meter body was solid and heavy across his back. The climb-pack lightened some of the guide's weight at this setting, but not nearly enough. Amarson felt the drag of the weight when he stood up, and he had a little trouble balancing the guide's mass. The twenty-five meters or so to the cliff was a staggering lurch, not a walk.

As he set a climb-hook in the first hand hold, Amarson opened the pack valve almost full. He held a reserve. . . Oz's tank was leaking. The extra buoyancy might be needed before he reached the top.

"Fill your pack, Oz!" he ordered. "And hang on."

He heard the guide's pack inflate; heard the ominous hissing of the leaking balloonet. That wouldn't help much.

Amarson started to climb. He set his hooks deep and sought broad ledges for his feet. The climb-packs, his and Oz's, were just barely equal to the job of holding his weight, lightened fifty percent. They helped, undoubtedly. Amarson could not have carried Oz without them. Still, his arms and legs had to reach out, set the hand and foot holds and lever his body up to the next stance. It was a type of exercise he wasn't used to. But he climbed—one hand; one foot; one hand. . . .

He was over half-way, before Oz's weight began to drag down on his back. Not much further on he began to feel the strain in his legs.

"Bahrun, you're not climbing in balance," Oz said. "Even the rocks have to be met with an even rhythm. Do not fight your own muscles and the cliff, too.

"Balance, Bahrun. Balance!"

"You balance!" Amarson grunted. "I haven't the time."

Oz began a chant. There weren't any words, not even religious cant—just four sounds; then another four; then another. Never the same set, but the same rhythm.

Ara eee ha oue
Dah noah tcah beay
Bea ssan vro meak.

After a while, Amarson realized that he was climbing to the chant; moving arms and legs to the sound, and the work went easier for a time.

"Your pack's stopped lifting," he managed to say, after another interval. Talking seemed to take as much effort as climbing.

"I cannot tell from this position," Oz said. "But you are likely right. The hissing be stopped."

"Your balloonets are full," Oz said, a moment later.

"Uh. No, they aren't." Amarson was trying to see the top of the cliff. He'd climbed down so fast. Why was it taking so long to go up?

"Reach my valve, Oz!" he ordered. "I have. . . got a little. . . gas left. . . . need the lift."

"Try, " Oz said. "Can you stop climbing?"

"No. I couldn't get started again."

Oz didn't say anything to that. His weight shifted and Amarson could feel him groping for the valve.

" 'Tis all," Oz said. "Full turns."

Amarson didn't feel any difference, but he kept on climbing. His muscles were moving without direction, all by themselves, but they never decided to stop moving entirely.

"Ameerson! Bahrun! Ameerson!"

Amarson barely heard Oz yelling at him. Dazedly, he realized that he had been reaching his right hand up into the air, groping for a hook-hold. Groping and groping. Something seemed to be tangling his arm.

"Leon! Leon!" Ameera's voice, dim and wavering.

He forced his eyes to focus, and found himself looking across the meadow. His eyes were at grass level, but his left hand climbing-hook was locked in the ground at the top of the cliff. He'd reached the top. That's what Oz was trying to tell him.

"Leon. Come on. A little more."

He turned his head wearily. Ameera was tugging at his other arm, pulling, trying to drag him up over the edge. Her pale fur was ruffled and matted, streaked with dirt. The leather of her huntdress was grass-stained and stuck with leaves and bits or rock. . . . But she was the most welcome sight he could remember.

He stopped fighting her pull on his arm and let her bring it down to sink the climb-hook in the turf.

"Now pull!" she said and grabbed at his shoulders, her legs kicking and scrabbling to pull his weight over the cliff edge.

He used the other hook, pushing it out ahead of him, letting his arm fall and sinking the metal deep. He had to pull with his arms to get himself moving; his legs didn't seem to be of any help. But he did pull himself over the edge, and one or two weak, crawling pulls clear of the cliff; then he was through, and lay flat, just breathing heavily.

He felt Oz groping for the knots of the straps locking them together, then he saw a flash from Ameera's knife. She cut the guide free, pushed him roughly off Amarson's back and pulled the Baron close to her. Amarson turned limply, his arms flopping out of control.

He wasn't unconscious. He hadn't been climbing long enough for that sort of extreme fatigue to attack him. This was just a muscle-thing. The quivering of his legs after the down-climb had been a warning. Riding the seat of a flier, the long campaign against the Draks, didn't condition his muscles to climbing. Jungle Patrol exercises kept his strength focused, available for combat-stimulated effort, but this had been draining.

He felt Oz slump to the grass and heard the noises as the guide unbuckled his climb-pack to see if it could be repaired, but Amarson didn't open his eyes. The guide's tanks were probably empty and nothing could be done about that until they were recharged back at the camp.

He leaned back and felt the warmth of Ameera's body.

2

The Younger Sun was stopped in the sky. The grass and the leaves were shining with the hard, yellow light. The tent ropes and the poles of the awning were showing a twin-vee shadow of First Passage. Amarson heard Oz begin the ritual for *Point of Pausing*, but he didn't get out of the camp chair to join him. He watched the red color come up on his boots and deepen. The Father Sun was rising higher.

128

Amarson greeted this evidence of another day by continued inspection of his out-thrust feet. The light deepened, the twin shadows became crisper; one deep-dark, the other pale. The pale shadows to the tent ropes began to move. *Point of Pausing* was over and the Younger Sun was traveling through the sky once more. The shadows of the Father Sun were moving too, but only to get shorter; not so easily seen.

Oz's changing voice finished the ritual.

Amarson saw him come across the camp area and stop at the cook fires. A small swirl of smoke clouded him and then the fire caught and burned clear. The way Oz's fires always burned.

"Oh, good. He's made the fire this time," Ameera came out of the tent behind Amarson. "I was getting tired of the smoke. My fires are always smoky."

"His limp is gone. You'll probably be relieved of the hunting, too."

"Leon, that was no chore. We needed the fresh meat, and you stomp around too much to get close to the small game around here. Besides, this is a friendly forest. I like walking in it. Not like the jungle around Fort. I could stay here for a long time. Except. . ." She looked up at the canopy roof. "I don't like my tent under these trees. I brought along this light canopy so that the sunlight would come through."

"You know why I did that, Lady. I could see this nest of rainbows from above the thermocline. I'm a flier, remember. I see the ground the way a Drak would."

"You're still worried about one Drak?"

"Somewhat."

Ameera came around and sat at his feet. "Leon, you came up here to get away from the Drak fighting. Mitch told me. You've been flying missions all over the valley. Hunting Drak every hour you could get a flier in the air. He said. . . ."

"Did he tell you I hadn't found any?" Amarson leaned forward. "Did he tell you that the Drak have stopped fighting our patrols. *Did he tell you that*?"

"No." Ameera gripped his leg, her claws came out. "Our war's over? No more Draks?"

"Ameera. I've forced our people to attack. Attack! I built

129

flier fields deeper and deeper into the jungle. The Jungle Patrol bases were pushed further up the mountains. Further and further. Wherever I could meet the Draks and strike.

"But the Rivermen stayed with their river and the Valley People stayed with the Harvest. . . because we cleared the Draks from their sky.

"Riverman; River. Valleyman; Harvest. The Marchlands have the Draks. There are always Draks in *our* skies."

He slumped back.

"Then my patrols started coming back with no kills. Then, no contact reports at all."

Ameera turned her head and pointed out across the campground and to the long, clear view down the mountainside to the valley below. She said, "Those are the skies over our Marchland, Leon. We are not Rivermen or Harvesters. The Warrior's Code runs deep. All the People followed you when you built the Fort. . . and those new flier bases. . . Families, merchants, children, Administrators. The Marchholders live beside your bases and behind Jungle Patrol perimeters. Yours is our sky, my Baron. If you have driven the Draks away, the sky is still ours. Are they really gone?"

"It would seem so. They haven't really been hunting in large packs for two years now. We flew strike missions against all their swarmings. Whenever scouts sighted them. . .

"But our patrols have been coming back with no kills. . . no contact sightings at all."

"But a secret? Why, Leon? No one in Fort knew. I would have heard."

"I can't hold it much longer. My fliers think the Draks are massing for a big swarm, and they held the news secret. . . . As long as I kept them flying searches. But the Jungle Battalions will rotate six units out of the mountains on relief a few days from now. There will be no secret then. If my skies are clear, the Jungle Patrol will have no kills either."

"But why hide it? No Draks. Your fighting is over, isn't it? Why hide?"

"Because I don't know what to do!" Amarson pulled his legs back, and stood up roughly. "If the Marchlands aren't fighting Draks. . . *what will they do*?''

"They will follow you, Leon."

"Will they? Already, in Riverton and in the Valley, there are those who have found other ways to live than by fighting Draks.

"Oz!"

The guide looked up at the call, and padded over.

"My cooking be about down, Bahrun. Food will be ready in a hundred heartbeats."

"Very well. But I want something else. Oz, I need men from your village. Men who know these mountains. Hunters, trackers. As many as you can get.

"Burn the signal fires!"

"No men, Bahrun." Oz started to turn away. "The food be hot now."

"Never mind the food. I want hunters. Get out there and start the smoke columns. Talk to your Elders. Have them send me men."

"I will burn the fires, and so you ask it. But no hunters will come. The Elders will not take men from the fields."

"They won't answer our signals?"

"Here on the mountain I have shown you the ways that trees and grasses grow in balance to shelter and feed the ground animals. In the fields and harrows of our village the grain has grown this high." He swept his hand across his shoulder. "The food-heads be balanced heavy, and the stalks are drying and stiff to hold them. They sway as the air moves and the People are ringing about their food-fields for the cutting. That is part of the balance, too, Bahrun. The rhythm of the fields in the swinging blades.

"You understand, Bahrun! My Elders will send no one from the fields while the food-heads dance."

"Forget the dance. I want hunters! Get them up here. Light those fires!" Amarson grabbed the guide and shook him.

"Leon, stop," Ameera said. She came up off the ground and gripped his shoulder. Her claws came out in the stress of her move. She knew why Amarson wanted the Valley hunters. "He's talking about the *Harvest*. They don't let anything stop the *Harvest*. Not even swarming Draks."

131

"I'm not talking about a swarm. Just one. One Drak. I need hunters."

"I be the only hunter in the mountains."

"You're wrong, Valleyman. I'm here. And I'm hunting!"

"No, Leon!" Ameera said. "It's only one Drak. Why?"

"Because the Draks are gone from our skies. I couldn't find them over the Marchland. But up here. . . Ameera, the Draks always made their henges in the high mountains, until we poisoned the land against them.

"This one Drak can tell me where the others have gone."

"The high mountains? We can't go there, Leon. Not on foot."

"No. Not there. But I can hunt these ridges. Oz, will *you* guide me, if I go hunting that Drak?"

"Oh, aye. I'll guide you, Bahrun. But I will not hunt the Drak. I hide from Draks."

"You find him for me. I'll make the kill."

"I can guide you for that. The words have been said, and I be in the hills to guide your hunt. That is a balanced thing.

"We will go after eating. The food be hot on my fires." The guide turned to go back to his cooking , then stopped to say, "Bahrun! Lady. Do you pack warm cloaks for we must spend the dark-cycle on the ridges. . . afore we can return to camp. I would not want to build my fire up there."

"I wouldn't let you. We'll go after eating."

"Then, let's eat," Lady Ameera said. She looked sadly at the gay, colored cloth of her tent. "I should have left this tent at Fort. The vacation is over."

"Over? Far from it. You'll enjoy a walk in the mountains. I'll show you the sky I fly through. We can look down on it.

"Aii hee, Warrior Lady," his voice took on a swinging lilt.

Warrior Lady lift your eye
Let me show you all my sky.

3

They weren't stalking this time, but walking easily, using the climb-packs at quarter inflation to lengthen their stride. Oz, leading, was bouncing along in time to his little four beat chants. He wasn't tracking anything. In fact he kept up a running commentary, between chants, on the signs he saw.

"Before leaving I could fill up the game-bag," he said. "The Bahrun come up here to hunt. I can have dinner for tonight and a bit. The *c'narle* lairs would be over there. I have seen their night trails crossing ours.

"Warm furs for your lady? The *rock-vair* have littered. Hear them! You can hear the pups bark."

Lady Ameera laughed cheerfully. She'd heard the high pitched barks; wondered what they were.

"Your word was to guide me to that Drak," Amarson tried to cut off the hunting tips.

"I get up on top of this rise, then I can see."

"You said that about the last rise. Up one ridge and down to the next. Is that the way you track Draks?"

"The Drak flew this way, Bahrun. Let me get up high, the Drak may be visible when he flies again. I do not know another way to track a Drak that does not leave a trail. D'you, Bahrun?" Oz kept on hiking up the ridge as he talked. After the last question, he went back to his chanting.

Ameera walked over the top of the ridge, found a rock and sat down.

"Let him do his looking alone," she said. "We don't have to follow him around. I can see anything he can see from right here.

"Leon, which way is Fort from here?"

"That way. South and east. The jungle hides it. All you can see is the top of the jungle."

"There's no jungle out this way. What is all that?"

"I don't know, Ameera." Amarson was looking around, trying to fix his bearings. The alp mass was south, on his right as he stood with his back to Fort. To the left, long kilometers up from the range, were the old Drak henges. "We must have crossed over the range. Those hills there, lead down the other watershed."

They were looking down a narrow sloping valley that gave them a view through the mountain ranges into a far away shimmering.

"It's flat and wet looking," Ameera said. "But the color isn't right. Looks more like jungle trees."

"The mud sea looks like that from very high up. But, as you say, the color is wrong. It looks big enough to be another sea though. Goes on as far you can see."

"Can you get a flier out to look at it?"

"No. Not enough range for the return trip. We can fly up into the mountains, over them, but, to cross the alps and get out there. . . . No. It would be a one-way trip. You're looking a long way, Lady. The air is clear and that shimmer is really way out there."

"I've got more important things to look at right here, and how. Where did Oz go?"

The guide had been up on a rock knoll near this high point. After a few minutes survey he'd jumped down and gone prowling toward one of the shallow intervales. At the moment he was out of sight.

Then Oz re-appeared.

He came quickly around the bulgy knoll down at the bottom of the intervale. He was walking light, a scrabbling run with his climb-pack balloonets inflated. When he saw Amarson and Ameera up on the ridge he stopped short and waved; beckoning them down. His arm signals were excited.

"He's found something," Ameera said, pointing out the gesturing guide.

"He was hunting the Drak," Amarson said, pulling his

134

huntbow around to the ready. "Maybe he didn't have time to hide. Let's get down there."

He led the way, Ameera following at close spacing. The rearguard position was secondary now. If Oz had found a trail, the enemy was in front of them. If he'd found the Drak. . . .

"All right, Oz. We're here. What have you got?" Amarson pitched his voice in low whisper-tones, because, for all his jumbling and waving, the guide hadn't called to them or made a sound. If Oz had found something serious enough to keep his flap-tongue quiet, Amarson intended to talk softly too.

"You would not believe me, Bahrun." Oz matched his whisper. "Just follow."

"Drak?" Amarson had to know—before he followed the guide.

"No. *Hourn*." Oz went slowly around the curve of the knoll.

Amarson hand-signaled Ameera, *Alert* and *Follow*: then he walked after the guide. They seemed to be walking on a path. That is, the ground was level and there was room to walk, despite the bushes and low grass. The rock knoll rose to the right and dropped away to the left as they walked around the curve of its flank, and into a wider intervale beyond.

Out in the center of the intervale was a clutch of seven *hourn*. The animals were grazing quietly. The guard male lifted his head when he saw the movement, then kept his head and nose-horn pointed at Amarson's party. But his move was watchful, not aggressive.

The *hourn* were penned in by a circular wall of thorn bushes, higher than their heads and wide enough to keep them from jumping.

"Seven of them," Ameera breathed. "And we spent days tracking one. Oz, and his balanced mountains. . . . I may break his limping leg."

"Oz didn't build that pen," Amarson said shortly. His ears were erect and he moved the huntbow in wide arcs as he scanned the tops of the hills. This intervale hadn't been visible from the ridge where they'd rested, or he would have walked down into it. It was a wide valley, closed at the end by the knoll and the ridge they'd just left, and lined on the right by the rising flanks of a still higher climb of mountain ridge and a broken cliff-face. The valley sloped generally in the direction of the other watershed of the mountain range and was closed at that end by more rising hills. But the valley was wide enough for a flier to maneuver in.

Amarson's practiced eye followed the flight path he would take to come in, circle the valley, and do a wing-turn to come back. The valley had flying room, plenty of it. And the three of them were standing in the short grass, clearly visible, with no cover.

"Oz! Take us out of here! That way! To the cliffs!" His eye had followed a water channel break to an erosion cut in the cliff-line and he pointed directly to it. "There! Fast!"

Oz followed his gesture and nodded, then began to run. Amarson jogged after him, moving fast, but keeping his climb-pack pumped down. He didn't like to fight light-weight.

They reached the cleft quickly without being attacked by anything. Amarson stopped abruptly; he'd almost run into the guide. He'd almost shot him, too, coming around the corner and finding him standing, instead of still moving.

"Aarahah!" he growled, then swore.

Ameera coming in after him had turned to guard the sky behind them and didn't see him stop. She heard his exclamation, however, and whirled, bringing her bow up to firing position.

Oz was looking at a bloody carcass lying on a shelf above the floor of the erosion-cut.

The bloody bundle was about a meter-and-a-half long, and a meter wide. At first glance it looked like a headless torso. Amarson's curse and Ameera's scream had been drawn by the resemblance to Drak kills they'd seen before.

A closer look, and Amarson saw the thin legs and the skin strips tying them all together. The horned head was missing, but the bloody mess was an animal carcass.

"A *hourn*. Aye, cleaned and skinned. Good butcher. No

wasted meat," the guide confirmed.

"One of those from that pen back there?" Amarson said. "Or the one the Draks stole from us?

"A Drak that flies away, and doesn't come hunting the three of us. A pen full of tame *hourn* grazing themselves fat so they can be butchered. And wrapped up in a package. This is one Drak that has changed a lot of its habits."

"It will be hard to track," Oz shook his head and looked around vaguely. "It all be in balance here. There be no trail in or out of the thornbush ring, Bahrun. No trail. Nothing disturbed. If a Drak is here, it be living in simple balance. We are the ones to walk wrong here. . . out of balance. The Drak can track us more easily than I can track him. I think we best hide."

"Bloody. . . ." Amarson looked at the carcass again. The surface blood was dry, but the meat was still blood-colored. "Fresh! Just killed."

"Oz, we won't have to track this Drak. It can't be far away. Up this canyon. Right ahead."

"Bahrun. I will not hunt the Drak."

"Then stay here! Ameera, stay close. . . enough to keep me in sight. We'll find the Drak on the ground if it is here. . . too narrow for flight."

The narrow cut-canyon had water in the bottom, a meter-wide stream which made enough water-noise to cover their footsteps. Amarson took care not to cross it or step in it. Drak ears that had been living near this stream would hear a break in its noise pattern.

He moved up the left stream-bank and around a buttressed rock.

The Drak was standing ten meters away.

The end of the canyon was just in front of them. The water was coming down a three-meter fall from a source inside a low cave in the rock wall. The Drak was standing on the dry-ledge at the top of the fall; standing motionless looking at Amarson. A food-fire was burning at his feet with some cooking sticks braced over the flames. A fighting knife gleamed in the stones, partly covered by a slab of meat. Two pointed poles leaned against the rock five meters from the

Drak—fighting spear—but the Drak was weaponless. And it made no move.

This was the strangest Drak Amarson had ever encountered. It penned *hourn*, butchered them. . . . And this cave and fire was a permanence that Amarson hadn't thought of in connection with Draks. Not since he'd flown that one spray mission for Scientist Lewyll. . . long ago and high in the alp-henge. Since then he'd fought Draks on the wing, as they attacked. . . .

This Drak was not attacking.

Amarson moved his huntbow slowly, bringing it into line for a shot. He moved the bow a bit at a time, muscles tensed for full-speed if the Drak sprang. He was sure he could fire first if the Drak tried for the spears. . . . But he was acutely conscious of the Drak's curved beak and talons; deadly natural weapons that the Drak could launch in a wing-swirling dive. The huntbow couldn't stop a ten-meter fighting dive. And Amarson had little room to dodge. The narrow canyon trapped him, too.

But the Drak didn't move.

It stood, blocking the cave mouth, and made no move at all.

Puzzling. The continuous combat tactics of Amarson's flier squadrons had driven the Draks from Marchland skies. Was it possible that the years of combat had also battered them to the point where they wouldn't fight at all? Very strange.

Amarson's bow was up, lined to fire.

"No, Leon!" Ameera said sharply. "Don't shoot! Look!"

Another Drak came out of the cave. It moved slowly, blinking in the change of light.

Amarson held his trigger.

A female! That's why the Drak hadn't moved. It was blocking Amarson's fire into the cave. Protecting the female with the bulk of its body. *Aeehii*! A proud thing to do. Warrior's Right. Amarson had kept Ameera close behind him as a similar protective tactic.

He met the Drak's eyes across the ten meters. He saw no

138

dull stare of defeat. The Drak's eyes were clear, shiny with alert instinct. The Drak knew its own killing ability in that short fighting distance. It knew the deadliness of Amarson's dartbow, too, because it had stood to guard the female from the quarrels.

"Amarson!" Ameera's voice was a low breath.

A third Drak had come from behind the female. A small chick-Drak. Not more than a meter tall with immature wings.

"A young Drak," Amarson's voice cracked. "That's impossible." He heard the voice of Scientist Lewyll explaining once more the deadly effect of the spray he'd flown to the high-alp henges. "*Wherever it falls, no Drak will be born. . . ever again. This will kill Draks, Baron.*"

In the years since, Amarson had seen the hunters, and attacked Drak camps, but he had never flown to the henges to check on infant mortality. The Drak swarms had become smaller; they did not reproduce. The March men killed them in the air, and Amarson had supposed Lewyll's spray had killed—was killing them in the henges. He didn't fly to see.

Now he was facing two fighting Draks. The female with chick. . . . was as deadly a threat as any hunting male. His huntbow steadied.

And still the Drak did not fly.

Amarson was held by the Drak's eyes again. The same beak and crest he'd met in the air; the same defiant glare frozen on the mounted head above his headquarters battle-map, but this Drak was different. This Drak. . . . These Draks were confident and firm, standing guard on their own territory. They weren't hunting Amarson and they wouldn't fly away from the helpless chick-Drak. Amarson felt that, this time, he was the invader—the hunter-killer in the Drak's sky.

The stand-off went on for more long pulse-beats; soundless so far, except for the falling-water noises. The Drak made no sound, and Ameera had read the tension in Amarson's back and shoulders. She kept silent, too.

Then Amarson's back changed. It was only a meter from Ameera's eyes and she saw his shoulders relax.

"No." he said. "In the air and armed, but not this way.

Back out. . . slowly," he ordered. His voice was low and even. A sudden move, or loud sound, and the Drak still might charge. Either one of them.

Amarson moved back warily, one step at a time, until the canyon curved and the rock wall cut off his sight of the three Draks. To the last they hadn't moved. The small chick-Drak had shifted behind the female, but the two adults were stolid, unmoving statues. It was easily the strangest sight he'd ever seen—two passively defiant Draks.

Once he was in the blind area he whirled to find Ameera kneeling behind two rocks with her huntbow ready. Her eyes were wide and dark with fear, but the huntbow swung through a precise arc so that it wasn't pointing at him.

"Out!" he waved her back. "I want to get out of this ditch. Now! Move." He followed her at a fast-jog. He felt some of her fear too. The canyon was constricting.

They came out into the grass intervale, but this open area didn't feel any safer than when they'd crossed it the first time. The circle of piled thorn bush and the peacefully grazing *hourn* seemed to be full of menace.

"Keep going," Amarson said. "Straight across. I want to get to high ground. Where's Oz gone to?"

"He said he was going to hide," Ameera said. "Leon, we can't leave him."

"I won't. He'll find us," Amarson said. "Pump your climb-pack to half-weight and move out."

He turned around once, and gave a single hooting call. Oz would hear and meet them on the trail. He wasn't worried about the sturdy guide. He was concerned about leaving the Drak's territory, and leaving it now! He followed Ameera, walking light and hurrying.

At the rock knoll, on the rim of the valley, he turned once more, his huntbow raised. He half expected to see a flying Drak, but the valley was still peaceful and uninhabited, except for the penned *hourn*.

He shivered slightly at the strangeness. This was what the war with the Drak had finally come to. That Drak and its female had been driven from the Marchland skies and found this high valley. The thorn-bush pen insured them a food supply; the cave, shelter and water; the location, peace and safety from Amarson's fliers. This intervale was the Drak's territory just as surely as the Marchlands and the flier-patrolled skies were Amarson's. And the solid, unmoving defiance that Amarson had met was a final defense of that territory. With its eyes and unbending resistance, the Drak had said; "*This is my last place. I will not leave it*!"

Amarson had flown one mission to spray Death to the Draks. He had fought their swarms in the air over the March-lands until there were no more flying there. . . but this one Drak. . . .

If it wanted to live in the high valley. . . Amarson had left it alive. One Drak was no threat to Riverton or the Marchland compact.

And Amarson would do the same thing. He would move the Marchholders again. Move them south away from River-ton and carve out a new land to claim for the People. Build a new city—a new Fort—a new Marchland for the People. *Their* final place. And they would not leave it.

"Oz!" Ameera's voice called out. "Leon. Oz is here."

"Hoo heh! Lady. Here's the trail. The way back to camp." Oz's voice was unmistakable. "Hoo heh! This way. Call the Bahrun!"

Amarson laughed. His moodiness was shattered by the guide's calling. He turned and jogged around the rock knoll.

"Lead off, Oz!" he called. "Back to camp. We'll go back to Fort tomorrow. Lead off!"

"No more hunting, Bahrun?"

"No more hunting. I've got things to do." He came up to Ameera and put a hand over her huntbow to safety it. "No more hunting," he said softly.

FIVE

Herald Be My Voice

1

The two target balloons had risen to a safe firing height, both fliers were curving in with the red disc of the Father Sun at their backs and the Younger Sun high in the sky, near the mid-point of its first passage. The firing pass was ideal; Baron Amarson signaled Captain Rydier to make the run and tucked his flier tight into the wingman position. The two fliers tightened the curve, rolled out, flattened into a firing run and attacked the balloons savagely.

Baron Amarson swung his flier slightly to the left and broke away from the two-man pattern. He was laughing hugely. The flying darts, rattling out of wing mounted launchers, had exploded the balloons most satisfactorily. Captain Rydier's savage attack was generated by his complete miss of his first balloon. That, and the fact that he was shooting with his Baron, Leon Amarson, Wing Commander.

He probably thinks I'm checking his bowmanship as part of my inspection tour, Amarson thought. *Well, I am. And I've seen enough. The guy's good.* He circled his flier and when Rydier drew up beside him, Amarson pointed blithely and innocently to the one bobbing balloon, dancing and weaving in the turbulent air currents at the thermocline above

them. Like the heavy lower air, the balloon couldn't penetrate the thermocline to get into the lighter upper air.

"We can't leave the sky all cluttered with trash, can we?"
Amarson said into the windshear. "Go sweep up and let's go
home."

Rydier knew instantly what Amarson's near-mocking
pointing meant. He went to full combat climb and took his
flier almost straight up, his anger evident in the overcontrolling he was doing to hold on to the target balloon in the
thermocline turbulence. When he fired, the balloon burst, but
the recoil of the dart launchers stalled his controls, and the
turbulence knocked him out of the air. His flier, tail down in a
vertical climb, stalled off on one wing, and spun down—
twisting toward the landing strip.

Amarson curved into a vertical turn, slid off on a wing and
followed the other flier down. Rydier wasn't in trouble, he
was just using the spin to lose height and he finally straightened into a flare out above the field and slid into a short
landing curve. Amarson followed him down in a more con-
ventional landing spiral and rolled up beside the cargo flier
that was parked in front of the hangar.

Captain Rydier had rolled into the hangar before turning
and shutting off his engines, but Amarson would be leaving
almost at once, so he parked outside and signaled the
groundsman for a refueling.

That worthy was just finishing the fueling of the cargo
flier; he acknowledged Amarson's signal with a wave and
sent the fuel truck backing over to the combat flier.

Amarson undid his straps and slid out of the body-pod. He
stood waiting for Captain Rydier to come out to him. Rydier
was walking through the hangar, followed by the pilot of the
cargo flier—a pilot, Hariegh, whom Amarson had met briefly when he had landed; just before the balloon-bursting
flight.

Rydier strode up briskly. His eyes were gleaming with
humor and there was a grin on his face. Whatever his anger or
emotions had been at missing the target, they had been wiped
out by the involuntary acrobatics at the end. His sense of
humor was back again, and, since Amarson had thought the

last shot and spinning *were* pretty funny, Amarson was glad to see him laughing at himself.

"I have to report, sir," Rydier said lightly, "that I have just been shot down by a balloon."

"You have at that, Captain," Amarson chuckled. "And since you have the only combat flier on Base XII, here, the base is undefended. Maybe you had better release more balloons, heh?"

"As you order, Baron."

"Hiee, Pilot Hariegh. Join us." Amarson included the cargo pilot. "How did you like our combat games?"

"A good show, sir," the pilot said. "Who won?"

"The balloon did," Amarson said laughing. "Base XII has no Commander. He got shot down. Do you want the job, Pilot?" He noticed Rydier stiffen, all the humor fell out of the moment. Rydier had remembered that Leon Amarson, Baron Rufus, was Wing Commander and *could*, in fact, replace him; send him home for missing a target.

"No, sir! My orders are to take that cargo flier to Riverton. It's a scheduled run, sir. Due in today, sir." The pilot, glancing at Rydier, was also aware that Amarson could elevate him to command rank. Pilot Hariegh was a soft, almost sloppy pilot, and he didn't want command. He was anxious to get away from this situation. "In fact, my flier is fueled; I'm on minus time tick now, sir."

Amarson leaned against the side of his flier. His heavy broad shoulders were relaxed, casually turning his back to the noise of the refueling truck. He was trying to give an appearance of informality to his conversation with the two men standing before him. However, his ears were erect, to catch their words and block the pump noise, and the red light from the morning Father Sun had lined harsh shadows on his face. The result was not comforting to the pilot or Captain Rydier. Amarson could see that in Rydier's stiff back, and hear the dismay in Hariegh's speech.

"Do you fly this schedule often, Pilot?" Amarson probed. As long as they insisted on taking him so seriously instead of relaxing, he would get some information, then shove the pilot along.

"About every third trip, Baron," Hariegh answered. "I like the duty. These big fliers are clean in the air."

"How do the Rivermen treat you?"

"I land at the field at Theiu's factory. . . excuse me. Ambassador Theiu. He almost always meets every flier, still. Sometimes just standing and watching, sometimes a word or two."

"His men bother you any?"

"No. They're friendly enough. Especially when I bring test pilots down to pick up new fliers. They are more interested in the flier, than in me, though—polite, but not cozy."

"Much the same as it has been since we pulled out five years ago, heh?" Amarson observed. "Well, they didn't want March People around their cities after the Draks stopped flying and they still don't, I suppose. They weren't friendly then, I can't expect them to improve with age. Do you go into Riverton?"

"No, sir. We stay at Theiu's. Sometimes he asks me to fly out to the Valley towns to pick up perishables. . . medicines. They have a clear field there. . . I do it."

"No friendlies there either, I suppose." The pilot shook his head. "No. They have everything packed, as if they have been waiting for me. They load it and leave, so I take off. No words spoken or needed. Valleymen live in another world altogether.

"Excuse me, sir," the pilot was glancing at his flier. "I really should leave, or I will be late at Riverton. I like to land with the Younger Sun still in the sky. I ask your pardon, Baron, but my bowman is aboard. . . and I. . . ."

"Of course, Pilot," Amarson let him go. "Take off in your own time. Thank you."

"Permission to leave the Base," Hariegh asked Rydier rapidly and at his curt nod, turned and almost ran to his flier. In moments, as Amarson and Rydier silently watched him, the pilot had his big, single-winged cargo flier at the end of the flight strip and was rolling it for take off.

"Relax, Rydier," Amarson said when the engine noise died away. "You are the Commander of Base XII, this duty

146

shift, not me. I admit, being a Base Commander when you are the only pilot on the site, with ground crew of seven to command, is not a high honor, but the rank and pay are good, heh? You've got the job now. You wouldn't have wanted it when I had it—back during the Drak swarm days. You would have been up throwing your flier all over the sky; killing Draks and screaming when you had to land for fuel and darts, heh?''

"I suppose so, sir," Rydier said. He wasn't in the mood for old combat tales. The Draks were long gone from Base XII's skies and he had never flown against one. "It is hard to forget that this was once *your* base, sir. I keep thinking what it must look like to you; empty like this."

"Like an old coat, Captain. An old coat. Comfortable and friendly, but shoddy at the seams.

"No criticism of your command, Captain," Amarson waved a hand. "My inspection was thorough, and you are quite correct in maintaining only the one hangar and barracks. Keep the rest locked, as you have done. By the way, your two active buildings were spotless. You have a good groundsman."

"Phetres, yes. He's great with the flier, too." Rydier nodded. "No defects, since I've been here."

"Good," Amarson said. "One point about your flights— something I've gathered from other bases with one flier cadres—keep your flights short and either stay in sight of the base or set up a rigid schedule for your return."

"I stay in sight," Rydier nodded. "The groundsmen worry otherwise."

"Hmmm uh." Amarson realized his caution wasn't needed with this man. He could use his brains. "They tend to feel left alone when you are in the air—lost. You can escape the boredom of this duty with your flier. They can't remember."

"Yes, sir." Rydier smiled. "When I fly too much, Phetres has a way of taking the engine apart to clean something. He keeps me honest."

"Good man. You need him." Amarson put on his gloves. "Don't worry about your shooting. We'll consider that was for pleasure and not part of my inspection. For pleasure; my pleasure.''

"Thank you, sir.'' Rydier said. "I was surprised at how rusty I'd become.''

"Me, too.'' Amarson admitted. "I missed several passes at first with the balloons. I will see about sending around a target tow flight, so you can do some high altitude work in the thin air above the thermocline. Even though the Draks don't fly against the Valley anymore. . . . We are Warriors, heh. *The claws should be kept sharp against the need*, as the Heralds sing.

"In fact, that is my next task, when I leave here.''

"Sir?''

"Sharpening claws.'' Amarson gave a chuckle as he thought of the next item on his inspection agenda. "I've got a flight doing a night-cycle patrol—take-off in the dark to fly a hologram mission at first light. I am going to leave Refueling Base II before they take-off and be waiting at their rendezvous point when the Father Sun comes up. Pounce! Aahrrgh! I ought to scare their claws out.''

He climbed into the yellow flier and leaned down for a final word.

"I approve of your command of my Base XII, Captain Rydier,'' he said. "It is in good hands. I will send down a work crew, to handle the minimum maintenance on the rest of the base, so it will not worry you—broken windows, weather protection, and the dust and sand inside. I want to keep Base XII as sharp as any claw I have on the Marches.'' Amarson smiled at his image and remembered the other one he had used. "We can't let our old coat get too shabby, can we?'' he finished.

"No, Baron,'' Rydier said stiffly.

He's got his back up again, Amarson thought to himself as he worked the flight controls to test the flying surfaces. *He just won't let anyone get informal with him for long. Well, I can't blame him. Using two images, claws and old coats, in one breath makes even a Baron sound like a senile oldtimer, even to myself.* The ritual formality between Baron and Base Commander that he had used during the inspection was a better line to take with this young Captain. The value of rituals was that responses could have ritual form as well as questions: both preventing emotion, or channeling it, as required.

"Permission to depart from Base XII?" Amarson decided to make his departure abrupt and returned to the ritual at the same time.

"The Commander grants permission," Rydier called, completing the formula and stepping back clear of the starting engine. His relief didn't show on his face, but it was plain enough.

Amarson tugged his helmet down over his head and scanned his engine instruments. It was custom to ignore anyone on the ground after the departing ritual, so he concentrated on his flier and rolled it out onto the field with quick bursts of power. He checked the fuel tanks; both the main and long range tanks were topped full; so he could fly almost straight back to Base II. Good, his one month inspection trip, hopping from base to base around the old March perimeter, had been too long. Now he was in a hurry to get home. One day to the refueling base, the short hop to pull his surprise shake-up of the hologram flight, then he was through—no more. Suddenly, he was in a hurry to get back to city Fort.

He put the engines up to full take-off power and took the flier into the air. He lifted straight off the end of the landing strip and climbed steeply, then curved into a fighting turn and flew back over the base once more.

The flight strip was empty again; the whole base still and dusty looking with no one in the streets. Even Captain Rydier had left the landing strip.

Amarson snarled angrily at that, rolled his flier onto his planned course, then jerked it up toward the thermocline and cut his engines back to penetration power.

"Hiding again," he yelled into the windshear. "Why can't you stay out in the open anymore? There always has to be a roof to get under; to hide. There aren't any more Draks in the sky, you fools. What's wrong with the sunlight?" He pounded on the body-pod in frustration. This hiding habit was a growing thing with the March People and he couldn't stop it. He was half-afraid that the habit was the first showing of cowardice in his Warrior cubs. He didn't want to believe this, but with no more Draks to fight, there was no way to test them. . . or to test himself. And the cold dread that he too might be hiding under a roof, or hiding at all, drove him to harshness and anger whenever he saw the signs.

The People of the Marches had fought the flying Draks for years and they had not been afraid to stand in the open and fight—with dartbows. The Jungle Patrol had their favorite weapon, a one-meter fighting knife, which could only kill at close range. In those Drak-swarm days, guarding the Riverton marches, they were proud to stand under the sky and kill Draks.

Now. Now, the City Fort had domed roofs over the streets and everybody was hiding.

"Arragh!" Amarson growled at the strangeness he didn't know how to combat and brought his thoughts back to his flying—where he knew there was no fear. . . in himself, or his skill.

His height gauge told him he was approaching the thermocline and he began the flier's chant to bring his body reactions up to the swiftness needed to control the flier through the turbulent air. Here at the lower altitude, the heavy air did not mix with the lighter air of the higher altitudes. The thermocline formed a familiar barrier through which he must force his flier to get into the freer air above.

He reached the end of his chant, timed to penetrate the thermocline, and the flier, bucking in the turbulence, flung one wing up. He controlled the flip with smooth, quick motions and rolled the flier back level and through the rough air to send it climbing up into the clear sky beyond.

The Younger Sun set at its mid-passage, changing the light and appearance of the ground below him. He settled the flier on his course, reduced power to give him his longest range and settled down to trim the flier to fly straight through the sky with the least amount of effort on his part.

Amarson's course led him out to the end of the great mountain range, around its shoulder and down the coast to the new site of the city Fort. He would make that leg early tomorrow, when he was flying out to surprise his perimeter patrols, but he still had a long way to fly. He began the ritual chant to relax his body for the long flight, but broke it off in the second measure. The chant had put him in mind of the Heralds and their store of ancient ritual. There might be a solution there.

He lifted one hand from the controls and touched the little orrery hanging from his instrument board. His finger set it spinning in the light of the Younger Sun and he murmured the prayer as the planet disk spun and sent the lights from the jeweled representations of the two suns dancing through the cockpit—the bright, yellow jewel of the Younger Sun and the thin, red disk of the giant Father Sun. *By the two Suns*, the prayer went, and it could be that somewhere in the ancient rites, the Heralds could find a key to turn the March People out of this. . . hiding sickness; *By the two Suns*.

"*Herald, be my voice*!" he said, straightening himself at the controls. "Help me to keep our people together; to keep them still warriors; to honor the Ancient Compact with River-man and Valleyman: even though the price we have paid is that we must be alone."

He glanced around him; looked up at the great mountains. His last words had reinforced the fact that he was flying alone. Normally, he enjoyed being alone in the sky, but now he found himself wishing for the sight of a Drak. The sight of the dark flapping wings, the beaked head and gleaming hunting spear of his flying enemy would be. . . welcome. Loneliness *was* a price.

His course was along the old patrol perimeter and his flier was armed. He checked the racked belts of darts leading out under his upper wing to the dart launcher on both outboard panels. Combat fliers flew fully armed, even after two years of inaction. The years of peace left Baron Amarson with his own kind of loneliness, when he was in the air like this, and brought on thoughts of Draks. He was a Warrior who could feel the ultimate sadness; he had no enemy in the sky with him. No Drak to kill.

He shuddered his mood away. The Younger Sun was well above its second *Point of Pausing*. It had made its stop,

151

halting in the sky as it did just after its rapid rise, and was now moving on toward its mid-passage setting. The flight was going to be a long one, the Younger Sun would rise again before he reached the refueling base, so Amarson began, again, his relaxing chant, and drifted down into the near-sleep condition wherein he could control the flier with tiny motions of his fingers and conserve energy.

The yellow combat flier swept through the sky, solitary and alone; or perhaps. . . . Amarson's drifting mind conjured up the pleasant fantasy—perhaps, paced by ghostly Drak hunters who winged up to fly an honor guard beside an old, lonely enemy.

2

Amarson was flying fully alert now, his blood and nervous system charged by a high protein combat ration just before his take-off from the refueling base. He was about to try something dangerous and he wanted to be at a peak when it started. He was at high altitude, flying in the dark cycle, waiting for the Father Sun to rise. His eyes and his flying skill were centered on two Riverman instruments, one on his panel and one on the side of the cockpit by the power controls. They were curved tubes, containing a dampened bubble, lit by dim red lights. The Rivermen used these to guide their fishing boats under the river water, and here they told him the tilt of his wings and pitch of the flier's nose. They let him fly in the dark cycle when both suns were set. His course and flight were timed to navigate him down the coast and arrive over the position of one of his own patrols flying from Fort. He had flown past the point where he should have turned inland to reach the flight strip at Fort; past the area on the coast where Mardon's Jungle Patrol battalion was surveying for a new landing strip: his time had ticked off each of these invisible navigation points down below him in the darkness. He had actually flown a 360 degree curve over Mardon's battalion to set up this last leg of his course, grinning down at the dark ground as he visualized the effect of engine noise would have on Mardon's sleep.

Now his timer told him that the flight from Fort had taken off, also in the dark cycle, and would be at the point to begin their patrol when the sun rose. He would be there too, at a higher altitude, and would try to catch them off guard.

That was the dangerous part. He wanted to spot the patrol and dive on them without getting caught at it. However, his timing had to be just right. The patrol had to have time to see him and recognize him after he started his dive. If he surprised the flight leader too much, the man might open fire; turn and fight before he saw who was attacking. The patrol fliers *were* armed. Amarson was playing a game with cubs armed with deadly dart throwers. It could be a dangerous game.

The sunrise was beginning. Here at this altitude the light was growing. Already, he could see the dim red shadow of his flier. Down lower, where the patrol flew, the sunrise would be faster. The Father Sun's gigantic disk arced across a full quarter of the sky when it first came up. It was a trick of the thick air on the horizon, but one that should let Amarson spot his patrol first.

The dawn light grew, then suddenly, in the space of ten heartbeats, the Father Sun came up. The first great limb of its arc jumped above the horizon, filling the surface of the sky for hundreds of kilometers. Then the giant sun began its slow climb. It wouldn't rise very high this time of year, the top of the sun arc would barely reach the zenith before it began to set again, but even now, the glowing red light would let him see the mapping patrol.

Amarson tipped a wing down, looking over the side of the body-pod as he curved alertly through the air. They should be down there, somewhere. . . his cubs.

Yes! There. A flash of wings in a fast turn. . . . They'd spotted him first, then?

No. He could see all three now. *They were diving to attack*! Attack what?

Frantically, Amarson searched the sky and the jungle ahead of the three darting fliers, even as he dropped his own flier into a dive. The three, an orange, a red, and a blue flier, were lined out in a screaming combat dive below him. What was wrong?

Then he saw! His eyes following the path of the fliers, picked out their target and recognized the arched beating wings and the body attitude in an instant of coldness that was both fear and joy. Draks! Winged, hunting Draks. A whole pack.

He kicked his flier's tail up in a vertical dive and fed in full combat power. His glove hand armed the dart-launchers switches with the old familiar reflex. He heard himself yelling, screaming a challenge, as the flier fell down the sky.

After five years, it had been five years, and the Draks were back. From some hidden henge, they had survived to build up to hunting strength again. Whatever the reason, they were here, now, and his patrol was right on top of them. What was more important, he, Amarson, would be in on the kill, too. At least he would if he got down there fast enough.

Then he saw the other flier and the challenge cry died in his throat.

The Draks, five of them, were circling around a pale, brown flier—a flier with impossibly long wings. One he had never seen before. And they, the Draks were attacking it. He could see the flier swing in the air to avoid their dives.

Where were his cubs? Where was that patrol?

Aiiee, there they were! He saw the bright-colored wings roll right and left as they slid into the Drak fighting circle. The roughness of their flight pattern told him that they were down below the thermocline.

The thermocline! Now, suddenly, his hunting dive was dangerous. He had lost all the height he dared. He eased the power back and began his pullout, lifting the nose as fast as the straining wings would allow.

The height gauge gave him a bare hundred meters above the thermocline when he was level, and he shoved over again to penetrate and join the fight, scarcely noticing the turbulence, as he controlled the flier through it and curved right to pick up a target.

The Drak he lined up on, chose that second to close his wings and stoop on the long-winged flier—the stranger. Amarson had the open-beaked head, dark-veined wings in his sight for an instant then, with a gleaming slash from its hunting lance, the Drak struck the flier.

Amarson swung away in a tight spiral without firing. The Drak had hit the wing and body-pod of the weird flier. Its pilot would have to fight hand-to-hand—fighting knives to beak and lance. Amarson caught another Drak and lifted slightly to shoot. The darts rattled out of his launchers.

At the same time, another flier, the blue one, shot from another angle, triggering a brief burst then rolling over Amarson's wings in a close pass. Amarson could swear he heard the pilot's yell of surprise over the engines.

The Drak, hit by two cones of streaming darts, tumbled in the air and dropped its lance. It fell face up, wings crumpled and broken, down and behind Amarson as he swept by and looped up to look for more kills.

But the fight was over.

The other three Draks were still in the air. The over-eager pilots had missed their first pass. They were flying away, fleeing with rapid wing strokes, but they were bunched close, and the red flier with the leader's streamers cut two of them down with a quick level pass. His wingman opened out to the left and took the last Drak with a climbing shot and flew over the falling body with a snapping roll.

They hadn't forgotten all of their lessons, those cubs.

Amarson pulled his throttle back and looked around. His climbing loop had taken him up near the thermocline and he had to let down about fifteen meters, to get clear air. As he was coming down his eye caught a speck of movement.

More Draks! His attention was on the speck instantly. It was far off and very high, but no, it didn't fly like a Drak. It moved in a circling pattern and then suddenly dived steeply.

It was just a glint against the disc of the Father Sun and then it was gone. Lost against the great red light. But it had been there—a flier.

Amarson curved back to find the strange flier. He didn't have any patrols in that direction, and high. . . . A picture of his situation map back at Fort came clear to his mind. But the strange flier. . . . Where had it come from? Where was it?

"Arrgh!" The growl came out unbidden. The Drak had made a kill after all. That long-winged flier was down. It had crashed in the jungle.

The coldness returned, and Amarson twisted his head about to find the three fliers of his patrol. Had any of them. . . ?

No. No casualties. They were all there. The blue one that had shared his kill was orbiting over the wreck and the leader and his orange wingman were coming back for their chase. No casualties. Good.

Amarson slid his flier down to join the patrol pattern as the leader swung into the orbit circle—at close range Amarson could recognize the markings on the red flier—Flight Leader Wyllym, a top pilot. The three pilots widened their circle to make room for him and waggled their wings gleefully.

Well, they had a right to be proud, Amarson thought, waving an arm in salute. They had showed their claws. All they had had for five long years were training exercises, and now they had gotten their Drak kills like veterans. The people in Fort will honor them today, no doubt about it.

But, now, Amarson wanted to break off this patrol and look for Wyllym. He wanted to get the flight back to Fort for a briefing and a resetting of all the patrols. The Fort had to know about the Drak party. The information was more important than this training, mapping exercise. These cubs had passed the course.

The leader was flying a tight orbit over the wreck and Amarson could see the long lens of a hologram camera. Great. The patrol had been sent out to get some pictures for Mardon's Jungle Battalion and now Wyllym was changing his mission for something much more important. Pictures of that wrecked flier were going to be an unexpected bonus.

156

Amarson was going to be very interested in that flier. He wanted to see more of it.

Wyllym finished his picture taking and swung up beside Amarson and looked across at him.

Amarson made a *Survivors*? hand sign at him and got a negative reply, so the next signal was: *Return to base*.

The flight leader nodded and made his own signals. The blue flier pulled up on Amarson's right. The orange flier dropped two bright marker panels on the jungle and took up a station off the wing of Wyllym's red flier.

With everybody in position Wyllym put on power and headed up toward the thermocline, signaling: *Straight ahead*, with one hand.

Amarson looked at his course indicator and marked the time. He could send another flight back to orbit the wreck. It might make sense. The Draks might return. But first the task was to get back to report in triumph on the first Drak kill in five years.

He held his station on Leader Wyllym and followed him up through the thermocline. As he jinked out into the clear air Amarson flew automatically, forming plans and rejecting decisions, filled with the one big fact of the pack fight he'd just been through. The five years of peace were over. The Draks had returned.

3

Striding into his office, Baron Amarson swiftly cleared the stacked papers off the chart table. His Second Commander slid a rolled chart across to him and placed weights on it as it unrolled. Amarson read the briefing marks and arrows on the chart in two sweeping glances, as the flier pilots came in and

157

ranged themselves in front of the table. He looked up. The three men were still in their flight gear, holding their helmets and fighting knives in casual rest.

"Tell me!" Amarson commanded softly. "Tell me, Wyllym." The flight leader's name came easily to his mind as he matched the man's strong face with the symbols on his flier.

"We flew out on our planned course," Wyllym spoke clearly, repeating the report he had already given Commander Mitch in the briefing. "And by time and course indications we were at altitude in the area where the Jungle Patrol wanted air maps of the ground. We were in position at first rising of the Father Sun. I was looking for landmarks on our mapping sweep and Tymmda here, saw them first. Not more than half a hundred pulsebeats after first light, sir. Five Draks. Here." He touched the map. "They were attacking a flier at low altitude."

"Not of your flight?" Amarson questioned. "You were able to tell that from the first?"

"No, it wasn't one of mine. My cubs had come up high and closed in tight as soon as they could see me. They weren't more than half a kilometer away from me at any time after the Father Sun cleared the horizon.

"No, sir. It was a new type of flier. Not one of ours at all.

"I took the flight down and attacked, but we couldn't save the. . . stranger. He crashed in the jungle. He took one Drak with him, though. You and Tymmda got one, sir. We took out the other three," Wyllym stated this with no sense of pride. Four high-powered, armed, combat fliers against four Drak, flying with their own wings and carrying only a single lance, did not call for pride. Killing Draks was his business; what he had been trained for. If a Drak had escaped it would have been noteworthy. "I took holograms of the crashed flier and broke off the patrol to bring them back. I left markers to help locate the wreck." He made no mention of Amarson's orders to break off. The patrol was his command, the orders were his. Leader Wyllym took his responsibilities seriously.

"Let me see!" Amarson was still keeping his requests short. He took the four prints from Commander Mitch and laid them down on the chart.

158

"No survivors, think you?" he asked after a moment.

"Not while I took these, nor up to the time I left," Wyllym answered. "The broken wing asssembly covers the cockpit area of the body-pod. . . . And there is the Drak body on top of the wing. . . . I would like to see a flight of fliers orbiting the wreck as cap cover; to drive off any more Draks, should they come out. We would want to see the bodies I should think, before the Draks had a chance to feed on them."

"Two fliers were launched on your recommendation, Leader, to fly that cap cover. It is a sound idea," Commander Mitch said unasked. "Another flight will relieve them. Also, I sent a message drop to Senior Mardon. His battalion is two march days from the wreck, but he can reach it as soon as any party leaving from here." This was to Amarson, briefing him on decisions taken in his name.

"Right. That's only a few degrees off Mardon's planned survey direction, isn't it." Amarson traced a taped line on the chart. "You thought to have him build the new temporary landing mat near this wreck, instead of at the planned site," Amarson nodded. He seldom disagreed with his Second, Mitch. The man had trained himself to think and act like his Baron, and Amarson had a high regard for his skill. Amarson was only considering whether he wanted to ask for a detail briefing on Mitch's plans. No, he had other problems.

"I agree," he said after a bit. "Cut firm orders to that effect and get them out to Mardon.

"Now, what are these others?" He spread out the two remaining holograms. They were blurred smears of terrain.

"Two frames from my mapping lens, Baron. That was all I had time for before Tymmda signalled. Use the magnifier, sir. That lens is set for broad field."

"Uh hmmmn. Blurry."

"I turned away . . . " Wyllym offered in wry apology. "A little too fast."

"No matter. We can re-fly the mission. What's this?" Amarson refocused the magnifier, moving it toward one corner of the hologram. "Look, Wyllym."

The pilot came around, leaned over to look without mov-

159

ing the lens. "Dust," he decided. "Wind? Is it in the other frame?"

"I doubt it. The horizon's tilted half across this one," Amarson said. "You were pulling around, weren't you?" He took the lens from the pilot. "It's still there. The dust shows up on this frame too. A long line. . . going back. . . almost out of range. And it's not a storm, there isn't a cloud in the sky. Look, Mitch."

"You're right. It can't be wind."

"Draks moving for a mass attack?" Wyllym said, his voice mirroring the alarm the idea suggested. He'd fought his way to a quick dread for the Draks. Meeting them in the air had that effect.

"Draks don't move on the ground," Amarson said. "Not to that extent. Not even a Jungle Patrol battalion could make that commotion. A fire perhaps. We'd better get a flight out to look."

"And look at more than that, Leon," Mitch said. "This frame. . . the sky is clear to the horizon. . . . "

"Uh huh. No clouds."

"No mountains! Look! You don't need the glass." He ran a finger along the slanting horizon line in the hologram. "That ground out there is flat. A wide flat. . . valley."

"Ahh yee! You're right. Wyllym, where were you when you took these. . . before you turned to fight?" Amarson walked to the big wall map. "Show me!"

"Ahh. . . my course was. . . . " Wyllym came over to the map. "Along here." He traced a line from Fort's position. "Mardon was about. . . here."

Mitch passed him the two holograms. The pilot turned and tilted them to orient the frames to the map. Finally, he held one picture against the map. "About here. . . . " He looked from one frame to the other, and back to the map.

"Baron!" His voice deepened with excitement, his ears erected. "I was turning here. . . back into the Father Sun's light. The camera took this before I turned. *It* was pointed this way." He jabbed his hand up along the map, away from the Fort, away from the mud sea, straight south at the unmarked, unmapped section of the wall chart.

160

"That plain, sir! *We were flying clear of the mountains!*"

"So it seems. I should have scouted this way long ago," Amarson said. He was remembering a glimpse of a large, open plain. . . once, long ago. He moved closer to the map.

"I was about here. . . . " he said, still remembering, but this time the memory was keen enough to bring his claws out. He put one hand up to mark the map area.

He'd let one Drak clutch live. . . by walking away. Had he let others live by not flying around a mountain?

"What, Baron?"

"Heh? Oh, I was up here. . . five, six years ago. . . hunting. I'd crossed over to the other watershed. . . . And from up there I saw a flat wide plain. Just like this one you hologramed."

The same one? Why it's . . ."

"Bigger than the Valley, or the Marches, or. . . . " Mitch let his voice slide into silence, too.

"The Draks had stopped flying then, we were flying searches all across the Marches. Looking for any last clutch or hunt-pack. And, too, none of our fliers had enough range to cross the mountains and fly back. I was deep in the planning of our cub-training disciplines. Trying to build something that would breed us pilots like Wyllym and Tymmda. Something to keep us from turning into a pack of Marchland raiders replacing the Draks in Riverton's skies.

"In a year, I'd forgotten I'd ever been in the mountains." Amarson spoke slowly; an apology for a mistake.

"We could have flown down the coast. . . and been flying that free, wide air. Long ago. Years ago."

"Mardon and his battalion are out there now," Mitch said, frowning at his Baron's moody attitude and speaking of practical matters. "At least he will be in two days. And he'll build us a landing strip, too. Unless you want to change the orders. . . . Because of that dust cloud?"

"No. No change." Amarson, stiffened out of his dark humor by Mitch's pragmatism, took the holograms out of Wyllym's hands. "I don't think that dust is Draks. If it is. . . . Well, our cubs have claws!

"Two days, you said?" He thought a minute more. "Let's

keep a cap over out there until Mardon gets the landing strip built. It will be a good operational mission. With the news of Draks in the sky again, you will have plenty of eager volunteers. Keep them busy.''

He gestured their attention back to the map. ''Put out a widespread scouting sweep as far out into that plain as they can range, '' he ordered, looking at his Second. ''Here, and here! Scout that plain! Fly at least one sweep a day, Mitch. Use up the volunteers, but keep half the Wing's fliers here on the ground and combat ready. You know the tactics.

''One other thing, Mitch. Orders to all pilots;—Wyllym, Tymmda; you gentlemen can spread the word through the mess. Orders: If anyone contacts these long-winged fliers, they are not to fight—not ever. Don't even get close. Get a bearing on their direction and come home fast. That's a firm order, gentlemen. Those fliers are friends and I want to know where they are; and I want to know it fast. Got that, Mitch?''

Mitch nodded and noted the order on his pad.

''I also want to be notified the minute Mardon can take fliers down on his new landing mat,'' Amarson went on. ''I intend to take a combat flier up there and ground it, so I will need a second pilot and a transport flier to carry fuel. Assign this gentleman for the combat pilot, please, Mitch.'' He pointed to Leader Wyllym, who smiled. ''Schedule his cap cover flights so that he will be available.

''That should be all then, gentlemen,'' Amarson terminated the briefing. ''Two days and then we can see, heh?''

He looked at the holograms once more, then up at his men. ''I will keep these a while, thank you,'' he said. ''Remember, about these new fliers; their pilots are fighting Draks too. Kill all the Draks you see, but not long-winged fliers.''

''That will be all, gentlemen,'' Mitch said. ''Return to your duties, please.''

The room cleared, leaving Amarson standing, fingering the prints. He was looking at a picture of a flier with fantastically long wings. Even though they were torn and bent by the trees and the crash, the length was easily visible in the depth of the hologram. They were easily three times as long as the wings on *his* combat fliers—and they had some symbols and obvious numbers on the outer panels. The body-pod was short. It must be broken, even though it looked intact. The engine was missing and the tail group had separated—it was behind the wreck a distance; showing the direction of impact.

Technically, Amarson was noting the details of the flier. It must have landed at a very slow speed, for the damage was slight for a jungle crash. His eyes saw, his mind registered these details, but a greater realization grew and spread into the forefront of his thought.

He was looking at a flier that had never been manufactured by a Riverman. The small, soft, incredibly talented Rivermen had built all of Amarson's fliers; combat and cargo, and he was thoroughly familiar with their design tricks. No Riverman had conceived, or built any part of the wreck. The pictures alone showed a strangeness, and he knew the wreck site, when he visited it, would show the same. . . unfamiliar . . . nonRiverman design in the flier.

Mitch came back in carrying a compartmented box of map symbols.

"I want to put the kill reports up on your map, Baron," he said, moving to the wall. "They've already posted the big chart in operations. Wyllym and his wingman are in the middle of a mob by now."

"Kill report?" Amarson looked up. "Oh, yes, of course. Come ahead, Mitch. I was looking at the holograms—the new flier."

Mitch went across to the big wall map, found the reference point and put up the five black symbols, small fighting knives with wings, that marked the Drak kills Wyllym had reported. He stuck a banner pin in the map with Wyllym's flight number on it, and stood back to admire.

"Now you have a combat situation map again," he said. "It looks good."

Amarson leaned back and considered the map. "This wreck almost drove the thought of the Drak out of my head. That's our first kill in five years, isn't it?"

"Since the Winter Swarm over Base III," Mitch nodded. "It's the very first for this Fort location, too. But you'd think we were back in the old days at Riverton, the way the Flights have tightened up and switched to combat schedules. Oh, the pilots are a little wild about it—parties and bottle-flying; bragging and betting. But I've got twenty volunteers for perimeter patrol and not a single complaint about the flight postings. Their discipline is worth every day of training we've thrown at them these long years.

"By mid-passage I'll have Chief Mencsar up here screaming at me to get my cubs off his back so he can repair fliers."

Amarson smiled. "Every pilot with a flier in the repair tents will be right behind him with complaints of prejudice and laziness," he said.

"Right. It will be a two day wonder," Mitch said. "Wyllym even asked me for permission to send a dart reward plaque to Mardon's battalion. 'Just for luck,' he said."

"Ouch! Mardon will have a whole battalion of Jungle Patrol out there in two days." Amarson considered the request. "Offering *them* a reward for returning fallen darts is asking for trouble. There were four fliers shooting darts at those Drak. The Jungle Patrol is bound to find some darts. Does Wyllym know how far away from valley *frooge* we are? The nearest still is two kilometers back at Riverton. . . . . And has anybody told him how thirsty a Jungle Patrol battalion—in the jungle—can get?

"Oh, let him send his plaque," Amarson waved an arm. "He's got to learn respect for the ancient traditions in some way."

"They will find darts," Mitch said, grinning. "If you are going to base fliers out there."

"Now, Mitch. Watch that close. Call it off by then. We don't want to bankrupt the boy. Besides, someone will get hurt trying to steal the belts out of loaded dart launchers in the fliers."

Mitch nodded. Mardon would police that for him. He turned his attention back to the map board. Framing the two top corners of the map were the dark veined wings of a long-dead Drak. A fighting trophy of Amarson's early command. These long, leather-like wings and the two short lances beside them were the Drak's main fighting equipment. The Draks flew, using their own wings, and hunted by

164

stopping with the short lance. At close range, against a flier's cockpit, the wings and lance were deadly. At long range, baffled by a combat flier's speed and rapid firing dart-launchers, the Draks were helpless.

Mitch who remembered the battle map from long ago, was considering the vacant spot, above and centered on the map frame. Here a mounted Drak head had hung, its cruel beak open in a fighting scream, eyes flashing fire into the minds of cubs and warriors who came to Amarson's office to plan sorties and defenses. Four years ago, when the Drak flights stopped coming from the western alps and the perimeter flights around Riverton had become mere patrols, Amarson had taken the head down. He angrily claimed he couldn't look at it anymore and sent it to the Flight Mess to hang with the other battle trophies.

"Forget it, Mitch," Amarson rasped. He had seen the direction of Mitch's glance. "I won't have that head back. Five Drak kills don't make a swarm."

"They are the first Draks we have fought for five years, Baron," Mitch said, as if that was a reason for remounting battle trophies. Then he changed the subject.

"Do you think Riverton is safe?" he asked. "If the Draks are returning, I mean."

"I want to call a full tactics meeting tomorrow," Amarson said by way of answer. "Our planning must consider that along with other matters. Our scouting sweep may come up with some more information by then."

He got up and came up to stand beside Mitch, studied the map for a minute then pointed to the indication of the mountains. "We have come south around the curve of the western alps, Mitch," he said. "If, as you think, these five Draks are long-ranging hunters from a new hold. . . . Where would they be, do you think?"

"Back north again," Mitch spread one hand up the map along the spine of the alps, "in the mountains."

"Exactly. On the other side of the alps from Riverton." Amarson put a finger low down on the map-path of the great river; north, behind them. "Riverton is here. A whole day's flight away by cargo flier. We have left the Rivermen behind us, Mitch." He pressed his finger against the map until his claw came out with the pressure. "We cleared their skies of the Drak hunting packs once, Mitch. The little water-loving Rivermen and the Valley farms are no longer providing living food for the Drak hunting packs. The whole west watershed and the River Valley is Drak-free." He swept his hand along the map. "My flying cubs gave them that, and kept the Ancient Compact.

"But the price we paid, Mitch. . . . " Amarson said. "They don't want us in their cities anymore. Riverman and Valleyman, they have their peace, but now they are afraid of the March People. They don't know what to do about a warrior people with nothing to fight."

"They still supply us with fliers, dart-launchers and our weapons. They still trade, Baron," Mitch answered.

"You know my views on that," Amarson said. "They still keep the Ancient Compact. So do we. Our cubs still fly to keep the skies free of Draks, Mitch. Even though they no longer swarm. When a Riverman looks up from his fishing to watch wings in the sky, they are our wings—engine driven wings of combat fliers." He curved his fingers along the blue arc drawn around present base and location of the city Fort.

"The March People still guard the marches of the River Valley. That is our honor by the Ancient Compact. But look at the map, Mitch. My perimeter patrol is a long way from Riverton. We've moved outward in these last five years. The border we guard is now *our* border. This time when we fight Draks we fight to protect our own skies. . . . our own marches."

"No one argues it, Baron," Mitch soothed. "The cubs at least will be glad to fight Draks again. They were hard to keep at the training exercises."

"They will have more than Draks," Amarson said, dropping his thoughts of the past and coming back to pick up the pictures of the wreck again. "They have these new people to meet. And you heard Wyllym's report. Here, look at this picture. They can fight Draks too, Mitch. They are warriors; not wet, small Rivermen or placid Valley crop raisers. By the

166

Two Suns, they are warriors! They fly the free air and they are Drak killers.''

Mitch took the hologram. The body of the dead Drak, wing-crumpled across the top of the wreck, proved Amarson was right. ''So you have found a reason to go flying again, Baron,'' he said.

''Yes, by the Younger Sun! Yes.'' Amarson pulled open his jacket pocket and threw his flight helmet and gloves on the desk. ''I have been good for two years. You run the wing operations better than I do. I have able administrators governing Fort who always argue with my decisions. There is no reason for me not to go back into the air with the combat flights. This is a time when I must fly my own missions.'' He laughed. ''I can still remember how to fight, Mitch. It was a short pack fight out there, today, but it felt good again. I was alive. Even if that cub Tymmda did beat me to my kill,'' he finished ruefully. ''Give him the kill, Mitch. He was ahead of me by whole pulse beats.''

''Leave it, Baron. He is prouder to have shared a kill with you than if he got one of his own. His honor is intact. Let it be. You should let the cubs do the flying anyway.'' Mitch tried once more. ''Think about the people here in Fort. You've already got a full battalion away from their homes. If you go flying out, the city will believe that you are planning to move the wing again. You know the resistance we've been getting. The people don't want to move.''

''I know that, Mitch,'' Amarson said. ''But they've got to move. Have you noticed the way they hide from the sky? Watch them, Mitch. We haven't had a hunting Drak in our sky for years, but this habit our people have of staying under a roof gets worse. Fort is a domed cave. The Jungle Patrol stays in the forest, under the trees. Even our pilots land and run into the hangars before they stop their engines.

''Look out there now, Mitch. Look at the field. You say your cubs are excited about the new Drak kills, but look! You can count the men in the open on one hand.

''Our people are sick, Mitch.'' Amarson's voice became somber. His eyes darkened in worry. ''And I don't think the sighting of five hunting Draks will bring them out of it.'' He shook his head. "They were never like this when they were fighting Draks. Never. I've got to start them building a new flight strip. . . a new city, if I have to. I must do something to bring them out from under their roofs.

"Besides, the new flight strip will be further away from the Rivermen. And the next city we build will be permanent. Up along the mountainside."

"Further away from Riverton?" Mitch said. "Our supply lines are too long now, Baron."

"Right. We must fly in everything." Amarson nodded. "Our fliers are the only skill we have, beside the Warrior Arts. Our future is in long trade lines by air. That is our skill. . . .

"Mitch, you know my policy as well as I do," Amarson said tiredly. "We must use our fliers to develop a trade line one day. The Valley and the Rivermen must grow to like the speed and distance we can cover with our wings. We are warriors, true, but half our people live in Fort—on the ground. Our fliers must work for them, too. And not just as weapons. Mitch, the Draks are back, but remember the last five years. . . . If, and it will happen, the Draks come down on us and are beaten back again, we *must* fill the next period of peace with more hope and a better use of our flying skills. We *must*, Mitch."

He looked up at the situation map. "Those long-winged fliers mean something new, you see, Mitch. Out there. . . . " He walked over to look closely at the coastline beyond the markings of the perimeter patrols. "Out there, somewhere are other people fighting Draks. They are strangers, but friends. By their actions they can't be anything else but our friends, Mitch. Think of it.

"*Someone else; and also fighting Draks.*"

The hope flared in his eyes for a minute, then he turned away from the map and went back to his paper work. The administration of the city Fort, still partly military in nature since the six combat flights were based here—and the Jungle Patrol battalion, was technically based here until they set up the next flight strip—seemed to take more paper work every day. The work would fill the time, though. It would be two days before the field was set up and he could fly out to the wreck site. Then he could get away into the sky again. In the meantime, he had other business to consider.

For instance, the flier modification factory his Chief Groundsman, Mencsar, was setting up. He wasn't up to manufacturing a whole flier yet. Amarson was still dependent on the Rivermen for that; but there was an interesting modification to help with short jungle landings. . . .

4

The Lady Ameera was looking out at the horizontal arc of sky and jungle that the window of her living area possessed. Her face held an expression very much like the one Baron Amarson wore earlier, before his wall map. Ameera had spent seven years of her life with Leon Amarson, Baron Rufus of the Marches, and, except for the fineness of features that was her female heritage and the pale, gold-white coloring that was her beauty, she was habitually able to duplicate most of Amarson's expressions. Some expressions, as now, her face took at rest, as her thoughts patterned themselves after the man she knew so well.

Amarson was in the next room arguing with the two chief administratiors of the city. The argument was sure to be one she had heard before: the city Fort was stable, almost self-supporting, so now Baron Amarson wanted to move it.

This time Ameera didn't agree with him. This time the women of the town were building for permanence. More and more they had found places to look at the sky and the towering mountain to the east. The Draks came hunting no more and the women had found time to see a beauty where their men saw only struggle and tactical problems; or supply and trade.

Ameera had been visited, by two's and in small groups, by most of the women in Fort. She took no decisions in the administration of the city, but her position was useful. Amarson knew of the meetings and listened to her voice because he knew her words came from a vital part of his community. Sometimes, he or his administrator asked her to test a plan, by asking advice from her meeting. By this means, the women knew she was passing their words up to the administrators. They also learned, by testing, that she filtered complaints and favors. So she earned their respect as they used her. The women did not tell her secrets directly, for Ameera was open about her role as ears and voice for Amarson, but Ameera learned these secrets too, for she was also a capable and intelligent woman, and as subtle, covertly, as she was transparent in her public role.

Now, it was these two sides of her diplomacy that held her staring thoughtfully out into the jungle. When his arguing was done, Amarson would ask her to support his decision to move again. This time she believed he was wrong.

This city on the shoulder of the mountain with its view of the sky and the places where they could look up at the sky should be built into a permanent city for the March People. These were the things that the people of the city cherished and, given time, they could build Fort into a rival of Riverton.

Ameera frowned slightly, her ears coming slowly erect as she considered the words she would have to use to sway the mind of Leon Amarson—words and persuasions. She put her tongue out delicately between her lips and turned to consider her room judiciously. It was a calculated part of her persuasion.

The soft curve of the domed ceiling was as high and as gentle of arc as the builders could make it, to give space and lightness to the room. Small circlets of lensed glass pierced the dome at intervals, letting in the day and refracting the ever-changing patterns of the two suns into dancing spears of light. The light spears were caught by, and spun away from, a slowly turning crystal hanging in the center of the dome; refracted into drifting discs of color which floated through the room.

The effect was repeated and enhanced by the crystal food service on the table near two low couches. All of the outlines in the room were softened and blurred by this moving light play. Even Ameera's gown was slashed and ribboned to add to this illusion, making her seem to float in the wind as she stood by the window. This was her way of bringing the outside, the breeze and jungle-sifted sunlight into her room. It brought a calmness that she loved; a calmness that even Amarson's vibrancy couldn't dispel.

She kept this room so different from his office—or his flier—as a place where he could be with her alone. The light from the outside world came in, but very little else.

The rumble of the argument died away and Ameera put up her ears at the lack of sound. The meeting was over.

She moved smoothly down to the table and checked the heat of several dishes with her hand. If they kept him much longer, Amarson would want the dinner recooked.

The door opened and he came in, slowing his pace unconsciously as everyone did when they first entered Ameera's drifting light display. He was wearing a long robe, colored and cut to be in harmony with the room; a habit he had affected as long as she had known him. Even when the room had been the rough-log Lodge on the River valley marches.

"Leon, you're laughing," she said, reading the unexpected expression on his face while she heard the quick-measured rumbly bubble he made in his chest. "You are laughing at them. Oh, Leon. You aren't going to move everybody out of Fort, after all. You've changed your mind."

"Yes, I've changed my mind. No. They have changed it for me." Amarson came into the room and gripped her shoulders. "You should have heard them, Ameera. There is no reason to move, now. No reason. The Draks have come back again, and more."

"The people that flew the wrecked flier?"

"Yes, the story about it is all over the city. You should have heard the arguments I've been getting: plans for strengthening the city against Drak attack; volunteer lists for duties at the Jungle Patrol barracks; complete inventories of all supplies in the city. . . . I didn't know anybody was keeping that up to date; it ran to three volumes.

"Ameera, they're alive again. Our wonderful March People, they've got a purpose."

"Five Draks make a purpose," Ameera shivered a little, reacting to his intensity.

"They make a start," Amarson said. "The Heralds will sing all the old combat chants again and, while my cubs hunt the skies for more Draks, the people here at Fort will build a spirit they were losing. You'll see, Ameera. This time we will be a warrior people guarding our own marches— protecting the city Fort; not Rivermen. This is a new Compact; from ourselves, to ourselves. Aiiee! Watch it grow!" He pulled her into an embrace.

"Fine words." Ameera relaxed in his arms. "Grand philosophy. And you have an excuse to go flying again, so off you go. Piff! Spaat! . . . While your great civilization grows up behind you. Fine words for a man who just likes to play with fliers in the sky."

"How well you know me," he laughed. "Do you know the drinking song my cubs sing?"

> "Warrior Lady tell me why
> You so sadly pass me by.
> Warrior Lady lift your eye;
> Let me show you all my sky."

"I know that verse and several others you don't have to bother to sing," she said squirming out of his embrace. "Come and eat before the food cools. We have the second passage all to ourselves before you fly out. . . . " She guided him to the table.

"Food?" Amarson questioned. "Maybe later, not now. I'm too happy to eat. Too excited, Ameera. I feel like a cub again. As if the flight out to Mardon's battalion is my first combat trip. My instincts are aroused again, as they haven't been in years."

"Now, that I do not believe," Ameera laughed, sliding down to the cushion beside him. She never sat across table from Amarson as a habit, alway at his side, but then, too, her gown was not designed to be viewed at a distance. She sat close.

". . . and your arousal has been a care of mine, Leon, should you remember." She was chiding him.

"Remember?" Amarson caressed her with his eyes, looking where the gown lured him to look. "Ahh, but today I plan to fly. . . against the Draks, perhaps. Warrior Lady, you should be afraid of my instincts, today."

"Afraid of *you*?" Her laugh was clear and delightful. "Oh, dear Leon. Fear you. . . ?" She sucked in her breath as he brushed her back against the cushion, then went on: "Afraid of you, Leon? Why no. You are just a big, soft. . . . " She rolled herself into his embrace, greeting his caressing hands with glides of her body that were bursts of intense delight. The susurrus of ripping cloth mingled with the low rumble of Amarson's soft laughter—his rapid drone of care and love.

5

Amarson took his big cargo flier into the circle of the cap cover fliers and started to set up his landing spiral. The combat fliers slid out to make room for him and his slower air speed. The jungle landing mat was below him, a raw scar in the red light of the Father Sun.

Mardon had cut the opening in the jungle with explosives and hadn't wasted any time on niceties. The torn trees and broken growth of the landing path was a puzzle jumble, already crisping with defoliant powders. There was another cruel scar on the take-off end of the mat, but between them lay the neat flatness of the flexible landing mat. Mardon's battalion carried this mat with them in sections and they could surface a landing pad for combat fliers in a very short time. This mat was longer than standard because it had to take cargo fliers, but it was complete; including the bright banners of the landing markers and the wind indicator.

The landing mat was ready and waiting. Amarson slid around his downwind turn and headed in at the landing slot. He widened the flier's wings to give him more lift and take-off power. The flier sank in toward the landing mat. From this angle and direction, the mat was no longer smooth. It had a definite up and down waviness. Mardon had made no attempt to level the ground under it. There was no need. The flexible mat would take the weight of the flier and spread it out, distribute it throughout the mat, absorbing the landing shock and letting the flier settle and roll as if it were on a smooth grass field. Mardon and his men had built landing mats like this before—they were good at it. . . . And Amarson had landed on them before; the bumpiness of the mat didn't bother him.

The flier sailed over the end of the mat and Amarson widened the wing again, pulling the inboard trailing edge down to its maximum lifting shape. He added power as the nose came up and the flier settled into the mat. The wheels hissed across the mesh with a whirring shriek; the power cut back to shorten the roll and Amarson was on the ground.

Mardon, himself, was standing to wave the flier off onto the side mat. Amarson looked up quizzically at the overhead covering. They *had* killed three Draks here, but the flier cap cover should be protection enough. Why was Mardon hiding?

"I brought a full load of fuel," he called down, after he cut the engine. "Get it unloaded and you can call down the combat flier that came up with me. He will hold here on the ground with you."

Mardon nodded and waved up a work crew.

Amarson unbuckled and slid down to grip Mardon's arm.

"You're being a little conservative, aren't you, old friend," he said. "Are you hiding everything? Don't you trust my cubs any more? Trouble?" He knew Mardon had a good reason for his precautions; fear and distrust weren't the reasons.

"Nothing positive," Mardon answered. "You were up there. You must be able to see what's ahead of us. I had three patrols out all across my front. Baron, if your pack fight hadn't diverted us into here we'd have marched out of the Jungle yesterday. My battalion would have been camped out in the middle of that grass obscenity."

"Obscenity? It's beautiful, Mardon. It's wide and free and all sky as far as you can see. I could fly all day and never see the end of it."

"I could walk all day, never find cover to fight from. No jungle. No mountains. Your maps didn't show. . . that."

"We've come past the mountains, Mardon. Out from under the threat of the Drak henges. I didn't plan on this when I sent your battalion out to string landing pads down this way. But the plans changed.

"We're filming maps for you now. You'll get the holograms. But the next landing strip will be out there. How far can you march in a day, out on that flat land?"

"How far do you plan to fly in one day?" Mardon said.

"I'll have to find out whether I can get a squad to follow me beyond the Jungle. That is if we're allowed to get any further than this."

"Ah yaha. The Draks," Amarson switched out of his dreams and back to Mardon's realities. There had been Draks killed. And Mardon had to believe there would be more Draks. His life of fighting them, like Amarson's, told him that.

"Have you had any more contacts? Seen anything out on the plain?" Amarson suddenly remembered that moving dust cloud.

"Not yet. But I've got everybody set for anything. All around perimeter. They'll come in from the mountains, I guess. Draks wouldn't like that plain any more than I do."

"You've got lookouts on that side?"

"Lookouts? Amarson, I stopped playing cub-tricks years ago. I've got four sections—dug in tight. I'll have the whole battalion dug in by the time Father Sun has set. All the cook fires are underground now. I'll have a full perimeter out all through the dark cycle, and I hope they remember how to handle a ground attack. They haven't had anything but training maneuvers for too long.''

"Maybe you had better tell me what's got you nervous," Amarson said.

"Come and see the wrecked flier first," Mardon answered vaguely. "We haven't touched anything except some maps and paper. It will be dark soon. See the wreck first, Baron, then you can read the pilot's combat report."

Amarson nodded and followed him off the mat and along a well-cut trail until he was standing at the wreck.

He found himself drawn toward the two bodies.

The one in the front of the broken body-pod was torn and broken—only the helmet and goggle-covered head untouched. The other was sitting erect, staring forward. This one wore no helmet or goggles, his eyes were open, his face undistorted by pain. The head was completely covered by a heavy, soft fur that blew in the wind. There were two wide circular ears, also fur-covered, and of course the fur made any attempt at reading facial expressions impossible. However, the wide-open eyes, clear and still undesiccated, made the body seem still alive.

Amarson felt the hair lift on the back of his arms and his claws ran out unconsciously. He moved closer to see how the furry one had died.

A Drak lance was driven through the instrument panel and had impaled him to his seat. Amarson clenched his teeth—it was a painful way to die. He noted the heavy, furry hands and a long, curved, flight control.

"This was the pilot, then?" he said.

"Yes," Mardon said. "His name is Bryn and he had been flying that thing all night—in the dark cycle—to get here."

"He was alive when you got here?" Amarson asked harshly. Even an alien stranger was entitled to some medical. . . .

"No. Quite dead." Mardon said. "That lance started to kill him the minute it went in, but he lived awhile. One day, perhaps. He wrote a complete combat report. Here on the ground, while he was dying.

"Bryn," Mardon said softly. "Very small and impossibly furry; but he had a Warrior's Code. I would have liked to have know him."

"Hmmm," Amarson was looking at the controls and the broken instruments. "Mardon," he called, his voice oddly strained. "Look here." He reached in and lifted out a small shining disc. It was a religious orrery.

"One of your men must have put it here," he said. "I thought you told them to leave things alone."

"No, Baron," Mardon said. "Look again. The colors are all wrong on the World disc. That is his. His orrery."

"It can't be," Amarson shook his head. "Nobody has ever heard of these furry people. There would be legends at least, if we had ever. . . ."

"I'm beginning to wonder how old our old religion really is," Mardon said. "Make it spin. It works just like ours." He watched his Baron thumb the orrery and listened to the automatic prayer chant Amarson whispered.

"He would have said the same thing," Mardon said, referring to the fuzzy pilot. "His combat report was written in church cant. My First Soldier can read it. He's the one who's got the troops digging in."

"When my flight leader pitched into the pack fight, this flier was already being attacked. at first rising." Amarson made the association, forgot the religious curiosity and went right to the military problem. "He. . . what did you call him? Bryn? This Bryn flies in the dark cycle, and you think the Draks may have learned to fly at night too."

"He fought something at night, sir. He thought they were Draks. It is all in his report." Mardon answered. "We are on guard against what he fought. . . or," he paused, "another night flier who finds us camped around a wreck and shoots first. This is a Jungle Patrol battalion, Baron. We grew up suspicious."

Two fliers roared over the field at low altitude, rattling the silent jungle.

"There goes our cap cover," Mardon said. "They will

just have time to get back to Fort before the Father Sun sets. We ought to get in, too. I don't want a light out here after dark. Besides, I want you to read that report."

"I'm more than anxious to," Amarson said turning to follow. "You can begin dismantling the wreck tomorrow. I want it charted, numbered and carried back to Fort. Chief Groundsman Mencsar will want every piece to play with.

"There are body sacks in my flier, too. Have the numbers and symbols there on the wing fabric cut away into death banners. I want to rebuild the flier, but those two did kill a Drak and they're entitled to have a part of their weapon burned with them."

Mardon disappeared into the ground ahead, down into the command post dugout. Amarson followed him and found a First Soldier setting out food and drink in a room that had been cleared for his, Amarson's, use.

"I want the Baron to read the pilot's flight report," Mardon was saying to the Patrolman. "Set the perimeter and then come back, please." He had lifted a small bound book out of a chest.

"No need for an interpreter, Mardon," Amarson said. "If you have reported right. I can read church cant; it's been an interest of mine for a long time."

"The Baron will have no trouble," the Patrolman said. "It's a soldier's report—simple, with no priestly arguments. The language is old, but I've read harder."

Amarson smiled and opened the book. The writing was bold and the phrasing was not what he was used to. The old religion went in for internal rhyme and mystic symbolism. There was none of this in the report, so at first the phrasing was strange, but soon the words of the pilot came clear from the page.

The First Soldier came back in and reported: "Perimeter set. Full dark out now, sir. No lights. We landed one combat flier. It is refueled and spotted to fly at first light."

Amarson, interrupted and now used to the narrative style of what he was reading, leafed back a page and began again.

6

Bryn dropped the nose of his flier out of its climb and began a wide circle to let his observer pick up the navigation points. The yellow Younger Sun and the giant, red Father Sun had set before the night patrol left the ready-wagons. Bryn's take-off had been directly from a darkened catapult-wagon into the blackness of Frieland's starless night. From the catapult launch, the flier's tiny engine had pushed it up to the navigating altitude in a series of timed turns, carefully charted to avoid the seven other fliers of the Herd-patrol, maneuvering in the darkness.

Bryn balanced his forty-five kilos against the flier's turning and sat up tall in the body-pod's rear seat; the pilot's station. Standing, Bryn was just over a meter tall, so he had to sit high in order to sense the flier's movements and control its flight. Over half of his body had to be above the windscreen of the pod when he sat at the controls. He erected the fur on his arms and shoulders. The vibrations of the flier's wings and the movement of the air past the pod came to him through the sensitive fur. With the engine popping, his side ears were buried deep in the protective fur of his head. The engine noise made them about as much help as his eyes. His eyes were fully dilated in the darkness, but there just wasn't much to see. The thin wing above the pod, and the one below, stretched out to the left and right. The vibrations of their working spars and taut wires could be felt, but they were not visible. The tail boom behind him was, likewise, beyond his sight. The direction instruments glowed a soft green inside the flier. Bryn could see these phosphors and the dim shape of the observer in the pod in front of him; the rest of the flier was lost in the night.

Bryn stretched a hand out and touched the little swinging shrine in the corner of his instrument panel. The shrine was a gold and green sphere of The World, around which the two suns rotated. The Younger Sun was a yellow jewel and the Father Sun a disc of red gem stone almost as large as the green planet. His wide fingers pushed at the disk of the Father Sun and set the shrine rotating on its pivots. The gearing in the arms that held the sun jewels sent the Younger Sun whirling in its orbit around The World. The jewels caught the soft light of the instrument fluorescents.

We know The World revolves around the Father Sun, Bryn thought, but the shrine will never change. The Father Sun, gigantic and so far away, could never be sculptured in its true stellar scale in any case. The old religious artists had pictured a divine balance for their symbol. The shrine symbol has come down to us unchanged, as we use it today; *In the name of the Father Sun, the Younger Sun and the Darkness*. He turned the World sphere as required in the prayer. He couldn't see the shapes carved on its surface, but they hadn't changed in generations, either. The planet globe had three great continents on the other side to balance the one known continent on this side.

More divine balance, Bryn mused. No one from Frieland has ever flown across the mountains of the sun to look at the other side of The World, but our shrine is sculptured to balance. If we ever do see that side of The World, I wonder who will be most surprised, the map-men or the priests?

The flier rocked in the air. The observer was shifting in the front part of the pod. Bryn corrected his controls and glanced at the folded map strapped to his leg. The instrument glow-lights fluoresced the inks on the map to show him the route of the Great Animal Herd for the night patrol. Bryn's course was a long patrol forward toward the Herd's leading edge and across to ride the mountain air currents. Seven other fliers patrolled the night sky over the migrating herd ahead of Bryn and above him, but none of them would fly north tonight. Bryn would be alone on that loop.

Despite the length of the flight, the Herd Commander had delayed Bryn's flight until last. The Commander had waited until all of the day patrol reports were in and examined. He wanted final assurance that the Drak were not flying, before sending Bryn up.

Bryn shared his commander's worry. The food-herd migration of the Frieland Commonwealth had been virtually free from Draks when Bryn began to fly for the Herd Guard seven years ago. In those seven years, the attacks had begun. At first there were scattered strikes against the Northern herding patrols. The strikes had increased slowly, until Draks were attacking anything that flew in those far Northern skies. Then, a year ago, the Kraal-lands on the main trek-way came under constant raids by Drak hunting patrols. The Draks were winged, they flew out of the mountain canyons in packs of eight or ten and struck and killed, then they flew back.

Bryn had flown some of the combat patrols against them and he had seen the results of their raids. He had seen the beheaded, cooked and partially-eaten bodies the Draks left— when a Frieland rescue flight arrived too late.

Like other Frielanders before him, Bryn became single-minded about Draks after seeing those butcherings. He attacked them in the air whenever their obscene wings brought them within range. The Draks, for their part, were equally fanatic and a single Commonwealth flier usually brought six or eight warriors up out of the jungle, beating their wings in violent combat climb. The Draks attacked with spears and even by boarding Frieland fliers. Bryn was armed with rockets and carried a fighting knife in the pod, against their boarding him.

The Draks always attacked the fliers, as they raided, in small packs. Sometimes they grouped two or three of these packs into bigger parties to attack the Kraal settlements. One of these war parties had struck at the Miera-Kraal garrison at dawn this morning. Miera was the northernmost Kraal of the Frieland Commonwealth. Bryn had seen the second passing report from Meira-Kraal, too, and that was part of his worry.

Very suddenly the Draks had changed their standard way of fighting. Three days ago they had disappeared from the sky and a lull had begun. No Draks flew anywhere. Then, this morning, at the rising of the Father Sun, Miera-Kraal was attacked and destroyed. How many Draks did this, no one knew. Only one scout survived and Colonel Siith's rescue flight found no Draks. Both the lull and the hit-and-run attack were something new for Drak warriors.

The migrating Herd would reach Miera-Kraal lands in two more days. There it would mill out and settle down for the calfing season. The Herd would cover hundreds of square kilometers, expanding the patrol range of the herding fliers and holding the Herd-Guard in a single location—near the mountains and the Draks.

Also the Commonwealth. . . all the people traveling alongside the migration would move into camp at Miera-Kraal. All would be prime targets for Draks when they attacked. And they would attack.

The whole Herd-Guard was on alert tonight. Colonel Siith thought the Draks were being driven back on the Commonwealth by an enemy from the north. He was very noisy about this. The Herd-Commander thought the Draks were planning a night attack. He believed they had begun to fight at night; and attacked Miera-Kraal at night.

Bryn didn't believe the Draks were able to fly at night. The total darkness would ground anything that flew on its own wings, like the Draks. However, if they weren't flying by day, they must be doing something by night. If that something was an attack against Frieland, it could come from the north where the high mountains were closest to the main trek. Bryn's night patrol was going looking for Draks up there, if they were to be found.

The darkness grounded the Draks, but it didn't ground the silent, long-winged fliers of Bryn's night patrol group. He flew his flier in the darkness with a sure knowledge and instinct for flight. He didn't need to see much. The flier was fitted with special invisible lights under the pod that were used to track the Herd animals on ordinary patrols. Tonight they would let the observer, and Bryn, see the mountain canyons; see Draks. They wouldn't be used , much, until the patrol crossed the coast. The observer used them to observe and to check his navigation points, but they were there to let Bryn hunt Draks if he needed them.

The flier was safe in the dark, high in the thin air of the upper sky, but the business of the night patrol wouldn't keep. The flier couldn't stay here with its engine popping fitfully. For one thing, the fuel gauge was half-empty and fuel weight was needed at the end of the patrol. For another, the Draks were north, over against the alps, down on the ground, not up in the safe dark air.

Bryn made a final check of his flier. On course? At altitude? Everything checked against his own efficient instincts and balance and told him that the flier was holding steady and flying well.

He reached out and turned off the engine.

The nose of the flier dropped. The push of the engine mounted behind the wings no longer held it against the sky. The flier began to build up speed as it slid down the sky. With speed came the control he expected and the nose lifted slightly.

The noise of the engine was soaked up in the darkness and gone. A soft rustle of sound, a humming and vibration began. This was the sound of the flier working against the sky. It was a noise Bryn knew and loved. The engine sound made him a little uncomfortable and slightly sick, but this. . . .

His ears lifted and opened and began to move around. The hair that covered his face and head began to fluff out as the tiny muscles at their roots started receiving signals of vibrations from the air. All the fur on his body was doing this, but the green instrument light only shimmered on his face and head. His eyes, widening in an attempt to see in the blackness, picked up the reflected glow from his face hair and he could see his mustache stiffen and puff out. He put out his wide, pink tongue to wet his nose and settled down to fly the patrol.

The observer in the body of the pod ahead of him moved the cover from the map board. The flier rocked as the long twin wings deflected with the observer's movements. Bryn's senses picked up the vibrations through the pod and the movement of the wings. His ears heard half-a-hundred creaks and sighs. A change in the tension strumming of the rigging wires told him the attitude of the wings. He corrected slightly with his controls and continued the flat dive down the sky.

"Lights on. Begin the patrol," the observer said.

"Silence!!" Bryn snapped. "Sound discipline!"

His ears had flattened painfully against the protective fur of his head. The observer's voice was several hundred decibels higher than the sky sounds. When Bryn had his ears erected and attuned to the small noises, voices were painful. Worse, they cut off his contact with the flier.

His eyes were on the instruments, now. He controlled the flier crudely until his hearing returned. His luck was good tonight, the air was smooth and the flier handled itself. But what kind of an observer had he drawn tonight? Talking on a night patrol. Unbelievable.

Bryn shook his head slowly. His ears came up with this movement. The sound of the wind moving changed as his head turned and his ears moved to pick up the new sounds. The murmuring of the flier came back through the darkness as a friendly thing; Bryn relaxed slightly. His ears were very sensitive to the sounds of the wind and movements of the flier, but he quite literally couldn't fly and talk at the same time—not in the dark cycle.

The flier rode down the wind and felt delicately for the thermocline. Minutes before they had climbed up through the heavy air. Now, Bryn was sliding down toward it again, listening for the motion of the air.

The lower wing shivered as it began to move through the denser air near the thermocline. Then the upper wing took up the soft humming. The observer looked around, briefly, at the noise. Bryn nodded in answer, to keep him from asking questions. They were riding near the thermocline. He eased the flier lower.

At this height over the plain, the light upper air and the heavy molecules of the lower air did not mix. Here was a border region. The upper air increased in density as it met the thermocline, but it did not cross over. Instead, it moved in circular winds parallel to the heavier air below. When the wings of the flier entered this dense moving air mass, the result was air moving over the wings faster, producing more

184

lift and the effect of an increase in speed. That was what the wing noise indicated.

Bryn guided the flier lower. He forced it down against the increased lift at a flat angle to the moving air. The air density increased and the wings deflected upward at the tips. Bryn's senses read the vibrations of the stresses in the wings and the sounds of the air. When they were at their maximum, he neutralized his controls and let the pressure of the lift build up until the flier reacted.

Its nose came up violently. The deflection in the wings threw it into a giant swooping climb. Up. Up. Up!

Bryn held the flier on the patrol course and let the natural dynamics of the lift carry him high into the thin air. When the speed dropped off, he controlled the flight into a long, flat dive that carried him back down to the thermocline.

This time Bryn knew the approximate height of the swirling winds and the maneuver was repeated with precision. Each swoop through the night covered kilometers of his course up the Trek-path toward the mountains. The night patrol was a series of silent, wind-powered hops, in and out of the thermocline's turbulence.

The course for tonight paralleled the migration route of the Herd as far as End Rock, then directly across the leading edge of the herd and out to search the forest slopes of the High Mountains. The observer would scan the ground for signs of Draks, and Bryn would keep the flier in the sky. He would fly the plotted search pattern, then come back, crossing the Herd to end back at the home wagon, just before the rise of the Father Sun. His maps were marked with the furthest-on point of the Commonwealth's night march. The point where landing signals and a field would be laid out for him.

The observer signaled a navigational checkpoint. Bryn slipped his night goggles down over his eyes. Below him the plain was illuminated by the invisible rays of the powerful lights mounted under the flier. The goggles converted the rays into frequencies he could see, and the deep canyon with its shallow sloping sides was plainly visible.

Also visible were the heavy backs of the Herd animals. They were already pouring down into the canyon, moving

185

easily down the slope. Generations of migrations and un-counted millions of animals had worn the passage into an easy grade, into and out of the canyon. Bryn could see the near edge of the moving Herd. See it quite well. . . even an occasional lifted head; a tossed horn. He couldn't see the leaders. They had passed further down into the canyon. He couldn't see the far side of the Herd either, that was five kilometers to his left. But his timer said he'd reached the front of the Great Herd, and the canyon was his check point. As it passed beneath him, Bryn turned the flier onto the second leg of the patrol.

Now he would go out across the moving Herd and ride the rising air currents up the cliffs of the High Mountain. This was where the day patrols usually found their Drak hunting. And it was here where the mystery of *no Draks* in the sky had first been reported.

The flier was high on the top of one of its hops. Guiding it up here was easy, so Bryn kept his goggles on for a few minutes. He was watching the ground below for End Rock on the far side of the Herd. This was a pinnacle jutting out of the plain and was a marker for the beginning of Miera-Kraal lands.

He saw it, and was satisfied with his course. The goggles were shoved up on his head. He wiggled them in his fur a bit so they wouldn't interfere with his ears. It was nice to see the ground, but he could only see places where the lights were pointing and looking over the side of the pod spoiled his balance with the flier. His ears, his fur, his feel of the vibrations, helped him guide the flier through the night. Bryn had an instinct for flight, let the observer look at the ground.

The air was clear, undisturbed by any weather cells, and Bryn's climbing, swooping progress became rhythmic. The rhythm allowing him to time his control moves and relax, in between, as the balanced flier flew itself from one high arc to another. Bryn was moving well through the night and enjoy-ing the responsive feedback from his wings and wires as they talked to him from the darkness.

He didn't even mind the pitch and jiggle of the observer's movement, right at the stall point on top of a climb. He steadied the flier into its power dive and took time to drop his goggles and look at what the observer had seen on the ground.

Forest. The flier was moving across the foothill jungle. Nothing special. The jungle was a navigation point on their course and the observer was just making his maps.

Bryn listened carefully to the sounds of his wings. The mountains were out there in front of him, and he wanted to be ready to turn when he felt the air currents.

He stiffened in his seat. His ears snapped open. *He heard a sound*.

He listened. He heard it again. Faint, far away, a tearing, roaring sound. He had never heard it before. This might be the Drak activity they were looking for. His back stiffened a little. The sound was very faint. He had not been quite sure of its direction, and now it was gone. One thing was sure—Bryn trusted his ears for sounds in the air—the noise was in the air with him. Not on the ground, but in the air.

The thing that made the little thrills of fear run up and down his back fur was the feeling that the sound, and whatever made it, was in the air *above him*; in a superior fighting position; at a higher altitude.

The flier shuddered into the upper edge of the thermocline and swayed as it struck a rough mass of air. Bryn heard the swirl of the air mass moving between his wings, corrected away from it, not into it, and felt the air quiver and fall off down his wing tips.

A wild air mass. You can't see those even in the sunlight, he thought to himself. That was close. The mountains began here. They rose out of the plain into towering alps and marched north in broken ranges far beyond the Miera-Kraal lands. The plains air moved steadily against this rock, was split around it, swirled and spun with turbulent mass, and rose up-slope in blasting vertical columns that tore the surface of the thermocline.

Wild air mass. The flier had dropped, almost unheeded, into this rough air, while Bryn listened to the faint noise in the air.

He gathered his senses together again and began to concentrate on his flying.

He let the flier dive deep into the thermocline. His wide hands were spread along the control bar, feeling and fighting the turbulence. He wanted to ride in as close to the mountains, as quickly as he could, to catch that mysterious sound. He held his dive and let the speed build up before the lift. The wing wires were howling, but the lift, when it came, took him high into the smooth air. Very high.

When the flier topped out, Bryn flattened his dive as much as he could and reached toward the High Mountains.

The turbulence above the rising ground worked for him. Only three hops were needed. Then the observer signaled that they were nearing the cliff line.

Bryn leaned forward, waiting for the signal to turn parallel to the rock ranges. Instead, he saw every hair on the observer's head standing straight out. Fright? Fear, up here?

The observer's hand jabbed straight up and made a circling motion. Enemy sighted! Right below!

Bryn growled in his teeth. The fur on his head was erect too. Draks! What a place to sight them. The flier was on top of one of its hops. It was almost hanging in the air, as Bryn had been waiting to turn onto a new course.

He drove the nose down to get speed to maneuver and lifted the wing in a tight turn back on their course. The observer caught his sighting again and indicated a direction.

Very well. That was away from the alps. If he had to fight, he wanted room.

Bryn swung right and let the flier lose altitude swiftly. His tongue curled out several times to wet his nose, as he dove for the invisible thermocline at combat speed.

The observer made circling motions again and Bryn's ears and tensioned nerves felt the shiver of the wings. He made his turn in the thermocline and controlled the lift into a tight climbing spiral that took them straight up over the same point on the ground.

He pulled his goggles into place and looked over the side. The lights were sweeping over the ground in swirling arcs, but he could see what had to be seen.

He spiraled over a camp; a large one. Ten, twenty tents and

several fires. Near the trees, his lights reflected from something hidden under the jungle growth. Out on the edge of his swirling beams it looked like somebody had been cutting down the jungle. Draks? A Drak war camp? No, too small. When the Draks swarmed, they came in thousands. This was the camp of a raiding party or maybe a scout for the main swarm. The Draks were up to *something*!

The mission north up the mountain's flank was changed, as of now. Better to take a look around here. He checked his time. Flight back, so much. . . time to sunrise. . . . He did his sums and came out positive. His patrol had to be back at the Herd by sunrise, but that left time enough for a figure-eight search here along the mountainside. About one hop on each leg. Good, let's go!

He swung out of the top of his spiral and drifted north until his wing wires whined with the crosswind vibrations. He kept his goggles on and tracked the jungle below him, ignoring for a time the mountains. He was moving parallel to the cliffs now and cutting the up-rising air pattern. The air sounds at this height told him he had safe kilometers between his flier and the crags.

Behind him the strange, rackety noise started up again and then faded. The sound was louder this time and this time it didn't stop. Bryn could still hear it when he looped around on the north leg of his figure-eight. It wasn't a sound he was used to hearing and his ears still could not locate it. The sound seemed to be moving. He had the uncomfortable feeling again, that it was coming from the air above him. High above him.

The observer signaled a sighting on the ground. Bryn looked over the side and saw a cut, crushed pathway in the jungle below. Something, somebody, had built a crude road. The observer was marking crosses on his maps, but to judge by his flier's instinct, Bryn would bet the road ended up in the camp back there on the coast.

He kept the flier on its search course and crossed the camp again at the top of one of his hops. The rackety noise swelled in volume and for a moment Bryn had to flatten his ears a little to filter it out.

A sense of dread began to raise the hair on his back. Something was wrong. What?

The unexplained noise swelled and then faded, as suddenly as it had come. Bryn's tongue licked out and wet his nose. His senses were strained. His ears and hair nerves had caught the faint impression of something passing over his flier. The erect hair on his back and shoulders, his sensitive, alert senses reacted to something up in the darkness with him. He stiffened for an attack.

Then it was gone. Bryn let the tension go loose. Was he feeling ghosts? No. The sound was really there, but, whatever it was, it was gone now.

The observer had noticed nothing. He had stopped marking his maps and was merely watching the ground below. The flier was sweeping into the southern leg of the figure-eight search, but this leg covered nothing but jungle.

Bryn held the flier into the controlled turn of the pattern and dropped it into the thermocline. When his climbing hop took him back over the camp again, he arced around into a tight spiral, and lost altitude as slowly as he could. The observer had time to record details of the camp in the jungle.

The boost out of the thermocline this time was a fast violent climb. At the top, Bryn dropped over into a vertical bank and rolled out on the course for home.

He trimmed the flier for the cruise back and let it drop smoothly through the darkness. They had seen this camp and mapped it, and now Bryn wanted to get home with those maps and the information. He was in a hurry.

The observer realized that they were leaving and turned around to make fighting motions with his hands. He had six war rockets under the body-pod and wanted to use them. Bryn shook his head angrily and let his teeth show in a growl.

You ought to be able to see that in the instrument glow, you squirmer, he thought. *Sit down and let me fly.* He was working the flier into the swirling air over the channel and the observer's movements rocked his control dangerously.

No fighting. He was going home.

The patrol had to get back with the marked maps. Let a war patrol come back and kill Draks. *Our business is maps, and*

190

mine is flying, Bryn thought at his jiggling observer. *Sit still and let me feel the air.*

Bryn put out his tongue and wet his nose, then he concentrated on the vibrations of the flier. He had to get back to the field before the suns came up. It was a matter of great pride for the pilots of the Night Patrol to finish their flights in darkness, just before dawn: they *were* the Night Patrol. More practically, Bryn wanted to bring his maps back before the Morning Patrol was launched; and they flew at the rise of the Younger Sun. Bryn's patrol time was running out.

The flier bumped and jerked in the air. Bryn cursed the observer. The man had the itch. Couldn't he stay still? The fool was actually looking over the side.

The flier rocked its left wing low and lost altitude. Bryn caught the fall with his controls and held his dive.

Now, the observer bounced back into the center of his pod and was peering into his scope and marking his map frantically.

Well, at least he had sighted something, Bryn thought. He swung the flier around in a circle and felt for the thermocline. That makes up for his itch, but when we get on the ground I'm going to put a few nets in him. He jumps the flier all over the sky.

The wings hummed the right note and the ship kicked up in its circular hop. Bryn dropped his goggles into position and took a look.

The jungle ended and the flat plain-land began in a sharp line off to the right. Below them was a small group of herd animals moving out into the plain . . . not more than fifty. But they weren't moving right. . . they weren't moving at all. And they weren't solidly bunched, the way. . . . He caught a wave of wide-spread wings. Wings! Wings meant Draks.

He dove down lower, forcing the flier into the thermocline and back up again in a maneuver that cracked the wings, but gave him speed and control enough to pull up and around in a tight turn. The flier stood them on their heads and the force of the turn pulled Bryn's ears down into his fur, but when he rolled out, the lights were centered on whatever was down

191

there on the plain. Bryn turned into a spiral and kept the lights centered until he could see plainly.

The group was Draks. . . two groups of them. Draks on the ground; not flying. In the concentrated light pattern, he could see fighting spears. . . weapons. *A raiding party*!

The pod of the flier shook as Bryn took it around in a third circle. The observer was bouncing again, pointing down and making fighting signs that were dimly visible in the glow of his map screen. Bryn nodded violently. *Yes, you blood-thirsty fidget. This one we will attack. A Drak raiding party on the plain is why we carry rockets. Now, sit still and let's get this done right.*

He took one more look to fix the position of the column in his mind and then headed the flier down through the thermocline in a fighting pattern. He couldn't fire his rockets accurately through turbulence.

The Draks were down below him on the ground. He reached out and touched the little shrine. The two sun jewels spun with his fighting prayer. He forced the flier's nose down further.

The flier lost height in a steep dive. He would not be feeling for the thick air this time. He was diving for penetration, and he wanted as much speed, afterwards, as his wings would take.

The pitch of the wires rose to a scream that flattened his ears. The wing deflections were sharp and violent, but he spread both hands on the controls and held the flier steady as it dropped through the thermocline barrier. The wing spars and struts groaned as they took up the stress he was forcing on them, but they returned to normal. The flier was through and in the heavy lower air.

The speed held in the dive and began to build when the airflow increased. Bryn dropped the goggles over his eyes for wind protection now, as the air flowing past his windscreen became almost solid.

The observer snapped his arm up. They were passing over the Draks again.

Bryn flattened his dive and began a measured count, then a controlled diving turn. At the end of the turn, he switched on

192

the two lights in the nose of the pod, and held the flier steady.

The observer bent over his aiming screen. This screen was now illuminated by the reflection of these fighting lights. Invisible, like the others, they pointed straight ahead of the flier and, in this fighting dive, they should pick out figures on the ground. . . . about, now. Now?

Now! The observer began signaling small course changes that Bryn followed as fast as they were signed. He threw up his goggles and leaned forward under the windscreen to see the signals more clearly. Left: left a little, and steady; the flier dove in on the Draks.

The observer fired!

Three of the rockets dropped out of their wing racks and fell away before their motors lit. Bryn felt their release and climbed the flier to get away from the flare. His night-adapted eyes blinked automatically when they fired. The flare was deep in red and would be almost invisible to the Draks, but it made Bryn's eyes close briefly.

He concentrated on his flying and threw the flier into the second leg of his combat figure-eight and dived back into the target. He held his line again and the observer fired the last rockets.

This time Bryn risked a look through his goggles as they went over the Drak grouping.

The rockets were set to detect the ground and break up at a certain height. They carried no explosive or fire. The rockets just broke up into many small rods which whirled through the air and tore into the target. They were silent and deadly; a perfect night weapon. The Draks would never know where they came from.

The lights under the flier showed the carnage as he went by. The first three rockets had spread and hit both groups. The Draks had made a narrow trek-track through the grass. Now the track was wider, distorted and crushed as dying Draks lurched and swirled brokenly in their dying. The first group in the marching column was down. Bryn could see bodies torn and broken by his missiles. He saw the second column beginning to run and mill around as they heard the dying screams.

That was all he had time to see, then they were over and past. The second stick of three rockets would hit and do their share of damage, but Bryn couldn't stay to see. He pulled the flier up in a steep climb and began to trade his fighting speed for altitude.

He bent forward to watch the height recorder on his instrument panel. There was no turbulence here below the thermocline to warn him of its location. He had to stop his climb just under the barrier, and do it by instruments. When he had dropped the two sticks of rockets, they left six gaping slots in the wing panels. The flier would still fly, but it would be dangerous to penetrate the barrier with the wings like that. More important, the flier would never survive a single lift maneuver *above* the thermocline. The wings would tear off.

Bryn got his height and leveled off. His course indicator was spinning from the maneuvers. Navigation would have to come from the front seat. He tapped on the pod side to attract the observer's attention. The man was looking down through his scope and checking a map. Well, maybe I've got a good observer, after all.

The observer signaled a course to the left; Bryn let the flier dive a little to pick up speed and turned into it. The flier was sluggish. It had lost most of its speed in the climb. He dropped the nose a little to get some control, then flattened his glide a little until the wings shuddered. Well, it would be close. He didn't have much time or height. The flier might decide to come out of the sky all by itself, before the suns came up. He concentrated on holding the course and losing as little height as possible for long enough to reach the home field.

His stick of rockets hadn't killed all of the Draks. They would be up, flying at the first light, flying to kill, and he didn't dare let them catch him in the air.

Bryn reached out and loosened his fighting knife in its clips. That knife was his only weapon, if the Draks boarded his flier. Now that the rockets were gone, the patrol flier was unarmed and no match in the air for a flight of Drak hunters. Especially angry survivors of those two groups.

. . . Two groups. . . . They couldn't be the only two. The

Draks were probably setting up a dawn attack like that against Meira. There would be more than columns of Draks. A night march across the plain would put them in easy flight-distance of the Herd. They were probably there, now, working their way through darkness; waiting to attack.

Bryn concentrated on his flying. He had to get back to give the warning. He had to be on the ground before the Suns came up. The Draks would strike at him if they caught him in the air. . . . And he had to get down out of the way so the Frieland combat fliers could be launched.

Time and usable height ran out almost at the same time. Bryn's instinct told him he should be very near the landing field, but this was a short cut. He couldn't be sure.

He felt the air burble under him with ground-effect turbulence. That would be the Herd below him. The rough air was common, turbulence and small thermal rises from the body beak of the animals, over the Herd. A shallow turn to locate the marker beacons, and he would be home.

The Sun came up.

The observer screamed. The giant red sun was straight in front of them.

Bryn snapped his eyes shut, but the pain came in anyway. His eyes, dilated for the darkness, were contracting to adapt to the light. He had looked directly at the giant Father Sun, directly into its red disc; the adaptations of his muscles were fast, and violent—and painful to his night sensitive nervous system.

The Father Sun! By a freak, a horrible mistake, he was flying straight toward the rock-cragged silhouette of the mountain spur. The Father Sun filled the canyons.

Bryn jerked the flier into a turn. . . away from the mountain *into the Sun*? Any direction. . . away from the rocks!

The observer had screamed with the pain.

He should have screamed in fear too, the fool. Bryn's anger welled in him as he fought the controls. *He turned us the wrong way.* Bryn's thoughts were chaotic. *We've been flying away from the Herd. . . going sunward. . . not south! Over the jungle. And low! We are too low! We are going to crash. . . . Should have hit the trees before now.*

The red light seemed to come through his eyelids, even the arm he had wrapped around his face. The pain under his lids was like sand, driving deep into his eyes.

The indicator? They were too high. The dial blurred before his eyes; filled with the sun's red after-image. They *were* too high. He'd forgotten to set it for the thicker air. *Aiiee! Two mistakes*. But this one gave him a little time.

The flier rocked and swayed.

Bryn fought to control it. The senses he needed were blanked out by the pain in his eyes. He could hear the wings, but not feel them. He didn't know where the ground was.

The extra height was good. Good: how much? Never mind! Spiral it in. LAND! Get it on the ground.

He leaned forward and tried to peer through his fingers at the jungle. How far off was it? The trees? How high were the trees?

The red light was brighter, now, and he blinked to keep his eyes open. They began to water, but the pain was going away. That helped: he could feel the flier.

He brought up a wing and tried to think. Had he seen a wide clearing down there? Or was it just a blurring of his eyes? Had he really seen it? No: they were too high. . . . He didn't know. . . .

Really, it didn't matter. The flier was going down. Now, the next minute!

Bryn closed his eyes, forgot about his blurry vision, and straightened his landing spiral as if to line up with the clearing he thought he had seen. Behind the darkness of his eyelids, he began his landing as if it were still night.

He leveled the flier and let it drop, feeling for the uplift of air from the ground; feeling for it carefully. The jungle was reaching up for him.

The observer screamed again; "Draks! Behind us!"

Bryn's sensitive ears flattened at the sound and he lost control of the flier. It dived. The jungle was further away than he thought. They didn't hit it.

Bryn jerked the nose up by reflex and turned his head. The word *Drak* had flooded his nervous system with energy.

A flight of five, maybe more! Draks above him and diving

to fight. He could see their heavy black wings beat open as they braked out of their combat dive. The red Father Sun glittered on the short hunting spears.

With the last of his speed, he twisted the flier through the air, dodging the dimly-seen Drak flying in at his side.

One Drak came straight in.

Bryn lifted the flier's nose and crossed his controls to spoil the Drak's aim. The Drak filled the sky above him. It dove into the top wing and stuck there.

The observer, standing in the pod with his fighting knife out, howled, "Drak!"

Bryn twisted in his seat, tugged his knife out of its clips and thrust straight out. He felt the knife bite deep, then the flier fell out of the sky.

His maneuver had slowed its speed. The added weight of the Drak slammed it down the few feet into the jungle with a crash and a tearing groan. The trees tore at the wings, ripping the lower panel away and back, and tripping the flier into a narrow gap between the trees. It slammed to the ground, slid half around, hit a group of close-bunched trees, and stopped.

Bryn felt a violent blow on one side and a white haze of pain in his legs, then nothing: no pain, no sound, nothing. His ears, overloaded by the tearing cracks of the crash were sunk deep in his head fur, deafening him.

He fought his eyes open again.

The Drak was dead. Its lance and arm had gone through the wing panel and the spear was locked in the pod. Bryn's knife thrust had taken it in the chest, just above the wing muscles. The Drak was dead and it looked like it was stuck to the section of wing still attached to the body pod.

A motion in the sky caught his eye, and he looked up in amazement. Numbly, he stared at a fast-moving flier circling overhead. A flier with tiny short wings, banking in impossibly tight turns. Swiftly it circled and, like a dream where all goes faster than life, it was joined by three other fliers. They were painted bright colors and they moved . . . so very fast.

Now, Bryn remembered. They had been in the air with him when the Draks attacked. He had seen the yellow one, just before the Drak hit and he had seen two of them kill a Drak just before he'd crashed. Kill it from a distance with some kind of a weapon he hadn't seen.

The memories had been driven from his mind by the crash, but the pictures were returning. He had to tell them he was alive; these fast fliers. They were climbing to leave him alone.

A dull pulling tugged at his side as he tried to wave and he reached down to unstrap his belt. His hands were blocked by a bar of metal and he began to lose consciousness—the color leaving his vision; turning the jungle and sky to whites and gray.

He came back to awareness slowly. The image of what his fingers and eyes had told him filled his mind, with the same thought he'd had as he fainted: *a Drak hunting lance smashed through the instrument panel and into his side above the hip*.

Bryn knew the lance was fatal, he didn't really need the coldness in his legs and feet or lack of pain to tell him. His body and his mind refused to move, accepting the spear and Death with an instinct that said any movement would quicken the process, and that enforced waiting and life were all that mattered.

Slowly he brought a sense of deep duty up into his surface thoughts. He had to finish his patrol and tell the Herd Commander. . . about the Draks on the plain. . . . And those new bright-colored fliers. . . .

A part of his mind shouted about the impossibles; he was crashed—in the jungle; the Herd Commander would know all he had to report—from others—long before his, Bryn's, report could reach the Commonwealth wagons; no other patrol would ever come looking for the report of Bryn. But another part of his being, drifting dream-like and forcing his hands to move, slowly drew a report book from the map pocket in the side of the body-pod and began forming words. His fingers found strength to write; slowly. . . slowly, as his body waited without feeling, neither of pain or emotion, for death.

7

Amarson awoke slowly. He had gone to sleep in the chair. Someone had curtained off the operations area and its planning table as a concession to his privacy. Also, he'd been covered with the light, foldmarked foil of a thermal blanket out of somebody's march pack—the First Soldier's, for a guess.

There was a low-voiced activity beyond the curtain. They were using soft combat tones, but whether they were doing so because of an emergency or because of his sleeping presence, Amarson couldn't tell. Mardon would have awakened him if anything serious was afoot and a whispered conversation would have triggered him out of his sleep just as quickly. He decided the low voices were kindness, not necessity, and sat up. Bryn's combat report spilled off his lap, thumped to the floor and brought memories of his reading streaming into his mind.

"Morning," Mardon said, sticking his head around the curtain with a ration kit in one hand. "The Father Sun is wide on the horizon. The Younger Sun will shine yellow light in a few hundred pulses. Are you ready to eat?" Then he noticed the report book and said, "He wrote quite a report, didn't he? . . . And all with that lance sticking in him. My medic says it probably cut nerves near his spine and he didn't feel anything. If it helps to think about it that way."

"Warrior's Code," Amarson said. "He deserved the honor, that one. He did quite a bit of fighting before he crashed."

"And quite a bit of dying," Mardon nodded. "Warrior's Code indeed. *Blood only stains the hands*."

"Aargh! A fine subject to talk about before breakfast."

Amarson growled. "Where's your First Soldier? I want to spoil his breakfast too. I intend to fly the bodies back to Fort for full funeral rites."

"Funeral? At Fort? We can bury them here, Leon. The First knows the Herald's obligations and chants."

"I decided when I saw them sitting in that flier," Amarson said. "I want our people to see these furry glider pilots, so they can learn to honor them too. They are fliers just as we are, Mardon. And think—if they can pilot a glider this close to us during the night cycle—Mardon, these people are really good fliers.

"We are growing away from the Rivermen, Mardon. Now that the Draks no longer fly over their cities, our compact to protect Riverton is lessened. The Draks are flying against this Bryn's Frieland. When we meet these furry people I want the Fort to think of them as warriors and allies, with honor, not as another race of Rivermen. A public funeral will do that and make my job easier when my patrol flights meet these glider-flying furries. The honor we pay their dead warriors will help make friends on their side, too."

"But a funeral, you mean Shrine rites?" Mardon asked.

"No. Although, judging by that orrery, their shrine rites are probably the same as ours. No. I will ask my Chief Groundsman Mencsar to devise a public ceremony using his Herald's calling, and saying the funeral is held by Warrior Rite, because we do not yet know the true Shrine rites of these glider people. It will serve, I think."

"It will certainly serve the pilot Bryn and his observer," Mardon said. About Amarson's other, political purpose, he wasn't so certain.

Amarson nodded. "Send in your First when he's free, will you?" he asked, then opened his ration kit. "I may have to spoil his breakfast with a body detail."

"No need," Mardon said. "He is out now, spoiling the breakfast of his duty squad, You told him about the body bags last night. Then too, he read the report—and also ranks as Herald in my battalion. He will have recognized the honor due those two. It should be done by now."

"Ahh, very well," Amarson said. "You can start on

dismantling the flier, then. I will send back cargo fliers and hologram equipment. Take enough pictures so we can put it back together again. The Frieland people *know* things about building fliers.''

''I understand. I have our survey cameras here for a start.''

''Don't put too many men on it,'' Amarson said. ''There is no hurry and I want this landing mat built up—developed. I intend to send in a combat flight as soon as I can fly them down to you. Then we can stop this orbit cover business.''

''You want me to start on a solid landing strip then?'' Mardon asked. ''You got permission from the Administrators to split the town, huh?''

''No. That policy may be dropped permanently. There doesn't seem to be any need for it now. Fort has gleefully gone over to a fighting readiness that caught me completely by surprise,'' Amarson admitted. ''But our air patrol did kill Draks out here, and that has sharpened up the whole perimeter. There is plenty of reason to set up an advance base out here. Remember the mention of the Drak raids in Bryn's report? There will be more Draks.

''Go ahead and build up this site, Mardon. The discovery of these Frieland glider people, their common religion, and the showpiece that Menscar will rig for Bryn's funeral will bring me enough volunteers to man it. I want to send them out here where they can be Warriors again; find some struggle again; and have a chance to meet these new people. We have to reach out to them, Mardon. They are our kind; Warriors. Drak killers. We have to meet. . . . ''

The air was filled with a screaming roar. A flier dived past the landing mat, flat-hatting on full combat power, and screamed away in a climb. It was a warning, violent and startling, in the morning air.

The men poured out of the command post.

''Captain Azlid!'' Mardon snarled. ''Put three scars in the head of anybody you catch in the open.''

''If the noncoms leave me bloodroom,'' the Captain said and disappeared to take charge of the camp.

''The First Soldier has a burial detail at the landing mat.

Send him to me!'' Mardon ordered to two officers headed that way.

"Have them hold that fighter on the ground!'' Amarson snapped. "I will want it for courier work.'' He noted approvingly that a duty section formed around the command post operations table. The men who ran out were going somewhere, not just rubbernecking at a noisy flier.

"Follow me,'' Mardon was ordering his Baron. This was his battalion, his fighting ground. "There is a covered path to the landing mat. We can see the sky. The trouble's there or the pilot wouldn't have buzzed us.''

Amarson nodded and followed the Jungle Patrolman.

Mardon's gliding run brought them to an elevated observation point about the mid-point of the landing mat's length. Amarson was almost certain that this bunker hadn't been here when he landed yesterday. Mardon's battalion could run these things up fast. Amarson swept his eyes down the length of the mat, saw the flier poised at the end. A patrolman ran up to the flier and Amarson saw the pilot, Wyllym, pound the side of the cockpit in frustration. He grinned a little. An eager cub, that Wyllym.

Then he was scanning the sky; looking in the direction Mardon pointed. He saw them at once. A flight of the long-winged fliers, their transparent covering making them glow in the red light of the Father Sun. They were high up to the south. Very high. The long wings and their unfamiliar circling flight made them look like straight fiery bars, whirling in the sky.

"Gliders from Frieland,'' he exclaimed. Gliders. Bryn's fellow pilots, riding the air currents at the top of one of the looping glides that he had described and coming out to look for a lost friend.

The swiftly moving pattern of the circling cap cover flight caught his eye. Two fliers had rolled out of the circle and were climbing hard for altitude.

"Quick, Mardon,'' Amarson said. "You have signal panels. Where are they?''

"Here in this bunker, Baron,'' a Senior patrolman answered. "This will be landing control when we are set up.''

"Mardon, put out: *Do not engage*, quickly!" Amarson nodded his thanks to the senior, but spoke to Mardon. The battalion was his; the orders were his to give.

Mardon hand signaled to the Senior, wasting no time repeating what they both had heard. The Senior tugged three panels out of a pack-sack and rolled out of the bunker. He appeared moments later out on the landing mat, still rolling, moving prone on the mat to display the panels. A combat habit, that. A running man can be seen from the air for long distances, a prone one is invisible.

"Those panels will attract their attention to the mat," Mardon observed. 'They' meant the strange fliers; Mardon expected Amarson's pilots to see the panels.

"If they don't see the scar you've made in the jungle from there, they are blind," Amarson said absently. He was watching the climbing combat fliers, calculating angles. "Ahhh," he breathed. "Good, they're climbing away from the gliders. Ahh, yes. That's Dymault going up. He's no cub, that one. He will know enough to avoid an attack. But I want the panels out. If the gliders do one of those swoops for power that Bryn wrote about, my cubs may think it is an attack run. I don't want mistakes at this stage."

"You don't intend to fight them?" Mardon asked.

"No! By no means!" Amarson was positive. "We have to meet in peace. Dymault will figure that out. Those aren't Draks he's flying against."

"He seems to have seen the panels at least," Mardon said. "But those pretty gliders have claws, remember—rocket racks in the wings."

"Hmmm um. They may be usable only below the thermocline. If the gliders start a low run. . . ." Amarson considered. "Well, we'll see. Our fliers are faster; the engines give them more control of the air and the dart throwers on our fliers will tear up those fragile wings: the advantage is ours and Dymault will hold off, honorably.

"Although I think those Frieland pilots could give us a fight. Hieee! Look at the way they handle those things."

"Any chance those are combat maneuvers?" Mardon was still suspicious.

"No. I don't think it's likely. Bryn's patrol is over-due some three days now. A combat flight from his base would have come looking for him right away. This has to be a rescue expedition. Maybe, with those gliders flying so very slow, they have a way of getting their pilots back out of the jungle. With a rope harness, perhaps. In any case, I'm convinced that they are friendly." He paused, realizing the battalion of Jungle Patrol here on the ground was placed in jeopardy by his inane statement. "At least they are friendly, until they start shooting," he finished dryly.

"I will keep my men dug in," Mardon said, looking up at the swirling gliders. "My thought is: you still have a job to convince *them* that we are friendly."

Mardon's First Soldier rolled into the bunker, signifying by his presence that the battalion was combat-ready, else he would still be out harrying the slackers.

Mardon pointed to the fliers and said softly, "They fire a kind of rocket in a low level attack. The battalion will stay under cover until they leave." That was all the briefing he was giving the First. In his capacity as Herald he had read Bryn's report.

"Mardon," Amarson asked, "may I borrow your Herald's services?"

"Huh?" Mardon looked at his Baron. "This is no time for religious services, Baron. . . . Or tricks, Leon. What do you have in mind?"

"Religious service," Amarson answered. "I want to show them," he pointed upward, "that we are going to honor their dead pilots. It may keep them from attacking."

"Go ahead." Mardon had his battalion in a safe position, he could spare the First Soldier for a time.

"*Herald, be my voice*," Amarson asked formally, using the ancient cant. He was requesting the First Soldier to take up his obligations as a Herald of the Ancient Rites.

"*By the Father Sun, the Younger Sun and the Way of the World*," the Herald answered. "I will speak ritual for you. But the Baron knows the ancient ways as well as I. What ritual do you require?"

"There is no ritual, that I know, Herald," Amarson said.

"I will need your support. I need a funeral ritual for those two glider pilots—Bryn and his observer. It has to be a ritual that *they* can see from up there, and one that they will know is an honor for their dead warriors." He clenched a fist and smashed it into his open palm. "We must do it now, and fast. And then fly word to Fort so that Mencsar can arrange a ritual too. He must put on a spectacle for the whole Fort to see. *Herald, be my voice.*"

The First Soldier was silent. He knew of Baron Amarson's reputation and habit of doing things suddenly on impulse, but this idea was a good one. He had worked with the bodies of the two pilots; read Bryn's story. The small pilot deserved Warrior's Rites, his Herald's sense told him that. His silence was because he was considering and rejecting parts of ancient ritual very rapidly in his head.

"The bodies are in the burial sacks by your flier, Baron," he began slowly. "I marked each with the letters and numbers from their flier. It was the only death banner I could think of since we don't. . . . " He stopped.

"The Death Banners, Baron!" he said, deciding that he'd found the answer. "Those number strips are better than four meters long. If we fastened them to the wing edge of your flier. . . . "

"And put the bodies aboard out on the landing mat where *they* can see," Amarson picked up the thought. "You've got it, Herald. The Frieland pilots will be able to see those numbers from their altitude."

"And you can fly the Warriors back to Fort, sir, so that they can be Presented-to-the-Shrine. Mencsar can revise that ritual to fit strange warriors. His Herald's skill is greater than any of us," the First Soldier finished his plan.

". . . And do it all out on the flight strip," Amarson was triumphant. This was exactly the effect he wanted. "If it works right, the gliders up there will follow us back to Fort and see everything. They will know we honor their dead."

"My thought is: they will also know where Fort is located, too," Mardon said. He was still suspicious.

"Of course. I don't intend to keep it a secret," Amarson said. "See to the banners, Herald," he ordered. "Mardon,

I'll need a messenger to take a written order to Wyllym out there. He must fly out just before I do, so he looks like part of our ritual."

"Write your message, Leon," Mardon waved up a patrolman. He had seen Amarson plan these instant maneuvers before and knew how unstoppable he could be. If you put up obstacles he simply changed the plan and hurtled off to complete his objective. "The Herald will help you, and my battalion will get to work building your flying strip. . . . As soon as you get those. . . . " He threw his head back to point with his chin at the gliders. "Out of our sky."

"They will follow me, Mardon, I'm sure of it." Amarson took the message pad that was handed him, then changed his mind.

"No, wait. I'll tell Wyllym myself. This will take too long to write. . . even longer to read. Herald, you go ahead and start the work at my flier, will you. *Herald, be my voice*."

"Take the Baron to the combat flier," Mardon ordered his patrolman. "Stay under cover; and bring him back."

The tight group in the bunker broke apart, each leaving in a different direction. The First Soldier rolled out of the bunker, still maintaining his combat discipline and headed for the flight mat, but already rehearsing his Herald's obligations—planning a Warrior's Rite that would be completely new; not Ancient Ritual.

Mardon started off on a walk around the battalion's position. He wasn't checking on his officers or noncoms, their defense formations would be well-disposed. He intended to let himself be seen by as many of the troops as he could reach—to calm them, cut down jitters. If any attack developed, his operations staff could handle it, until he got back to the dugout. Morale, steady influence, was more important for now. With those fliers overhead this was not a training maneuver, and his battalion hadn't *fought* for a long time. . . .

The walk around had barely gotten started when an alarm whistle went off: a wild warble that meant Draks.

Mardon slid into cover reflexively, then scrambled to a spot where he could see the sky. There was a crackle of running feet in the undergrowth and his four-man squad of messengers caught up with him. They had been following, he'd been aware of their movements, but they'd kept out of sight. Now, they were fanned in a defense pattern behind him, under cover, but near enough for hand signals or verbal orders. The corporal rolled up to him, said, "Commander," handed him a spare dartbow, then faded off to the right. The maneuver took seconds, scarcely distracting Mardon's attention from the sky.

The Drak flight was clearly visible. A large party. Fifteen or more; Mardon was quick-counting by threes. They were high in the air or he wouldn't have seen them at all; his vantage point had a limited sky view. High, above the thermocline? Yes, it looked like it. That meant they had flown in from somewhere, not risen from the ground nearby. Probably no danger of a ground penetration. . . not right away.

"Back to the flight line bunker, Corporal," he ordered, making his decision. "I can see more from there." He got up and led off, staying under cover, and ignoring the squad which deployed behind him, following his movements.

At the bunker, he found a messenger from the operations team waiting with the sighting report and a count. He glanced at the report and sent the messenger off to the end of the flight strip.

"Get Baron Amarson back here!" he instructed. "Fast!" Then he blew three blasts on his personal whistle, telling everyone where he could be found. His eyes went back to the sky, searching for the Draks.

"Watch your ground fire, Troops," he said in a low tone to the squadmen manning the four sides of the bunker. "Anybody coming in on the ground will be one of us. Steady down."

The corporal acknowledged, "Sir," and uncocked his dartbow noisily. Mardon heard the small noises around him as the other three took the tension off their bow wires and shifted to more comfortable positions. Then he concentrated on the pattern of winged Draks in the sky.

They were still grouped together, but beginning to spread out. They were also beginning to climb. They had seen the fliers up at altitude and were climbing up toward them. None of the Draks seemed interested in turning aside to head for the ground. Apparently, the battalion hadn't been seen yet; was still safe from the attack for awhile.

But how had a flight that large gotten so close? They weren't a thousand meters off. . . . How had the fliers up there missed seeing them? Why didn't they see them now? Mardon's thoughts were twitching from question to question.

A chirrupy signal whistle sounded; a rattle from a dartbow and a low bark of command from the corporal: Baron Amarson, his patrolman guide and the tagging messenger scrambled into the bunker.

Amarson came up beside Mardon and surveyed the sky. His chest was heaving with deep breaths. He had hurried.

"Messenger brief you?" Mardon asked.

Amarson nodded, turning his head to measure the air distance between his high patrol and the Draks. "This looks like I'm going to sit this fight out on the ground," he said. "I couldn't get up there in time, even if I could fight my cargo flier. Our training program starts to pay off, as of now."

"Your patrol must be blind," Mardon growled. "If that Drak flight had been hunting us they would have been here by now—on top of our heads. And your fliers don't see them yet."

"They were watching the gliders," Amarson said. "One trouble at a time. The lower cap cover would have handled a Drak attack on us down here."

"Yeah, what about that. I don't see the lower cap cover either."

". . . Spread out so they can fly at stragglers, probably," Amarson said. "They don't want to fly under a pack flight. The falling darts will be lethal.

"Aarfh! The gliders saw them first. They're attacking." He pounded on the parapet.

The gliders had broken their figure-eight pattern and wheeled into a rough line facing toward the Drak flight. This line dropped down at a steep angle, building speed, and getting steeper as they came down. They were headed at the Draks: in what was definitely a firing run.

"Their wing rockets," Amarson said. "See. No one is

flying behind another flier. They all have a clear field of fire. Come on, Dymault! Pull the cork! Surely, you can see what they're going after, man. Don't let them beat you to the kill!''

"There he goes!" Mardon exclaimed. He'd seen the flick of colored wings as Dymault had curved into a vertical turn and stalled down into a fighting dive. His wingman followed him faultlessly.

The two bright fliers, roaring full combat power flashed over the diving gliders. They had started late, but their engines were pulling them toward the Draks at twice the terminal velocity of the diving gliders.

"Don't get in front of them." Mardon found himself gritting his teeth, his ears up and his claw out.

"He's on top of it," Amarson said. "Dymault will realize they aren't flying in line like that to give everybody first stab with a fighting knife. He'll. . . . '' Amarson broke off as the two fliers curved up out of their dive. They made a firing run in a near level pass at the Drak pack and then separated, curving right and left, away from the line of diving gliders.

"Rockets!" Amarson snapped. "See the smoke." The puffs of smoke tore away from the trailing edge of the glider's wings, and then they too were pulling out of their dive.

"Your cubs got two," Mardon reported, even though he was sure Amarson could see the fluttering bodies falling.

"That may be all they get," Amarson grunted. "Those glider rockets have a terrific spread. And the Draks know all about them too."

The glider's swooping pass across the Drak grouping tumbled a good half of the hunters of the sky. The Drak pattern broke up; some spilling air out of their wings in frantic flight to both sides of the line of attack; others turning and beating their wings to climb and meet the gliders—actually flying to attack.

Dymault and his wingman made one more climbing attack, flying right through the shattered Drak pattern. The melee in the sky was too wild for Amarson to see whether they had made any kills on that pass, but he *was* watching with pride at the way Dymault was flying his attacks in support of the gliders. The cub was thinking.

209

The Frieland pilots had wheeled their loose line pattern and were sliding back into the Draks to fire another rocket salvo.

Phee-whirt-whirrble!

The danger alert whistle came from three points on the right.

Amarson snapped his head down reflexively and turned to Mardon. That worthy was looking out along the sights of a cocked dartbow.

"Drak," Mardon said in his low tone battle voice. "Straggler from up there maybe, if he's wounded. . . . Or a scout for another pack.

"Leon, check him."

Amarson lifted his head to look. The Drak was flying slowly, using long, wing strokes. It was just above the trees and probably curious about the flight mat. It was certainly close enough to see the mat and the broken tree lanes.

"It doesn't look wounded," he commented.

"Is your flier out on the field?" Mardon asked.

"Probably," Amarson answered. "You know your First Soldier better than I do. Would he waste time pulling the flier around, or get his men under cover? At your first alert, I mean."

"Your flier's out in the open," Mardon decided. "And our Drak has just seen it. There's his turn toward us. Hah! Wounds, see there! It is a stray."

"It held onto its lance," the corporal said. "Do you *have* to look in its eyes, Commander?"

"No ooo," Mardon answered, smiling at the corporal's eagerness. "Think you can hit it from here?"

"Hurrumph!"

Mardon picked up his command whistle and said, "Then let's get it before it starts poking holes in the Baron's flier." He blew a "Fire! Fire! Fire!" call on his whistle, then ducked furiously, dragging Amarson down behind the parapet, swearing and laughing at the same time.

The roaring snarl of a combat flier filled the air. The low cap cover flier had picked up the Drak, too, and was making his attack pass. The air was filled with darts.

"I forgot. . . . " Mardon gasped. "How many trigger

210

jerkers I have. . . in this. . . bush battalion.

"I may have to report. . . wounded roster on a one Drak
fire fight. . . . Hoo Ahh!"

The corporal came down off his firing step. He was laughing too. "We scared the pants off that cap cover pilot," he
managed to say. "He jinked straight up for ten feet. He must
have taken some iron, I guess. The Drak sure did. You
couldn't fly a cargo flier with all that iron in it. If the darts
didn't kill that Drak, the fall must have. It came straight
down. Splat! Action over, sir."

"The action's over up there, too," Amarson said, rolling
to his feet and standing up. "The gliders are back flying their
figure-eights and Dymault is showing off for them." He
watched the aerobatic flier looping and turning in celebra-
tion, high in the air. "They must have killed all that Drak
pack or they'd be running chases. Hummm. There have been
bigger pack fights, but this was about tops for sortness."

He stood up and shook himself. "Back to business, I
guess. They are holding my sky for me"—he pointed up—
"And we've showed them we can fight Draks. The next thing
is to show them how we can honor their Warriors. I'll go on
with the funeral ritual, Mardon."

"As you say, Baron," Mardon acknowledged, smiling to
himself. Not even a Drak pack fight could divert Amarson
when he was working on one of his plans. Mardon was
willing to let him go ahead. He had his own battalion to worry
about. Mardon wanted to get back to his command post and
see how his battalion had handled itself. This one Drak was
the first fire fight in five long years; the first ever, for sixty
percent of his youngsters.

"I know you are anxious to get back up in the air and lead
your fliers," he went on. "The pack fight was too short, you
couldn't have made it to the flier and joined them in time."
He was only half-thinking about what he was saying. The
thought of possible casualties in his battalion had just oc-
curred to him. There had been a lot of wild firing. "They did
very well, Leon," he continued. "Your cubs. You lose no
honor by being grounded while they fought. Your training
still led them."

"Led them? Me lead them?" Amarson looked at his friend. "For the past three years, all my training has been aimed at getting those cubs so that they *could* fight like that. Instant reactions; good tactics; and cooperation with an x-factor—the Frieland gliders. . . . I didn't train for that, Mardon. That was Dymault; thinking all the way. The victory was his, not mine.

"I still lead the wing, Mardon, and I am sure they will follow me, wherever I lead, but they don't need me to teach them how to kill Draks. Dymault, his wingman, even the low cap cover pilots who held their discipline; they've passed the course. Oh, they've passed it, my cubs.

"If you ever figure out who has a share in the bottle of *frooge* due on that trophy out there," he went on, "send the bill to Dymault, not me.

"Come on, patrolman. Take me to the cargo flier. You've got the pass whistles. I don't want to get shot up by this jitter-nit battalion."

A messenger slid into the bunker, preceded by the whistle-call that saved his life, and looked around at the corporal's squad, sheepishly uncocking their weapons.

"See what I mean," Amarson said. "Start whistling and go!" He pushed the patrolman playfully ahead of him, over the back of the bunker, and left Mardon.

8

Amarson held his flier on the end of the mat until Pilot Wyllym and his racing combat flier pulled off and disappeared over the trees. The message Wyllym was carrying had to get to Fort first.

Then with the mat clear before him, he looked once at each

side to check again that the stiff banners were clear of his controls. The banners were streaming flat with the symbols and number showing clearly. The Herald had trimmed the panels cut from Bryn's wrecked glider into narrow banners, however, the numbers were plain, and they would have meaning to the circling gliders. They already had, evidently, for Amarson's flier had been on the mat, in plain sight for several hundred pulse beats now and the furry fliers were still circling—curiously, he hoped. They had made no move, either to attack or to leave; fly home to re-arm. They were flying their power descents and swoops well away from the line of the landing mat and circling high in the sky, ignoring the two combat fliers, at their altitude, with some care. It might be that they had reserves of rocket ammo still, or, more probably, they couldn't come down below the thermocline without crashing or landing. Bryn's report had implied as much. If so, their circling watchfulness was the sort of tactical position that Amarson himself would have assumed, so far from his base and faced by combat fliers.

Amarson was still ambivalent about their peaceful intent, and tended to examine the combat potential of the gliders, even though he had committed himself to making contact with them, and not fighting.

He decided that nothing could be settled while he sat idling on the mat. The gliders had plenty of time to see him and the banners on his wings. If there was going to be a fight, they would have to start it in the air and the cap cover fliers would get him out of it.

He fed the engine full take-off power and started his roll. The high lift wings of the cargo flier took its near empty weight quickly into the air. Amarson climbed up in a wide curve, headed for the thermocline. He throttled back to penetration power and signaled for the cap cover fliers. Two of them were already lined out to follow him, and the one had remained, pulling into a tight orbit over the landing mat.

Better and better these cubs were thinking tactics, as well as if he had planned their moves himself.

He raised his arm and signaled for an escort pattern. They formed up and he led them through the thermocline, continuing his climbing curve, until he was on course for Fort, and then he leveled out.

He swung his head to locate the gliders and saw two of them sliding down toward him, but holding wide of his three flier pattern. From one of the two sinking gliders he could see a thin, white streamer. The pilot was holding it in a fist, streaming it in the windshear above his head. A piece of clothing or a torn map, but the intent was clear; he was acknowledging the symbolism of Amarson's streaming banners, however he interpreted them.

Ahh! He allowed himself to smile a little. They didn't want to appear to be attacking either, did they? Maybe this was going to work.

Amarson held his altitude to let the gliders sink past him on either side, and watched them dive into the thermocline, pitch up, and swoop rapidly in a violent climb. Bryn's report had told him about the maneuver, but he was surprised and excited at the speed generated by the dive and the climb. Aiihee! They were fast.

He tilted his head back and saw that Dymault was holding his two fliers at the high altitude. They had swung over and were following Amarson's course, but they were staying on top of the glider fleet. Amarson relaxed slightly. Combat fliers on top and at his back; his combat position was secure, even if it was never needed. He cut back on his power to let the gliders keep pace with him in their swooping, rising flight pattern. He didn't intend to run away from them, and Fort would need a little time to prepare the funeral ritual parade he had ordered.

The flight would not be long in any case, but he did not want to circle the base aimlessly if he could help it. A slow trip would give Chief Mencsar valuable time.

9

Ameera had come down to the flight line as early as she could without appearing to be worried. She had waited until the sunrise flight took off and longer, until the Younger Sun had risen to *Point of Pausing*. By this time, she knew the ground crews would have finished the morning meal and the *Point of Pausing* ritual. She came to the flight line to feel the open air and look at the clear, wide sky above the landing strip, to walk among the fliers with their bright, free colors and wonderful smells; to experience the wind and the dust and the sky.

"Good morning, My Lady," the gruff voice of the Chief Groundsman was mellowed by a friendship she knew was sincere. "I have just sent five fliers off to the advance landing pad. Two will land and remain there on station. When the flight comes back at mid-passage, it will not be relieved. Instead, I will send out a cargo flier with fuel and two groundsmen. This morning's flight is our last cap cover mission."

"You have one fighter on the ground out there now, don't you?" she asked.

"Yes. The Baron intended to ground one flier when he arrived. His cargo flier is also on the ground out there. There are, in addition, twelve combat fliers grounded on the line here, and three cargo types, plus one loading to fly to Riverton."

She spoke quietly of the weather and walked along the path to the flight line. The groundsman conversed with her easily. She made no attempt to dismiss him or ignore him. He was too good a friend to ignore, even though her only intention was solitude and relief from the roofed Fort. . . . And dismissing him was impossible. The flight line was his domain, and if the Baron's Lady wanted to walk the flight line, he considered it his duty and honor to be at her side.

Ameera had long been comfortable with him. She knew full well he could, and did, run the line from her side as well as from his office. And he had never been an intrusion on her thoughts or freedom. He had never ordered her off the flight line—he had the authority—even during a Drak attack. Once, he had swiftly provided her with a dartbow and two armed guards before leaving for his battle station. She had left, herself, that time, when the grease and fuel stains on the clothes of her guards told her they were needed with the fliers, not as a Lady's guard.

"Have our fliers explored all of the mountain?" she asked, looking out at its high cliffs and the red gleaming cloud at its top. The cloud always reflected the Father Sun, even at the high passing of the Younger Sun.

"Yes," he answered. "We flew scout runs on all the canyons. Our combat fliers can't climb over it, of course, not even the cargo fliers, but we searched it for Drak henges. There are holograms, if you would like to see them. Also the Jungle Patrol has combed the low slopes."

"It is so calm and serene from here. Beautiful." She smiled and was quiet for a time. "If we stay here at this location another year, someone must try to climb it. It would be quite wonderful to stand on the side of that mountain and look down on this field and city Fort." She paused, another thought occurring to her. "You could look down on fliers in the air."

"Yes, you could." The groundsman, too, considered the mountain. The idea was entirely new to him. You could see the wonder of it on his face.

Ameera heard his breath suck in, saw his eyes narrow.

"What?" she asked.

A flier," he said. "See. Low." He pointed. "Flying fast—full combat power and straight in on the landing strip."

He strode away to a flag stand by the parked fliers and

jerked two landing signals out of the rack. Ameera was close behind him, and he expected her to be, for he said: "Pull the alarm switch, My Lady. I'll land him here."

"Draks?" Ameera asked the dread question, even as she jerked down the switch and heard the bell sound in operations.

"Watch the sky," Mencsar answered. "See what follows him. Commander Mitch will hold the fliers on the ground if Draks are chasing him closely. Anything flying that low can be handled by our ground mounts better than the fliers."

The flier was sliding sidewise at the end of the field, cutting speed for a power landing. The groundsman began to manipulate his signals.

"What is wrong, Lady Ameera?" The voice behind her made her jump. It was Commander Mitch, Amarson's Second Commander.

"That flier," she replied, he could see which one, "coming from there. . . low and fast. Chief Mencsar says to use ground fire if anything is chasing him. Nothing is visible." She knew the value of short reports. Her eyes had never left the bit of sky and jungle where the flier had first been sighted.

"Very well, the ground mounts are manned." He raised his voice to command a man headed for the flight line. "Captain Arika! Hold the duty fliers on the ground!"

Then he spoke evenly to Ameera. "I have the duty, My Lady. Stand easy. Thank you." He had noted her intent stare, and used the combat ritual to relax her tension.

She looked from her patch of sky, blinked to clear her vision and glanced up at his face, but he was now scanning the horizon in his turn and she could read nothing in his expression.

The landed flier roared up to the groundsman's signals, spun around and cut its engine. The pilot slid out and was headed toward the operations building when he caught sight of Ameera's brilliant dress, recognized the Second Commander and swerved toward him.

"Verbal message from Baron Amarson," he said when he was close. "For you and Chief Mencaar, sir." He stopped in front of the Commander.

"Hold on," Mitch said, and yelled: "Chief!"

The groundsman was directing the men in setting wheel blocks on the parked flier. He turned and came up to them swiftly.

"Anything chasing you, Wyllym? " Mitch asked the pilot. "Are we under attack?"

"No. Definitely not," the pilot said, grinning. "There was a terrific fight. Twenty—thirty—Draks, I couldn't count them, but we got them all. Two of our fliers and the big gliders. . . the strangers. Ohee, can they fly!"

"Fight?"

"Draks? How many?"

"Gliders? What are you. . . . "

"Hold it," Mitch commanded down the questions. "Give me a short answer, Wyllym. Are we under attack?"

"No, sir." Wyllym, calmed down, reported clearly. "I was flying fast, not running away, sir. In fact the Baron ordered: No shooting. Absolutely no shooting."

"Senior," Mitch turned to one of the staff that had gathered behind him in response to the alarm bells. "Get the ground mounts ordered to standby and pull back the pilots from the duty fliers."

He turned all his attention to Wyllym again. "Now, let's hear the message, Pilot."

"The Baron is flying in with the bodies of two glider pilots," the man began. "From the wreck. He is also bringing or being followed by two flights of gliders flown by the same people as the dead bodies. Strangers. 'They don't know us; we don't know them,' the Baron says. But they helped two of our fliers fight and kill a big Drak pack. The gliders shoot rockets and they—killed—every Drak in the sky. I honestly don't know how many. I didn't count.

"The Baron is leading them back here to pay honor to the two dead pilots—glider pilots, from the wreck—he wants a fancy symbolic funeral parade . . . on the field. With as many people visible and with as much ceremony as we can get organized. And quickly!

"Wait." He had more. "The Baron said to tell Chief Mencsar that the symbol of our orrery in the temple must be

218

visible and that stretchers for the bodies must be used. I was to tell you, Chief, to use the Ancient Warrior's Rite, or as close to it as possible in a short time. And, remember, it all has to be visible from the air. . . from high up. Because the gliders won't land. The Baron wants you to use your Herald option , Chief. The ceremony must look solemn, even if it has to be irreligious from the temple ceremony.

"And, sir," he turned to the Commander, "the Baron ordered, to you: No shooting. Very peaceful. But he did say to tell you to 'keep our claws out, but hidden', sir." Wyllym grinned a little as he stopped. "That's all, sir," he concluded. "Here's a written order, but he passed most of it verbally, sir."

Mitch opened the message sheet and read: " 'Coming back, and bringing friends and bodies for funeral. Alert the base. Put out all claws, but hold hard. *Herald be my voice.*' You are right. It's mostly verbal."

The group was silent for a moment. Then Ameera said, "Of course. He wants to show them we aren't going to slaughter them like Draks, but will honor their dead. A funeral parade is honor in any language. Surely, there can't be any temple objection to that, Mencsar, can there?"

"Not to my mind, My Lady. I am a Herald, not a priest."

"How much time?" Mitch asked. "Of course, I will have my claws out. With unknown fliers in our sky, what else? But how much time have we got to hide the claws. . . and arrange the parade? Aargh! . . . Amarson and his instant schemes!"

"He was ready to take off right behind me," Wyllym answered. "He'll fly slow, but you don't have much time—not much time at all."

"All right. We are at alarm standby now. That will hold for awhile. The Warrior's Rites? Chief, that is in your providence as Herald. Advice, please?"

"Warrior's Rites." The Chief was thinking deeply; reviewing the ancient chants and rituals. "I see no need for Shrine Ritual," he said. "They wouldn't know ours, and can't hear it from the air. . . . Hmmmmmn. . . . And no worry about Temple conflict, My Lady. I am Herald for all here, under the Two Suns, Father and the Younger. I may chant honor for any warrior slain. A warrior's *death* sanctifies the ground where he lies. The ceremony be anything we choose it to be."

Ameera nodded. Of course. Mencsar would bring the same exactitude to his obligations as Herald that he brought to his job as a groundsman. There would never be any sacrilege in any ceremony he chanted.

A burst of wind swirled Ameera's dress, streaming the ribbons and scarves. She said brightly, "Mencsar, my dress. Banners! Bright banners and flags. . . the most unwarlike things you can think of." The idea flowed in her mind like the chord of a harp.

"Of course, My Lady." The groundsman took up the idea. It would serve. And a simple parade, beside.

"Look, Sir." He knelt to draw in the dust. "Push all the fliers to a line, here. Then a double line of men out onto the field. Bring the Baron's flier up to the end of the line and march the stretchers down to his cargo hatch, then carry the bodies in state back to here. . . . ''

"The orrery," Mitch anticipated him. "From the Shrine."

"Too long to take it out of the Shrine," Mencsar said, shaking his head. "But there is a prayer shield in the hangar. It is polished metal and big enough to see from the air—if we lay it on the ground."

"That would be false, Mencsar," Ameera said. "Have four men hold it. They can hold it tilted up, perhaps, but don't be irreligious, even in a hurry."

"My Lady," Mencsar acknowledged the correction.

"What about the banners?" Wyllym asked.

"Signals, wind pennants, marker panels," Mencsar answered. "I have lockers full. Each man will hold one in his right hand; extended up, like this." He gestured. "Barbaric, but very close to Ancient Ritual. Very solemn."

"I will get busy hiding my claws. I'll want some good noncoms on those ground mounts, so we don't get shoot-happy." Mitch started to turn away.

"One more thing, sir," the groundsman said. He had their instant attention. "My Lady Ameera, city Fort should help with this. And I think there is time. Can you ask the women to come to the field—I will give you a truck, if you can persuade them. . . ."

"For your double line honor guard?" Ameera clapped her hands in delight. She was visualizing the groundsman's impromptu ceremony so completely that it amounted to a rapport between them. "Oh, yes. About twenty, say. I'm sure I can. Where is the truck?"

"There, My Lady," he pointed. "And, Lady Ameera. . . have them dress as you are, so please you; but hurriedly."

"Dress like me?" Ameera looked down at herself.

"In banners," he said simply.

10

Amarson curved in wide on the upwind side of the landing strip and flew across Fort to see if they were ready for him. The precision line of the fliers and the rank of men standing in front of them was more than he had expected. The brilliant waving banners in the parallel line leading out onto the field told him where he was intended to land even without the *Land Here* panels on the ground. As he banked across the far end of the field and turned downwind, he looked up to find the gliders. They had curved toward the mountain and set up a long figure-eight pattern, one long-winged shape sliding after another. Apparently, they had found the rising wind currents on the mountainside and were using them to give power to fly this pattern without losing much altitude. They were looping over the landing strip and back in a slow drifting pattern. The pilots could see everything on the ground.

And they certainly had a show to see. Amarson's downwind leg took him lower and he could see details better. He saw the blowing dresses in the twin line—women. Mencsar had worked a miracle. There was the orrery. The Father Sun disc gleamed in the light and the yellow symbol flashed its shine at him.

Along the edge of the field, around the buildings, wherever there was room, he could see people standing. Men, women . . . the whole of Fort had turned out to watch.

Turned out. . . . They had left the roofs of Fort, were standing in the open sky with fliers and strange gliders in the air above them. A thing that he had thought was impossible for his people. Yet here they were.

The little dead pilot, Bryn, was doing more good than he knew. Amarson owed him a debt; more than a funeral could pay, perhaps.

The thought of Bryn brought back the nagging worry of those deadly rockets he knew the gliders carried in their wings. He turned his head up again. The figure-eight pattern was like the one Bryn had described in his combat report. . . . The worry grew.

The flashing curve of his high combat fliers cover slid into his view. There were four up there now. His two escorts had climbed to join Dymault. He was covered by four powerful weapons—killers—if he had to call them down, but the people on the ground. . . .

Now he noticed tactical details he had missed on his first fly by. The Younger Sun was glinting from idling engines and the rank of grounded fliers had pilots at the controls. He noted their wide spacing. They could all take off into the air on combat climb from their ornamental positions.

Mitch and Mencsar had staged a funeral, on his orders, but they hadn't forgotten any elementary combat precautions:

"Haasamh!" Amarson breathed out. The ground mounts were manned too: rapid fire dart throwers as powerful as those in the combat fliers. He had just flown over one and the bowman was watching the gliders, not his Baron's flier. Mitch had all his 'claws' out, and waiting.

Amarson relaxed and took the big flier, with its two silent bundles of cargo, around to line up with the landing strip and slid it down toward the funeral parade.

222

The funeral was staged wonderfully for peace, if the glider people understood it that way. If not: Amarson ran *his* claws out against his gloves, briefly. If not, Mitch was excellently prepared for a fight.

His wheels touched and rolled.

Lady Ameera stood quietly watching the flier roll along the strip to stop at the indicated spot, almost beside her. The engine blew at her dress for a moment and then the engine stopped.

She watched Amarson, her Amarson, loosen his straps and slide down from the open pilot's position on top of the body-pod; down into the inside of the flier. Soon, he would open the hatch and she would see him, close again.

A tugging sense of incompleteness nagged at her. She looked up at the strange, floating gliders weaving overhead. Not them; they belonged to the sky. They were right and good. She dropped her gaze and turned her head to look along the double line of men and women, the wild waving banners proudly erect. A good ceremony, though she smiled inwardly at what Amarson would say about the impromptu banners. A good ceremony—then what was bothering her? She wished she could ask Chief Mencsar, but he was standing at the side of the field, by the orrery, ready to perform his Herald's obligations when the bodies were carried up to him. He would chant something from the Warrior's Rite, he had said. . . .

Warrior's Rite. That was it! Two lines of men and women . . . banners. . . . But nothing to signify a Warrior. . . .

The banner bearers, the men, were all Jungle Patrolmen and all armed, of course. They were carrying fighting knives at their belts. Amcera's mind took the idea instantly.

She acted on the thought. Her clear voice gave two ringing orders, carrying to each woman in the long line and to most of the men.

She turned to the patrolman next to her and drew his fighting knife—a meter of sharp, polished metal. She held it upright before her, glowing in the light of two suns.

The man beside her looked startled and started to move,

but all along that double line there were whirling flashes of metal; he wavered.

Ameera cried one more command.

The patrolman beside her obeyed it. He stepped back three paces; and down the line, like a wave, the banners moved back away from the upraised fighting knives. Now, there were *four* parallel lines; the men, on the outside with the gaudy flags and stiffly upthrust arms; the women, all gauze and ribbons in the wind, with the silver blades shivering in the sun. Now the funeral path was right—a Warrior's path to the Shrine.

Amarson opened the cargo hatch. Ameera saw his eyes widen when he was fronted by the knives and the women. Then the stretchers were there, and hands helped him with the bodies. They lay on the stretchers, the tops of the burial sacks open so that the face of these furry pilots could be seen. Flight goggles covered their eyes, and the wide furry hands had been placed in repose—Amarson had been kind—but the head and shoulders were visible to all in the honor lines and to the watching gliders above; especially to the gliders above.

"Carry them to the Shrine," Amarson ordered, firmly. "And them back here."

The bearers moved down the line between the fighting knives, and Amarson came to stand by Ameera.

"The women and the knives were your idea," he said softly. "Chief Mencsar would never have thought of it."

"But he did, Leon. When Mencsar thinks as a Herald he doesn't forget ritual or the old ways. He remembered the women."

Somewhere to the left a voice began the words of the Warrior's Cry—a female voice—and another woman took it up.

"You hear, my Lord," Ameera said, using formal tones, but smiling in satisfaction. "Not only old groundsmen and priests know the Chants. Women remember the ancient ways too, in things that matter.

"Do you like the knives? *They* were my idea. They seemed so right."

"Right? They are barbaric. My ears turned stiff when I

opened that hatch. Barbaric? The sight is erotic.

"Ameera, I have a decision. When they come back with the procession, have them seal the bags and put the bodies back on board the flier. Then get Chief Mencsar and get in yourself. . . . Both you and the Chief aboard, understand. I am taking you both with me."

"Because of your lust?" Ameera was still stimulated by her success and chiding him a little. "There isn't time for that, do you think, my lord Baron?"

"There will be, you kit, there will be." Amarson too was elated and matched her mood. "But don't spoil the funeral. Just get the Chief and get aboard. I am taking the bodies back to their homeland.

"Where's that refueling crew?" He ducked under the tail of the flier and made arm signals up the flight line. The fuel truck rolled out onto the field.

"Amarson," The Second Commander was at his side. "Why the fuel, Baron? Trouble?" The unexpected ceremony and the drifting gliders overhead had the Commander on edge, and the slight break in Amarson's movements had brought him immediately.

"No, Mitch." Amarson turned. "But I want to take the Chief with me when I go. Get word to him, will you. And I'll need a bowman for the twin mount dart launchers this time. No. Wait. Mencsar can shoot as well as I can. Just him."

"The Chief? Where?"

"I'm taking Bryn. . . the dead glider pilot. . . I'm taking the two dead bodies back to their home. I want a full load of fuel cans so I can get back from wherever we go.

"Here, Mitch. Take this copy of a map." He pulled the folded sheet out of his flight coat pocket and handed it to his Second. "As soon as you can get long-range tanks on the combat fliers, send one flight after me; as a ceremonial escort to an ambassadorial mission. The course is plain on the chart—it belonged to that dead observer."

"Ambassadorial. . . " Mitch was reduced to awkward gasps.

"No time to explain." Amarson pointed to the pale wings over their head. "This must be done now; with those glider

225

pilots here to witness what we have done in ceremony for the dead pilot, Bryn. I must do it now.'' He turned and ran along the side of the flier to direct the refueling, leaving Mitch looking at Ameera.

"Snap out of it, man," she gritted at Mitch. "You have that map, Mitch. Look at the course, quickly. *His* flier will make it to wherever he intends to go. Do your combat fliers have the range? Quick, Mitch.'' She looked down the line. The funeral procession was almost back to them again.

Mitch dropped his eyes to the map, took out his pocket rule and measured the distance against the scale.

"Yes,'' he said. "We have flown further with special fuel tanks." He nodded. "Yes, My Lady, we can do it.''

"Then, Mitch, please do it!'' She was intense. "The instant we leave, start work. Send those combat fliers after us. The Baron may need them quite desperately, don't you see.'' Then she closed her eyes, drew in her breath and was her calm self again, as she turned slightly toward the Chief Groundsman who was leading the slowly pacing procession back to the flier.

"Put the bodies back aboard, Herald,'' she directed. "Seal the bags and load the flier, please.''

"The Baron's order,'' Mitch reinforced.

"Then you and I are to get aboard, also,'' Ameera said, undisturbed by Mitch's statement. "You to check the dart launchers, and I to ride, but we both go. . . Also the Baron's order.''

The groundsman looked at her, saw the slight figure holding the fighting knife at Present, with her scarves flying wildly in the wind. He was still steeped in the emotion of the ancient chants; more thoroughly a Herald in his sensitivities and feelings than a groundsman. The walk through the ranks of chanting women and naked blades had reinforced his sense of ancient duties. He respected Ameera's feeling for the sense of Ritual. The references to the Baron's authority were unnecessary. He nodded in response to her order, with a half-bow and began to direct the men carrying the stretchers. He followed the bodies into the flier and, after a time, returned to reach out a hand toward Ameera.

"You may come aboard now, My Lady," he called.

Ameera lowered the fighting knife and turned to the man who owned it, the flag bearer behind her.

"The Baron may want me to carry this knife during our embassy," she said. "I will use it in honor, if you permit it."

The man, a youngish Jungle Patrolman, one of the bowman trainees, turned solemn. His eyes darkened a bit with worry, but he said correctly, "My honor goes with the knife, My Lady." The depth of the double-edged pledge—to fight for the holder of the knife and avenge any dishonor brought by its user—was extreme. However, the boy made his response as though he knew what he was doing and took off the sheath to hand it to her. Ameera took it without comment, as was customary, but she felt the weight of responsibility on her shoulders. The Herald Mencsar and her Baron were not alone in their respect for Ancient Ritual; Ameera knew the meaning of her gesture.

She turned, accepted Mencsar's guiding hand and climbed into the flier.

The bodies were shadowed lumps in the front part of the cargo space. Mencsar guided her up to the opening of the dart launcher position and quickly adjusted the straps to hold her in the seat.

"Ride up here, My Lady, until after we take off. You can see better," he said, and left her.

Ameera sat with her head outside the flier, looking forward under the single great wing as it spread out to each side. She was behind the wing, the dart launchers had to have clear fire, and with most of her body inside the body-pod. She felt like she was part of the big flier, or the flier was part of her own body; she couldn't decide which. She spread her hands out from her body, inside the flier, trying to imagine what it would be like to have wings as long and as capable as the big panels in front of her.

Someone seized her hand and she laughed gratefully when she saw Amarson close beside her. He checked her straps with gentle care, then squeezed by her and into the pilot's position behind her.

"Ameera," he said. "Look over toward Fort."

227

She turned her head, first to look at him. Both their heads and shoulders stuck out above the body-pod on this flier. Then she disciplined her mind and looked where Amarson had indicated.

She saw the groups of people from Fort. When she had made her whirlwind truck ride collecting the women for the parade, the city had caught her excitement. They had followed her back to the flight line and had been drawn out of the city to watch the funeral ceremony.

"They are out from under the roofs of Fort, Ameera," Amarson said. "That is something I thought I'd never see; our people coming out under the sky because they are curious. This is one more debt I owe that small dead pilot, Bryn, up forward. Perhaps now, our March People will find the strength to build cities with open streets and forest places to look at the sky. Perhaps this is the first time."

He turned to share his emotion with Ameera and saw the excitement in her eyes.

"Also, for the first time, my Ameera," he said gently, "I will take you up into my sky to the world you always shared with me—but never before sharing it like now." He looked deep into her eyes, then lifted his head to the gliders curving over the field. "There is even a little danger to spice the delight," he said. His ears came up and he grinned.

Amarson laughed hugely and started his engine. The blast of noise and vibration startled Ameera into an involuntary clutch of stiffening fear. Amarson, seeing it, gave another bellow of laughter—anger at him would help cure her fear of the flier. He got a rude gesture in reply and laughed again.

"Aiihee, Warrior Lady," he said into the noise of his engine, even though he knew she couldn't hear him.

Warrior Lady, lift your eye:
Let me show you all my sky.

He pushed the power on full and the flier began to roll. Dead pilot Bryn and his navigator; Baron Amarson, his Lady Ameera and their Herald; all, were headed into the air where they belonged.

228

11

The flier held an easy height two-hundred meters above the thermocline. Amarson didn't go any higher because Ameera was unused to the thin air and didn't know any of the chants for high flight. He kept to the middle sky because he wanted to watch the swooping flight of the long-winged fliers.

One of them was guiding him by flying up and down in long slanting dives and climbs that carried the swooping flier ahead of Amarson. The other escorts flew near his flier holding station on him, despite their need to drop into the thermocline for power.

Amarson was also flying fully alert. He hadn't used any relaxing or time-stretching chants. The big, single-winged flier didn't need strength or increased muscle tension when it penetrated the thermocline, so even that chant hadn't been necessary. Amarson was aware of his surroundings, watchful of the swooping long-wings and completely aware of Ameera's golden head and air-twitched ears. She sat straight and brightly curious in the dart-launcher saddle just ahead of him. She was turning her head, leaning to one side and then the other as she looked at the ground. She would catch the movement of the leading long-wing as it went past the flier's nose and lean to one side so she could see to follow the glider down through its quick-flying dive and the lazy appearing pull-out.

Amarson was proud to see that she had as good an eye for things in the air as he did for the unfolding ground below. This was the first time Ameera had been in a flier, yet she watched the sky as much as the ground. And she could see the fliers in the air—not many of his pilots had that skill on their first flight.

229

The flight might be long, but Ameera would never find it boring.

Amarson checked the ground himself and found that they were back over Mardon's airstrip and battalion base. He leaned forward and tapped Ameera, then pointed overside.

"Mardon's Jungle Battalion," he shouted. At this engine setting they could barely talk.

Ameera frowned a little as she searched the ground, then she found the signal flags laid out on the landing strip and nodded with a grin. Afer that, she was able to pick out details. Not many details, because Mardon had dug his battalion into the Jungle to hide it, but the signs were there. . . the flier parked at the side of the strip, some earthwork revetments and one open-topped bunker that had been built after secrecy wasn't so important.

Ameera gave a little cry: "Leon! Is that what we look like. . . to Draks?" she said. "So open?"

Amarson looked down at the landing strip. He nodded. That's what we look like to Draks. He'd never thought of that before. . . . The grounded flier looked particularly small and vulnerable. But Mardon's battalion was invisible. The Jungle Patrol had done a good job of hiding. They had learned in long years of combat, how to stay out of sight of a Drak's aerial eyes. Their training had held up during the time when the skies had been cleared of Draks. During this one fast attack the sergeants and old patrolmen had gotten the battalion dug in, and safe. If Amarson couldn't see anything, neither could a Drak.

But Ameera was still looking. Her mind was down there in the jungle, soldiering again, and realizing as she never had when she fought with her squad, how small and helpless a ground trooper was when Draks flew.

Now they were flying away from the mountain peaks that marked the end of the alp-range bordering Riverton and the Valley Harvests. Out here, somewhere, the pilot Bryn had his night fight with the Drak ground column. Ameera might see signs of that on the ground still, if they flew near the place.

230

Amarson was looking ahead and away from the mountains. He was scanning the vast, wide plain ahead, searching for detail in a featureless flatland. His eyes were constantly trapped by the clear, level horizon and he swept his gaze from left to right along its line. The red arc of the Father Sun rose behind him, not across that table-top flat, unlimited horizon, so that for the first time in his memory, Amarson could see a horizon from left to right without the arc of the giant Father Sun. And a horizon unbroken by any rise or silhouette of mountains.

His eyes were continually returning to sweep the sky. Here also, the air was unbroken as far as he could fly and further. North, south. . . . Wherever he wanted to swing the wings of his flier, he would find unbroken sky to lift his wings and a smooth, flat land beneath them.

It was a heady sequence of sights. A wild, free feeling that he had known sometimes, on lonely flights when there was no combat and he'd flown the clear air of the Marchlands and patroled over the level Valley Harvest land. There were other uses for the sky besides as a hunting ground for Draks. . . a killing place. There was, at these times, free air, and sport, and pleasure in the sheer delight of flying.

It was during these free times that Amarson had started thinking of ways of using his flier for other things than combat. The air-carrying of food and supplies back and forth between Riverton, the Valley and city Fort had been born during one of these free-flying patrols.

Now, here in this great open plain, was a whole new world open to the wings of his flier. And to the wings of all his cubs and pilots.

But his pilots would need more range to cover this new land. The technique that he and Mardon had been using, that of building landing strips in strings to extend range, wouldn't begin to touch this plain. Ambassador Theiu's designers would have to increase the fuel-range of the fliers in some other way.

Ameera was pointing off to the right and ahead. Her arm movement brought Amarson back to the present and to an instant alert status. Her eyes were quite able to see details in the air and on the ground, and if she'd found something she considered important. . . .

Amarson lifted a wing so he could see in the direction of her arm. . . . And saw the moving mass of the Herd for the first time. He'd read Bryn's report and remembered the pilot's reference to a great herd of food-animals. From this distance, he couldn't see horns or legs, or judge size, but there was a shadow of dust to indicate that the animals were moving. The amazing thing, a fact that dawned on Amarson as he watched the Herd draw nearer, was that Bryn had flown away from the front of the Herd three days ago. He'd written that the Herd was headed for 'Miera Kraal' to spread out. Yet here, three days later, the Herd was still moving in a column across the plain. Either they didn't move during the dark-cycle or. . . . The alternative meant incredible numbers of animals in that herd; millions on millions of animals.

A movement in the air caught his attention. He had been looking at the plain and the Herd, but only at intervals during his habitual up-down-and-around sweep of the sky around him. He wasn't expecting combat, but there were other fliers in the air with him, the long-winged gliders, and he checked their positions every half-hundred heartbeats. During one such check he saw the guiding flier bank its wings high and change course. He followed the turn and checked his direction. They were headed North now, flying back in the direction of Fort and Riverton. But this time rising mountain alps blocked his flight back to those landing fields. He was flying parallel to the mountains and on the opposite watershed from Riverton.

He was also flying parallel to the course of the streaming animal herd. Ameera shifted her attention to the left side of the flier and looked back at him; a questioning look in her eyes.

"Food animals," he shouted. "The glider people herd them."

"So many. . . " she said. "They will never get hungry." She nodded to herself and went eagerly back to watching the ground and the moving herd.

Amarson was trying to see whether he could judge how

232

much further the guiding long-winged fliers intended to fly on this course. But he couldn't detect any change in their flight pattern. The long-winged glider still dove into the thermocline at the same angle and each of its swoops seemed to rise just as high into the sky above Amarson. There weren't any landmarks on the ground below or ahead. Amarson checked his fuel indicators. He was still above the half-weight mark so there was no problem, yet. He could fly his tanks empty on this trip because of the fuel can load he was carrying in the body-pod. At the worst, he would have to try a landing down on the plain to refuel, but that would be his turn-around point. There was no concern yet.

He held the course while the Younger Sun moved across the sky toward the mid-passage point where it paused before setting. And still they were flying along beside that gigantic herd of food animals.

His routine checks on that side of the flier had given him a chance to build a picture of the great herd, in small bits and glances. And slowly, the thought began to form in his mind— in bits and pieces. And then all at once, the ideas came together.

This Herd was solution to the problem of finding other tasks for Amarson's fliers and other jobs for his pilots. Here was food source for Riverton, and Fort, and yes, for the Valley People too. Here was an unlimited source of meat, to supplement the Jungle hunting, the Rivermen's Fish Harvest and the Valley Harvest. Amarson's fliers would be able to set up a good three-way-trade. Food would be the trade medium at first, then factory goods from Riverton and some from Fort's new repair sheds. None of the groups in the three-way trade route was starving, but new foods always had value when a people was living on one staple diet. There would be trade.

And it would have to be by air. Distance alone dictated that the cargoes be carried by air. Then too, the glider people moved around following the Herd. They would have to be found and tracked by air. Amarson's fliers would be valuable and needed again.

Thirdly, there were those gliders themselves. Amarson

wanted to try out a flight in one, just from watching the way they swooped through the air. And he knew several of his pilots would feel the same way. Amarson planned to trade for gliders. The glider people could build them. . . and powered fliers for Amarson, too. They could help increase the output of Fort's own flier factory and make the Marchland independent of Riverton in that respect.

One idea tumbled upon another. The least of which was the fact that there was now no reason to move the Marchland People out of city Fort. No need to relocate at all. The movement out onto this plain would be by flier. All done through the free, open air.

The Marchland People wouldn't need to hide once they saw that plain. There wasn't any place to hide on its surface anyway.

And that magnificent herd of food animals. They could be harvested from the air, too. They could be killed by launchers from low-flying hunting fliers, and then transport fliers could land right beside the herd to pick up cargoes. The Glider People can teach us how to do that, but they'll probably want to increase their kill-rate with our dart-launchers. And our fliers can carry more than theirs. . . .

Amarson's flashing thoughts were deep in planning things, jumping from wide general concepts to detail precision in the way he usually attacked a problem before he turned it over to his staff. He was so intent that he almost overflew the guiding glider.

That long-wing had swung up from one of its power-seeking dives to swirl into a steep-banked spiral to hold a stationary ground point position in the sky by rising swiftly up to its top-off height in a series of tight, full-circle turns. Amarson was holding speed and height and a straight line course and was almost inside the radius of the glider's spiral before he saw the change of maneuver.

The glider swept by close in front of Amarson, barely twenty meters out, and continued to climb away as it crossed his line and swung around in a turn. The flier's bank was so extreme that Amarson could look straight out across the top

234

of his own wing and see the entire body-pod and the top of the pilot's head.

"Hold on!" Amarson shouted to Ameera and banked his own flier around in a turn. With the fuel load he had aboard, he couldn't hold the big flier into the same kind of bank, but he did curve it into a smooth orbit-turn and let it come on around.

"What's wrong!" Ameera wanted to know. She had freed the dart-launcher mount and was trying to figure out the safety levers.

"We have arrived, I guess," Amarson said. "Leave the darts alone." He wasn't worried about her firing accidentally. Ameera knew how to shoot, and when. But he didn't want to land at the glider people's home base with his Lady holding loaded dart-launchers.

The flier had made a complete turn by now, and Amarson was puzzled. The ground was still unmarked plain. He could see no sign of a landing strip or any encampment of any kind. This wasn't any sort of a base.

But the long-wing that had been guiding him was definitely interested in something on the ground. The glider had stopped its spiraling and was dropping down toward the thermocline at an angle for penetration. The dive angle made that clear. It was the same penetration angle that Amarson's fliers had to use and the attitude of the flier was instantly recognizable.

"He's going down to land!" Amarson said. "Stay buckled in." He curved the flier in behind the glider and followed him down. He wasn't too happy about trying to land on the plain without a regular landing strip, but if the fragile long-winged glider could land, then it ought to be smooth enough and safe enough for Amarson's flier.

As they lost height, Amarson could see that there was something different about the ground below. The grass was taller, richer colored in a long, road-like strip, parallel to the Herd's path—about 200 meters out from it. Maybe that was how these people marked their landing strips; with a different type of grass.

No, the glider was stalling into a landing well to one side of the odd grass strip. Amarson watched him make the landing and them swept over the area on a slow engine setting to check the ground. The ground seemed smooth enough, although he caught an impression of outcroppings and low rocks hidden in the rich-grass strip.

He didn't intend to land there anyway. The glider pilot had showed him the wind direction and, to Amarson's mind, had picked out the best place to land.

He curved the flier back in a landing pattern and flared out to land beside the glider. With his wings widened for maximum lift and the engine throttled back as much as practical, he lowered the flier lightly to the plain and stalled it in so that the landing gear wouldn't trip if the ground was rough. The plain surface was hard and firm and the gear bounced unevenly, but the flier stayed on the ground and the landing roll was short. Amarson brought the flier to a halt and switched off the engines.

"The other gliders are following us down," Ameera said. "If you want them covered, tell me where the safeties are."

"This is a peaceful mission, you bloodthirsty lovely," Amarson said. "Move the launcher slowly so it points to the side and can cover us when we get out." His words were light, but, like Ameera, he felt the need for some sort of security. The mission was peaceful, but only because he had decided that it would be so. He hadn't met the pilots of the gliders face to face, and found out what their idea was. They hadn't attacked him yet, and the appearances were all peaceful. . . so far.

"As soon as all the long-wings are down," he went on, talking to Ameera but watching the circling gliders, "you and I will get out and see what they want. Mencsar can back us up and stay with the launchers."

"Why did they land us out here? There's no city."

"I don't know," Amarson said. "That's why I want Mencsar to keep the dart-launchers handy."

The escort gliders were curving in for their landings. It was an evolution that they did with flash and smooth skill. When they were all on the ground, Amarson counted and then looked overhead, to find that the last glider was still circling high up—above the thermocline.

"They don't trust us, either," he said. "Very well, let's get out and see why they stopped. *I* want this to be a peaceful mission, at least. So, I guess we get out first.

"Ameera. . . ."

She was already unbuckled and down in the cargo pod. Amarson slid down and joined her, while Mencsar squirmed by and took his position in the dart-launcher mount.

"Stay back of the wing," Amarson said. "Walk toward the tail of the flier, so that Mencsar's dart-launchers will have a good field of fire to cover us."

Ameera nodded and picked up the fighting knife she'd borrowed for the funeral ceremony. "Peaceful or not," she said. "I promised to carry this with honor. I won't leave it behind if we are going to walk into a fight. *Blood only stains the hands.*"

Amarson grinned. If there was going to be a fight, he welcomed the thought of Ameera guarding his back. The glider pilot might think that knife was ceremonial, but Amarson knew her Jungle Patrol skill with it.

He opened his cargo hatch and climbed out. He turned to help Ameera, but she had come down close behind him, so he turned and walked away from the flier, toward the tail, and waited for the glider pilots to come to meet him.

Each one of the gliders had a two-man crew and Amarson was somewhat surprised that only one of the pilots was walking toward them. The others were all headed toward the rich-grass growth, which, from ground level, turned out to be about three times higher than the grass where they'd landed.

The grass here around the fliers was a thin-leafed growth a little higher than Amarson's boots and seemed to grow in small clumps interconnected by an above-ground root system. The glider crew seemed to be looking at something in the taller grass. They gathered in a group, then moved to another place, then three or four of them began pacing off to the north, stopping at intervals to signal back, as though they were measuring the length of something. They walked away and went out of sight in the long grass.

Amarson would have liked to find out what they were doing, but the lone pilot was close enough now and began talking. Amarson listened solemnly until he finished.

"Thank you for whatever you said," he said. "I'm sure you mean well, but I'd really like to find out why we landed just here, and then get on to wherever we are going. I am Baron Amarson of Fort, this is Lady Ameera and your two pilots in our flier really ought to be buried very soon now." He made the appropriate gestures when he mentioned his name and Ameera's, but he didn't indicate the flier in any way. He didn't want to emphasize the location of Mencsar and the dart-launchers.

The glider pilot was small. About the height of a Riverman and completely covered by a heavy soft-appearing fur. When Amarson started talking, the wide, furred ears folded forward into the fur, accentuating the look of frozen surprise that his wide, brown eyes gave to the face. Amarson remembered that Bryn had reported extra-fine hearing, and lowered his voice toward the end of his speech.

"He wants you to come over and see what is in the grass, Baron," Mencsar called from the dart-launcher.

As the Herald called down the translation, Amarson realized that he had understood what the small pilot had said. The words had been unfamiliar because he had expected to hear a strange language, but the words had been in the ancient cant of the Shrine Rites. Amarson knew the cant, and he remembered whole phrases of it when Mencsar told him what the pilot had said. He had heard the words, but just not recognized them.

"Mencsar," he called softly, because of the pilot's hearing. "Come down out of there. I need you to talk for me."

"Coming, Baron."

Mencsar joined them quickly. He was still wearing the Herald's tabard with the Shrine symbol worked on it, and at the sight of this, the glider pilot's eyes got even wider. He put one hand to his head, between his eyes and bowed. He was talking very fast, but Amarson caught the phrases for the Father Sun and the Younger Sun. Then the pilot reached into a pouch and brought out a metal object. This went to his

238

forehead too, and then was handed to Mencsar. Mencsar looked at it and said, to Amarson, "It is an orrery, Baron. The colors are different, but the pattern is Shrine perfect."

"I've seen one like it," Amarson said. "It's in the body bag with the dead pilot we have on board."

"Find out why we landed here, Mencsar. And ask him what those men are looking at, out in the grass."

"That's what he's been saying all along, sir." Mencsar put the small orrery to his own forehead and returned it to the glider pilot. "They saw this long, straight pattern in the grass. And they haven't ever seen it before, in all the years they have been flying this way. So they had to land and investigate.

"Now he wants us to follow him and look at what they found."

"I got that," Amarson said. His ear was beginning to pick out sentences in the furry pilot's cant. "Tell him that I have followed him in the sky; I will follow him on the ground. Go ahead, act like I don't understand. *Herald, be my voice.*"

Mencsar nodded his understanding and repeated the phrase to the glider pilot. Then the three of them followed him across to the group that was still staring into the deep grass.

The glider pilot spoke to the group as he came up and Amarson caught his name, and Ameera's.

"Introductions," Mencsar said, as the glider crew repeated the hand-to-head gesture. "They want you to look at what is over there, Baron."

"Very well." Amarson went forward. The grass was head high to the small Glider People, but barely up to his waist. He parted the grass and leaned over to see.

There were bones. The jumbled fragments of several bodies lying together, and on top of one another.

He drew in his breath and half-straightened in surprise. Ameera, from close beside him, gave a little cry.

"Look Leon! The skull. . . . Drak."

She was right. Amarson saw the curved beak. And he saw another smaller skull. Then his eye traced out a section of curved wingbone and found two. . . three. . . tip hooks.

He stood up and looked at Mencsar. "Drak bodies," he said. "Long dead. How many are there? More over there?" He walked along the tall grass. He found another group of bodies. Another tangled bundle of bones. Here there were odd shapes of metal, some broken pottery and crushed remnants of baskets.

"Ask them, Mencsar. What happened here? They must have some record of a battle as big as this. Look! Those three have been walking out to find the end of it. Look how far away they are. Ask them, Mencsar."

The Herald began talking. Amarson didn't pay any attention. He began moving, finding one cluster of bodies and moving from them to the next. He didn't disturb the bones, or try to pull relics away. The tall grass was growing between and through the bones, tying them to the earth. He had no desire to try to break the hold and rip the bones from the grass. The grass could have them. What he was looking for was something he hadn't seen. Something he couldn't find in all the broken bundles.

"Ameera, there aren't any weapons. Knives and fighting lances, even broken bits, ought to still be here." He looked out along the strip of long grass again. The two glider pilots scouting in the distance were even further away. "A battle this large couldn't have possibly been picked clean of weapons. The dead weren't buried, and yet all the spears were collected. . . . Doesn't make sense."

"Leon, this wasn't a battle," Ameera said. "Where was the enemy?" She swept her arm along the direction of the grass strip. "What kind of a battle line is that? And Leon, have you seen all the little bones?

"These are all Drak bodies. Lots of children—chick-Draks. But all Draks."

"You're right. I can't find any weapons, because the hunter-males weren't with them." Amarson lifted his head and looked over toward the Father Sun. The craggy outlines of the mountains were featureless silhouettes against the red disc. He was reliving again in his mind a high flight in those mountains. He was seeing a falling spray floating down behind his flier. He was seeing the open-topped henges.

240

There weren't many hunter-males there either; females and chick-Draks, but only a few armed males flew on that day.

"Mencsar, tell them this was a migration," he said. "They'll understand a migration. Just tell them that.

"They'll never understand where the Draks came from. But they don't have to. The Draks are our Draks. I know where they came from."

"From our mountains?" Ameera asked.

"Eeaa. I sprayed death on their henges and they were walking away from it. Some instinct must have told them they were dying in those high henges, so they came down out of them. . . . And found death out here."

"But why?" Ameera said. "They must have known the herd of food animals was out there. The Draks would have gone out until they crossed the trail. But another time of year—if the herd was somewhere else. . . . They were walking parallel to the herd. The animals must have been here at the same time, and anything that flies could have seen it. Why did they die?"

"No weapons to make a kill. . . . "

"That couldn't be it. A Drak could kill food with beak and talons. But they didn't. They just walked alongside an unlimited food supply until they starved. Why?"

"I don't know. I don't know." Amarson threw his head back in exasperation, then pointed up at the circling glider.

"The long wings," he said. "If they were patrolling, the female Draks wouldn't fly away from the chick-Draks. The chicks can't fly and the adults won't leave them. They probably thought the gliders were our patrol fliers. The gliders never saw them, or they'd know about this. . .

"They just walked. . . and walked. . . until they died."

Amarson looked at the rich grass that covered and held the long line of Drak bodies. This then was the way it ended. Not the violent air-clash of a Drak dying in a flier's dart stream, but decade-old bones, grass-strangled, and unnoticed on the ground. Baron Amarson and the Marchland had survived. Riverton had survived. But the enemy had not fought to the end. The enemy had walked off onto this plain and just died.

Amarson could also see the group of glider pilots standing

around Mencsar as he translated. Despite his suspicions and combat caution, Amarson had to hold to the idea that these people *must* be allies of the Marchlands. It would be so easy to fly out to this Commonwealth herd and raid it for food animals. The momentary picture he'd had in the air, of hunting the horned herd from the air. . . that would be impossible now. Amarson knew, as surely as the rise and set of the Father Sun, that one single flier raid against this great migrating herd would lead slowly and surely to another line of starving people walking out onto the plain to die. He knew that he, for one, would never be able to see killed and butchered herd animals without remembering this Drak graveyard.

The people of the Commonwealth would likely trade their food animals, but they'd also have to do the butchering. Amarson was resolved to use his fliers for transport and never for hunting.

"*Your words say that all these died because they had food-need from our Herd?*" A group of three of the glider pilots around Mencsar were standing near Amarson. One of them had asked the question in slow, word-by-word cant. Amarson understood him well enough.

"*That is truth,*" he answered shortly. "*They were Draks, and my enemy, but this is not the way anything should die.*"

"*We know Draks,*" the glider pilot said. "*But we would have fed these with our animals if we had known their need.*" He looked down the length of the long trail of dead bodies that was hidden by the rich grass. "*This is no way for an enemy to die. Do you wish them buried?*"

"*It happened long ago,*" Amarson said. "*These are enemies no longer. I will remember the place. The ground is honored by their death. Let the grass have its way.*"

"*As you say. I will remember the place also.*"

"*But now, we will go on with our flight to Miera-Kraal, while the Younger Sun stands in the sky.*"

The group turned and walked back toward the flier. One of the pilots stopped to engage in some frantic hand-signaling and the far-scouting pair broke into a run, heading back.

The glider pilot that had been speaking said something else, but too fast for Amarson to catch the phrases.

"He says that the warriors you carry will be buried with honor," Mencsar translated.

"That's why I am flying him to. . . What was it? . . . Miera-Kraal. I'm ready to go on. Unless he is afraid after he has seen the way my enemies run away to die. Go ahead and translate that, Mencsar. I'd rather bluff him a little while he's impressed by the Drak bodies, than have him fly us into a trap at Miera-Kraal."

Mencsar hesitated a moment, then said the words. The glider pilot's answer was lost in the sputtering noise of the gliders. They had a small motor mounted so that they could take-off and climb to gliding height. The crews were starting up to leave.

"Ask him to repeat that," Amarson said. "I didn't hear."

"*I am not afraid of you as an enemy,*" the glider pilot said. "*We saw you honor our warrior dead, and there is no anger between us. You would not fly to fight, and bring your Lady with you. A warrior doesn't carry his women into a fight.*"

"You are right," Amarson said. "*I fly to honor your dead.* Shall we go?" He started toward his flier, conducting Ameera ahead of him. He approved heartily of the glider pilot's conclusion. Indeed, that was partly the reason he had brought Ameera along. He wanted to give an impression of a peaceful mission.

"He wants us to let his fliers take off first," Mencsar reported as they walked slowly toward the big single-winged flier.

"I agree," Amarson said. "They probably need a lot of sky to get up to gliding height."

He followed Ameera into the flier and left the hatch for Mencsar to close. Ameera headed straight for the dart-launcher and strapped herself in. Amarson slid by her into his seat and began his engine-start procedure. The flier's engine roared into life as the first glider wobbled off the plain and Amarson pulled his power levers back to idle. He waited while the other long-wings followed the first at long intervals. They certainly did need lots of sky.

243

Ameera touched his leg and hand-signaled that Mencsar was ready. Amarson nodded at her, pushed his power controls forward and rolled the flier into a take-off. He held the flier into a shallow climb and eased over to the course he'd been flying before. He still had to take the bodies of Bryn and his navigator home for burial. That was the mission of his flight from Fort and the graveyard of long-dead Draks didn't change the job. He would always remember what he'd seen, but now the job was to take the flier up into the clean air and away from the past.

Ameera, in the dart-launcher position in front of him, shook her head to gather in the feel of the airstream as it flowed past her ears, then she swung the dart-launcher into its lock position, so that she could see. Her ears began to ruffle and turn as the wind reached her fur.

Amarson smiled to see her pleasure. The Commonwealth glider pilot had seen just the outer woman, the female softness, of Ameera and he *had* taken her as a sign of peaceful intent. Well-and-good. That was the idea. But, '*A warrior doesn't carry his woman into a fight,*' indeed.

Softly he began to chant:

> *Warrior Lady, Warrior Lady,*
> *Hold your knife and stay your kill.*

He shoved the power lever to a higher setting and let the engine noise drown his song. The course was clear, he had only to follow the migrating herd.

Amarson hoped the furry glider pilot never learned how lethal Ameera could be in a fight.

> *Warrior Lady, Warrior Lady,*
> *Let me show you all my sky.*

244

JOURNEY THROUGH TIME AND SPACE

Send for a *free* list of all our books in print

These books are available at your local bookstore, or send
price indicated plus 30¢ per copy to cover mailing costs to
Berkley Publishing Corporation
390 Murray Hill Parkway
East Rutherford, New Jersey 07073

THE CLASSIC SCIENCE FICTION
OF ROBERT HEINLEIN

Send for a *free* list of all our books in print

These books are available at your local bookstore, or send
price indicated plus 30¢ per copy to cover mailing costs to
Berkley Publishing Corporation
390 Murray Hill Parkway
East Rutherford, New Jersey 07073